TAKEOVER

THE TAKEOVER SERIES BOOK ONE

ANNA ZABO

For Harris, who nudged me down the road.

CONTENT NOTES

This novel contains descriptive on-page consensual kinky sex, including bondage and pain play.

Characters consume alcohol socially.

There are instances of homophobia directed at the main characters, including a threat of outing.

The internalized homophobia of an off-page character due to familial and religious pressure is mentioned.

A past non-sexual assault due to homophobia is described.

CHAPTER ONE

MICHAEL SEBASTIAN SAT AT THE POOLSIDE BAR OF HIS hotel, nursed a gin and tonic, and wondered how the hell he could have spent the past five nights in Curaçao and not gotten laid. Here he was on the most gay-friendly island in the Caribbean during the last night of his vacation, sulking in a nearly empty bar rather than being out on the town.

Lack of sex wasn't for the absence of beautiful, willing men. No, there were plenty of those, even in the staid environment of the corporate hotel he'd spent his travel points on. A young man in a tight black t-shirt across the bar had been giving him looks all evening. Nice body, but too boyish a face.

The other nights he'd spent hitting the bars and clubs in Willemstad, flirting with men with rock-hard bodies and erections to match. He could have had any number of them, but he hadn't because he was too damn choosy, too *particular* about what he wanted in a one-night stand.

He stirred his drink, avoided the gaze of the kid across the bar, and wished he had a bit more gin in his tonic. Who the hell had checklists for flings?

Tomorrow, he'd fly back to Pittsburgh, where it was bound to be cold, and return to his desk job. Back to fighting with the VP of Software Engineering not to release half-baked, untested crap to customers, even if the board of directors wanted them to.

Shit. The office should have been the farthest thing from his mind. This was his first real vacation since—

Since being screwed over by Rasheed and Susan. Since his demotion. And he damn well wasn't going to dwell on what happened three years ago.

He should have taken up that tall blond's suggestion of getting a room at a nearby hotel. That man had been willing to do just about anything and his inviting smile had stretched so wide, dimples had formed in his cheeks. Probably moaned prettily, too. Except he'd never been into blonds or obviously submissive partners. What he wanted, what he'd hoped to find was a man of power. Someone in industry or politics. A decision maker. A man no one would ever expect would want to be bent over and taken by a guy who drove an old Honda and wore shorts and t-shirts to work.

There were plenty of suits on the island due to the density of hotels with conference centers, but few of those men ventured into the heart of Willemstad to sample alternative options. Michael couldn't blame them. The top echelon of business wasn't exactly gay-friendly. He'd known more than one closeted guy whose title started with *C*, but he'd hoped that he'd find at least *one* on the island willing to step out of the mold, at least for a night.

He didn't want to have to deal with a partner deep in the closet ever again, but for a fling? He could do that. Revel in it, even.

Or he could go with someone with no walls at all. The

young man across the bar laughed at something the bartender said. Michael looked up and considered his options. Stay and flirt with black t-shirt, head back to his room and pack, or ask for another drink?

He was still ruminating over his choices when a suit walked into the bar. Short dark hair, charcoal jacket and pants that looked as if they'd had been tailored onto the man's legs, crisp white shirt, and a power tie of reds, yellows, and oranges. Despite the confident stride, the suit's shoulders slumped forward a bit too much and his gaze was downcast. His hands were clenched, as if the weight of the world sat on his back.

Now, there was a man who needed a drink. No ring on his finger, either.

The suit sat down at the bar, eight stools away.

Michael flagged the bartender. "The gentleman who just came in. Give him the best brandy you have, neat."

A tiny smile crossed the bartender's lips and he nodded.

Yeah, it was an obvious move, but it would answer the pertinent question quickly.

When the brandy appeared in front of the suit, he looked up, and the bartender nodded toward Michael. The suit swiveled in his seat and looked at Michael.

A slight parting of lips and a flush to his cheeks, but he didn't turn away, didn't bolt. Even from down the bar, it was obvious the suit was considering. Weighing options. Pale eyes. Sharp nose. Long, sculpted face. Not too young. The lines of worry Michael had seen before smoothed over, and the man picked up his brandy, stood, and strolled toward Michael as if he owned the place.

Yes. For the first time since Michael had arrived in Curaçao, a shower of pinpricks traced down his spine. The smoky, intense expression etched onto the suit's face stiffened Michael's cock.

Blue. The man's eyes were pale blue. He sat next to Michael. "How did you know?"

"That you were gay?"

A nod.

"I didn't. I took a chance." Michael allowed himself to smile. "Besides, you looked like someone in desperate need of a hard drink." With any luck, that wasn't the only hard thing the suit needed.

"And here I'd thought I was hiding that, too." He took a sip of the brandy and smiled into the glass. "Thank you for this."

Silver glinted at the man's wrists. Cuff links. Everything from the cut of the suit to the glimmer of a gold watch spoke of money and power. "For the brandy?"

He chuckled. "Do you know how long it's been since anyone has bought me a drink? Or tried to pick me up?"

The tingling in Michael's spine spread to his arms and legs, and down into his balls. "I'm not trying to pick you up."

The suit stared at him.

He slid his fingers over the finely tailored fabric covering the man's thigh and let his hand rest on the inside, near the knee. "I've already succeeded in that."

The rope of muscle beneath Michael's hand tightened, and the suit's breath hitched. Not much, but enough. Michael had no doubt he was turning the man on. Michael's cock hardened.

After a moment, the man relaxed and took another sip of brandy. "I guess you have." His voice was low, with just a hint of surprise.

Michael slid his hand up, enjoying the slight shudder

that ran through the man. "You're not used to being in the passenger's seat, are you?"

A soft laugh.

"But you crave it."

Beneath Michael's touch, the man trembled. He said nothing, but took a large mouthful of brandy and swallowed.

"Your name?" Michael skimmed his fingers farther up and traced the hard length of cock he found.

Silence for a moment. "Sam." It came out almost as a moan.

"Sam." Michael tested the name on his tongue. Short. Sweet. "Am I right?"

The vein in Sam's neck fluttered wildly. Michael massaged the shaft beneath his fingers while waiting for an answer.

Sam traced the rim of his glass with a long, shaking finger. "No one has had the balls to even suggest it in a long time."

"You'll find I have rather large ones." Michael pressed his palm against Sam's dick. "But that didn't answer my question."

Sam raised the glass to his mouth and took another long draw before placing it back on the bar. "Of course you're right. Neither of us would be sitting here if you weren't."

Perceptive. He liked that. With his free hand, he took hold of Sam's tie and pulled him closer. Those pale eyes were wide. "I'm Michael," he said before claiming Sam's mouth.

Sam opened to him, parting his lips at the briefest touch of Michael's tongue. He tasted of good brandy and desperation. Though Sam held himself still, he shook beneath Michael's touch. Here was a man who needed—

and craved—a good hard fuck. Just the type of stranger Michael wanted.

He broke the kiss. "Take me to your room, Sam."

———

SAM ANDERSON COULDN'T STOP THE TREMORS running through his body. When he'd walked into the bar, he'd planned to order a beer to unwind after his flight, do a bit of people-watching, and relax enough to get his courage · up to go into Willemstad tomorrow—not get picked up for sex fifteen minutes after checking in.

Michael, the man who had bought Sam a drink, stroked Sam's erection through his pants and hadn't let go of his tie. The taste of gin mixed with brandy filled his mouth and Michael's last words tripped around and around in Sam's mind.

Take me to your room. It wasn't a question, it was a command.

Now it was up to him to obey or walk away. He should do the latter, but his body burned in a way it hadn't in years, every nerve singing out with need. All for a dark-eyed, brown-haired stranger with glasses, in a hotel bar. Sam still wore the mask of his suit and the trappings of wealth and power that told his colleagues—and everyone else—he was not a man to be trifled with, but Michael had seen through that.

There really was no other choice to be made.

Sam picked up the last of his brandy and downed it. "All right." He set the glass back down. This was the craziest thing he'd done in years. He had come to Curaçao to check out the gay scene, maybe indulge in some harmless flirting, not to submit to a fucking from the first man he'd met.

God, he wanted it so badly, needed to let go and let someone else tell *him* what to do for a change. Feel the weight of another man on top of him again. His life didn't allow for that, not anymore, not at his level. If anyone knew he was gay, let alone liked to bottom, he'd be fucked—figuratively more than literally, though he knew a few guys would attempt the latter. That was the kind of coup that would put Sam in his place.

But the man holding his tie had no idea who Sam was, which was *perfect*.

Michael let him go and stood. He was tall, taller than Sam had anticipated. Thin material of a rumpled tropical-print linen shirt covered Michael's broad shoulders and an obvious erection tented his colorful beach shorts. He was probably wearing flip-flops, but Sam wasn't going to look down to check.

"You're going to have to stand up." Amusement colored Michael's deep voice.

If Sam could. He hadn't drunk that much brandy that fast in quite some time. He'd barely eaten today, what with an early start, then meetings and presentations, then the flight from Florida. Michael had managed to undo him in record time. No one had ever turned him on so hard so fast. He wanted—needed—more of this. Sam rose on wobbly legs.

Michael gripped his arm, his brow creasing for a moment, as if uncertain.

"I'm fine," Sam said. "I'm just..." Gay. Drunk. On fire. Longing for Michael's touch. Sam swallowed. "You have no idea how right you are about me."

"I do now."

Those three words sent heat racing through Sam's veins. Michael pulled him, gently, toward the lobby of the hotel. God, he was so glad he'd decided to fly here rather than stay in Florida. If any of the board members saw him, he'd be out of the job he'd just landed. It had taken two days to convince William that he could do what he said and turn their suddenly sinking routing company around. But the ink was dry, he might as well celebrate. No one here knew who he was. No one cared if he was gay. Hell, he'd had gotten picked up in no time flat.

Michael's hold on Sam's arm was firm, as was the press of Michael's hand on the small of Sam's back. They walked to the elevator across the well-appointed, gleaming lobby. Michael hit the up button. "Floor?"

"Fifth." Sam took a deep breath. "The keycard is in my back pocket. Room five-thirteen." The image they presented in the elevator doors was a contrast in opposites. Michael was at least four inches taller, and Sam, at five eleven, was not all that short. One businessman, one tourist. One in charge, the other following, only the obvious roles were reversed. Sam's heart threatened to beat out from behind his ribs and his balls ached from the unfulfilled desire his hand could never quench. He had to be dreaming, because this could not be happening. He could not be letting a stranger take him back to his room for a fuck.

Michael slipped his hand into Sam's pants to retrieve the card. "Not a lucky number, thirteen."

"It is for me." This was thousands of times better than a drink. Or maybe worse. The pain in Sam's head had vanished completely. He didn't fuck strangers. Hell, lately he didn't have sex at all. Too much of a chance someone would find out he preferred cock to pussy. And he'd seen how the wolves around him ripped apart those who did step out of the closet.

Sam pushed away a momentary flutter of guilt. He'd seen what happened to that kid in grad school, and he'd run.

Though Michael had freed the keycard, he slid his hand into Sam's back pocket. Sam swallowed the moan that tried to escape. "Too bad we don't have a few days. I'd love to see how long it would take to make you come thirteen times."

For a moment, the floor underneath Sam seemed to lose solidity and his knees threatened to buckle, but the strong hands holding him up didn't let him fall. Michael chuckled and the elevator dinged. God. He was not going to survive this night if cheesy lines like *that* undid him. He stepped into the car, Michael right behind him.

"Press five."

Sam was more than happy to obey, utterly aware of how obvious they'd been walking through the lobby. Finally, someone not intimidated by his clothing or the attitude he wore. It was as if Michael saw straight through the trappings to the man inside.

Sam didn't even see that guy anymore. Hadn't for years, because he never ceded control in business, ever. It was a rule he'd lived by. It's why he got the job offers he did. He was a hard-ass who could outmaneuver boards, charm the pants off of workers, then sell off companies for millions. Always in power.

When the doors closed, Michael took his hand from Sam's pocket, spun Sam to face him, then pushed him against the back of the elevator. The car lurched up. Michael's hard length rubbed Sam's cock. This time, Sam couldn't hold back the wanton groan. Sweat trickled down his back, sticking his shirt to his skin. Every nerve wanted more of what Michael offered. Sex. Domination. Maybe even a little pain.

"Where were you four days ago?" Michael kissed Sam's neck.

The scrape of Michael's teeth sent another wave of fire through Sam and he shuddered. "In a meeting in Florida. I'm a—"

Michael claimed Sam's mouth and everything slipped from Sam's mind but the strength of the man in front of him. He gripped Michael's shirt and thrust his tongue and cock against Michael. The elevator slowed to a stop.

Michael broke the kiss, breathless. "No title. No last names. The only thing I care about is what you are right now."

High-powered CEO, technologist, ruthless businessman—gone in an instant. The elevator doors opened. "Yours," Sam said. "I'm yours."

"Good." Michael pulled him from the car.

Somehow Sam managed to make it down the hall. Quite a feat, given how badly his desire and the brandy in his blood had screwed with his ability to walk. Everything about this was decadently reckless and terrifying. Before Sam knew it, they were in his room—his luggage sat on the rack and everything was neat and tidy, the way he'd left it. The door clicked closed and Michael took Sam's mouth again. Gin and sex and power—a heavenly combination. The man tasted as hard as he felt. He gasped when Michael broke the kiss, and no amount of air made Sam any less breathless.

"You have condoms and lube?"

That question hammered home exactly what was about to happen. Sam froze. God, he wanted and needed this. But — But— To be fucked by a stranger in his hotel room?

He must have telegraphed his hesitation. Michael kissed him, this time on the cheek. "You can say no. It's fine. This is fast and intense."

Intense was too soft a word. Sam's nerves wanted to crawl out of his body and every inch of his skin flickered from numb to on fire. Pain and pleasure. "You've done this before. I haven't."

Michael loosened his grip on Sam's arms. "A man like you? Surely you've picked up guys before."

Sam grabbed Michael's wrists before the other man could back away. He would not lose this chance to his own apprehension. "Picked up, yes." In undergrad, before he'd learned the hard way that preferring men was more than frowned upon in the top echelon of business. "Been picked up? Never."

Michael's smile was slight, but warm. "There's a first time for everything."

Hints of gold colored Michael's dark brown eyes. That had been obscured by Michael's glasses before, but this close Sam saw through the lenses. Michael would let him go if Sam wanted to back out, that much was obvious.

How long had it been since he'd let someone take control? College? *High school?* Jesus. He pushed the knot in his throat aside to speak. "I have condoms and lube. In my suitcase." Because he hadn't come to Curaçao just to *flirt.* Heat blazed in Sam's chest and throat, but the impish grin on Michael's face washed away Sam's apprehension.

He'd do anything to keep that expression on Michael.

"Then get them and put them on the edge of the bed."

Sam released Michael's wrists and every step he took strengthened his resolve. He dug out the bottle and row of square foils. This had to be the oddest way he'd ever celebrated winning a new job—surrendering himself for sex. *You want this. It's been too damn long.*

He placed the items on the bed, then faced Michael. That smile still graced Michael's lips and there were tropical birds on his shirt. Good God, he was going to be fucked by a man with *parrots* on his button-down. Sam tried to bite back the laugh, but failed.

Michael's grin widened and he strode forward. "What's so funny?" He took hold of Sam's tie again.

The pull of fabric around Sam's neck tightened his balls. "You. Me. This." He gulped a breath. "How did you know that I'd say yes?"

Michael closed his fingers around Sam's chin. "I told you. I didn't. But fortune favors the bold." Then Michael's lips were on Sam's again, prying him open, making him lose track of the ground. Michael pulled back a few inches. "And you looked like a man in desperate need of a good hard fuck."

Sam couldn't breathe. His cock ached and he wanted far less clothing between him and the man holding his tie and chin. "Please." He practically whispered the word.

Michael stroked Sam's jaw with his thumb. "If anything I do gets to be too much, say 'yellow' and I'll slow down. Say 'red' and I'll stop. Understand?"

A safeword? Lightning ran through Sam's veins. He couldn't be that lucky. "Yes." Sam leaned into Michael's touch. "And if I want more?"

"You beg for it."

Sam's whole body ached. To be naked. Controlled. Entered. He couldn't even speak. The fantasies he'd jacked off to for years didn't even come close to this reality.

Michael chuckled and undid the knot in Sam's tie. "I'll need this later." He freed the length of fabric from Sam's neck and tossed it on the bed next to the condoms and lube, then slipped his hands under the lapels of Sam's suit coat. He caressed Sam's chest before pushing the jacket off and to the floor. The long length of Michael's body was so close that every breath he exhaled warmed Sam's face and made his limbs ache with the need to touch flesh to flesh.

Sam closed the tiny gap between them and found the waistband of Michael's shorts. He dipped two fingers inside it and caressed Michael's hot skin. They were both wearing too much clothing, but he wasn't about to beg, not yet. He still had his pride, if nothing else.

Michael redirected Sam's hand, pressing it against his erection. "Do you want me inside you?"

The floor vanished again. All Sam knew was the warmth of Michael's touch and the hard thickness of the cock beneath a thin layer of fabric. He'd never wanted to be fucked this badly, ever. To hell with pride. "God, yes. Please."

"Say it."

Every inch of Sam's skin blazed. Voice the desire— something he hadn't done in years. No turning back now. "I want your cock inside me."

Michael nipped Sam's ear. "Then take off your shirt." He backed away and waited.

It was all Sam could do not to rip off all his clothing. He focused on the bright feathers of the parrot to the left of Michael's heart and worked the links free from the cuffs of his shirt. Then he removed his watch. Going slowly meant he wasn't the only one in torment, judging from the flush of Michael's skin.

When Michael held out his hand, Sam placed the items into his palm.

Michael examined the links. They were flat, and round,

and etched with the Copernican model of the universe. "Nice. White gold?"

"Platinum." Sam started undoing the buttons of his shirt, from the top.

Michael set the cuff links and watch down on the dresser. He never stopped looking at Sam.

With each button Sam undid, his heart rate notched higher. By the time he finished with the last one, his entire body strummed with the rhythm of his blood. He pulled the shirt off and the sweat on his back cooled instantly. Trembling, he dropped the shirt.

"Shoes. Pants. Socks." Michael crossed his arms. The bulge in his shorts was enormous.

Sam kicked off his shoes, then made short work of his slacks, undoing the belt, then unbuttoning and unzipping. It took very little effort to push them off. Gravity did the rest, pooling them around his ankles. With care he stood on one leg at a time and removed his socks. Apparently yoga helped you balance even when you couldn't feel the floor beneath you.

No more suit. No more mask. Not quite naked.

Michael wore a brilliant grin. "Nice color." He unfolded his arms.

Sam's briefs were blue. Not navy, but the color of the sky in the tropics. He shrugged, though his cock throbbed in time with the rapid beating of his heart. "Seemed appropriate for the climate." And it got Sam off a bit to wear bright colors under his very conservative suits.

Michael's laugh was musical. He strode forward and tucked his fingers beneath the waistband of Sam's underwear then pushed the briefs over Sam's cock and off his hips. "They look better on the floor."

The scrape of the fabric against the crown of Sam's dick

took his breath away and pulled the desire coiled within him even tighter. At this rate, he'd shoot before Michael removed a stitch of clothing. "So do my knees." Brazen. Begging? Maybe.

Michael huffed a laugh, then sucked Sam's earlobe. His hot breath caressed Sam's ear. "Prove it."

Without hesitation, Sam sank to the ground. Blood pounded in his head, but he couldn't blame the brandy for making him dizzy. He looked up at Michael. *Please. Please say what I think you're going to say.*

He hadn't wrapped his mouth around a dick since undergrad. After his first term in grad school, he'd learned that sucking cock wasn't an acceptable pastime for the type of businessman he needed to be. Grad school had taught him that. Gay either got you ignored or the crap beaten out of you.

Hell, the handful of men who'd blown Sam since then thought he was straight, that he just got off on the power. That was the expectation at his level.

Michael ran a finger over Sam's cheek. "Take my cock out and suck it."

With pleasure. Sam's hands were remarkably steady as he undid Michael's shorts and pushed them and the white briefs out of the way and got his first look at the cock he'd only felt.

No wonder the bulge had been huge. Michael wasn't any longer than Sam, but his girth... *Jesus.* Before the night was out, that cock was going to be buried in Sam's ass. A wave of fire washed over him.

Michael caressed the top of Sam's head. "Don't disappoint me now."

Sam kissed the crown. The sharp tang of the fluid at Michael's tip tasted different from Sam's own. He couldn't remember what any of the others had tasted like; it had been too long. Sam pushed back the foreskin and took more of Michael in and was rewarded by Michael's soft moan and his hands twisting into Sam's hair.

Giving head was like riding a bike—you could be horribly out of practice but you never forgot the skill. Sam stroked Michael's thighs and sucked more cock in. The thickness of Michael's shaft stretched his mouth wide, making it hard for him to run his tongue over the thick veins, but he'd never backed down from a challenging situation.

Michael tightened both his hands in Sam's hair and tugged sharply. The pain sent a shower of sparks running to Sam's dick. His balls tightened, and when he groaned his pleasure, Michael thrust his cock against the back of Sam's mouth. It took every ounce of Sam's willpower not to gag.

There was no way in hell he'd be able to take all of Michael into his throat, even if he wanted to. And he did. Sam looked up. He wasn't inexperienced—just out of practice. Because men who ran companies weren't supposed to be the ones on the receiving end of a face-fuck.

"Sorry," Michael said. "You just look so hot." He pulled back and stroked in and out more shallowly.

Hot. On his knees with a cock in his mouth. Those weren't boardroom qualities. Sam's skin itched and pricked. But then again, he hated boardrooms and he missed this so damn much.

It didn't take Sam long to get used to Michael's rhythm, and it gave him the room to use his tongue more effectively. He pressed against the underside of Michael's shaft near the head and hoped that got Michael off the same way it did him.

"Christ." Michael withdrew completely, his voice rough

and breathless. "You're going to make me come if you keep doing that."

Apparently, the answer was yes. Sam filed that away for later, then his heart sank to the floor. One night. No last names. There was no later, no reason to remember what pleased Michael, because Sam would never see him again. *Shit.* He pushed away the bitter taste that rose in his throat. "I thought that was the point."

Michael snorted and ran a thumb that tasted of salt and spice over Sam's lips. "Yes, but not yet." He stroked Sam's cheek with the back of his hand. "Up."

Sam rose. One night. That didn't seem fair, now. Then again, he hadn't come to the island for anything but a fling. After this, it was back to the US, into a new job, and back in the closet. He nearly choked on his own bitterness.

"Turn around and kneel on the bed with your hands behind your back." Michael's command brought him back to the here and now, right where he wanted to be.

Sam did as told, the bed's comforter cool against the overheated skin of his legs. When Michael slid the tie off the bed, Sam's balls ached even more. Silk tightened around Sam's wrists and he gasped. He was so damn hard and dripping from need. Now he couldn't even touch himself. This was every one of his dreams come to life. One night. "Oh, God."

Michael responded with a chuckle that would have made the devil proud. He finished binding Sam's hands. "Too tight?"

Sam tested the makeshift binding. No way was he breaking free easily, but he could wiggle his fingers. "No."

"Good." Michael kissed the back of Sam's neck, then pressed him forward and down until his forehead touched the mattress.

Again, Sam's heart threatened to ram itself out of his chest and the breath that escaped his mouth sounded suspiciously like a whimper. He'd always wanted to be tied up and fucked, but had never found the right circumstances —or the right man.

"Spread your legs wide."

He did, despite the tremble in them. Michael nudged Sam's knees even farther apart and the result felt gloriously hedonistic. Bound and spread, his dick and balls hanging and easily accessible, his ass up in the air and the perfect level, he expected, for Michael's cock to enter him. The coil of desire in Sam tightened and he couldn't help squirming.

"Damn." Michael's voice was low and full of gravel. "If we had the time, I'd sit and watch you for a while. You're stunning, moving like that. You want this badly, don't you?"

Sam pressed his forehead into the bed. Yes, he did. Only, what the hell was he going to do when he returned to the States? This would never happen again, not with Michael. Not with anyone else. Hard enough to hide that he was gay, but *this*? Suddenly, he was very glad Michael couldn't see his face. It burned, but not with need. More of himself to hide when he returned. A thin part of his mind whispered one word. *Coward*.

He didn't hate himself for being gay. No, he hated himself for hiding that he was gay because it was bad for *business*. He'd seen what being out could do to a promising career. Swollen eyes staring back at Sam's. The stink of stale water on brick.

The caress of Michael's hand on Sam's ass drew him from despair back into desire.

"You're a runner?"

Sam turned his head sideways so he could speak clearly. "Yeah."

"It's your muscle tone" Michael said, answering the unasked question. "You've the legs, the thighs"—Michael slapped him hard—"and the ass of a runner."

Sam barely heard the last words. Every part of his skin flamed when the sting from Michael's blow radiated all over his body. He moaned. It hadn't hurt, but it had done more to tighten his balls and stiffen his cock than any mouth or ass ever had. *Holy shit.*

Michael grunted, as if surprised. Then another blow landed. Followed by a third. After that, Sam lost track, because the world turned white. The pain… wasn't. Each hit stung but also sang in his blood, vibrating him from the inside out. He twisted and rocked but not in any effort to get away from Michael's hand. He thrust against air. Every slap melted his bones and tightened his cock.

When the blows stopped, Sam cried out, but more from frustration than anything else. "Fuck. No, please."

Michael smoothed fingers over his backside. His breathing was as rough as Sam's. "You want *more*?"

Michael was surprised? Sam pressed his face into the mattress. Just this single night—no time to figure any of this out. He lifted his head. "Yes, damn it." His mouth was so dry. "God, I can't take the waiting. Please just—"

The blow came and shut Sam's brain down, and he dissolved into a wash of heat and light at the glorious sting of Michael's hand. Sam's balls drew up, but there was nothing around his dick but air. This close to release, every point of pain burst like fireworks in his vision.

Michael stopped. Again.

Sam tried to ground his teeth into nubs. His body shook and his throat was so parched, he couldn't speak.

Michael whispered into his ear. "I have to stop. I'll injure you if I keep going." His touch was both soothing and enflaming. He was kneeling next to Sam. When had Michael ended up on the bed?

"Sam?" Concern laced Michael's voice.

Sam's ears rang with the pounding of his blood. He swallowed moisture into his throat and spoke. "I'm here. I'm fine." Lies. He wanted more. That was a problem. After tonight he doubted he'd find anyone to scratch this itch—certainly not among his colleagues.

Yeah, that would earn their respect, Sam begging to be tied up and punished. Because he'd always wanted this. Dreamed it. All those videos.

He was sure some would love to beat him, but with fists, and hard enough to break bones. He knew that pain. Despised it.

This wasn't anything like that.

Fuck. "I'm fine," he repeated. "Please, I need... more."

"Sam." His name was a caress. "I wish I had met you earlier. That would have been better."

"I can take it."

"Your skin says otherwise." Michael's touch over Sam's ass made him twist and shudder. Michael moved lower and fondled Sam's balls. "There are other things I can do to you."

The afterglow of the spanking merged with Michael's not-so-gentle hold on Sam's sac. Sam groaned into the sheets. The need pooling in his core threatened to spill out into the rest of his body.

Michael kissed him on the back. "You're glorious," he said, then climbed off the bed.

Except I only get one fucking night! That thought vanished with the click of the lube bottle. Slick, wet flesh—Michael's hand—met Sam's cock and Sam gasped. But the sweet touch wasn't there long. Sam pumped against air and wished for all the world that his hands were free, and was glad as fuck that they weren't. He didn't have the control to keep from jacking himself off. He wanted this to last.

He suspected Michael did as well.

The sound of the lube bottle opening again sent a bolt of fire through Sam. When the cool run of liquid ran down the crack between his cheeks and over his hole, the heat in his stomach and balls rose out of control, pushing him to the verge. "I'm close."

"I know," Michael said. "It's written all over your body." He dragged a finger down after the lube, and circled the muscles at Sam's entrance.

Sam's vision blurred and his balls drew up. Lightning shot through his veins. *God, not yet!* Michael hadn't even fucked him.

"Let go." Michael massaged Sam's ring, coaxing him open. That only made his need worse.

"Can't." Sam spoke through gritted teeth. He held on, trying to stave off the building pressure in his balls and in his brain. His blood was lava.

"Sam." Michael's call was strong and real, like the finger he pressed into Sam's ass. "Come for me."

Michael's command shattered Sam's control and he shot his load, groaning long and hard into the comforter. Every nerve snapped and stung with each push and pull of Michael's finger and the haze of light returned. It was almost too much and it might never be enough.

Slowly, slowly, the world returned to Sam, as did the delicious sensation of Michael still stroking fingers in and out of him. How many? Two? Three? Hard to tell. Each push burned and stretched as Michael twisted and explored. Every touch kept the edge of Sam's vision blurry and his head somewhere above his body. He hadn't thought, hadn't expected Michael to keep finger-fucking him.

"Better?" There was a vast amount of amusement in Michael's voice.

"Yeah." His body hummed and everything—the heat in his veins, the coil in his core—was less urgent. His ass stung, but not painfully so. And Michael's fingers opened him. "That feels so good."

Michael picked up the tempo, plunging in a bit harder each time—three fingers, given the way they spread Sam wide. "You're nice and relaxed now. There was no way I was going to fit inside you, as strung out as you were."

Sam moaned when Michael withdrew his fingers. Foil crinkled and more lube met Sam's ass, and then the hot head of Michael's cock pushed into him.

That wondrous sense—the slight burn of entry and then the overwhelming feeling of being stretched and split and taken—engulfed Sam. How many years since he'd last felt this with something other than a dildo? He drove his hips back to meet Michael's forward stroke. Shameless.

Michael grunted and stilled; then the binding on Sam's wrists loosened then fell away. Sam gasped at the sudden freedom, and drew his arms under him. They ached, but they also gave him the ability to press back harder on Michael's cock, take more of him in. "I want all of you."

"Fuck." Michael pulled Sam up and rocked forward, thrusting in farther and hitting Sam's prostate.

Sam shuddered in Michael's arms, hardly believing the sparks of need coming alive in his veins. He hadn't managed to come twice in a night since he'd been a horny teenager, and yet his cock rose. He met each of Michael's strokes, taking more inside each time.

When Michael's thighs and balls met Sam's ass, it was

like being hit all over again. Only this time Michael filled him, claimed him, and stroked Sam's sweetest spot.

The burn from the slapping swept over Sam and his cock tightened. "Harder. Fuck me harder."

Michael's breath warmed Sam's neck and he obliged, plowed into Sam with long, powerful thrusts. Everything fell away. All that remained was Michael, his strong arms, hard body, and his thick cock deep inside Sam, ramming him where he most wanted to be touched over and over again. Sam opened his mouth, but only a thin cry escaped.

Fire didn't burn through him this time, it was ice cracking in his veins, wrapping his core with pain and pleasure and silence. Michael closed a hand around Sam's cock and pulled. "Stay with me." Hot breath on Sam's ear. "I want you with me."

There wasn't anywhere else Sam could be. His vision clouded as Michael's thrust became more erratic and the pumping of Sam's cock more frantic. He'd finally undone Michael, this unflappable stranger. That was enough to push Sam over the edge again and he came, every nerve firing at once. Michael slammed into him and his guttural moan mirrored Sam's. They hung there, suspended in pleasure, one being with two hearts.

Then the world slipped back between them. Michael loosened his grip and pulled out of Sam.

There were no words said. Sam didn't trust himself to speak. Everything he wanted to say sounded foolish. Or desperate. *Stay the night. Don't leave. Give me your phone number. Where can I find you again? I need you.*

The best night of his life would also be the worst. Sam remained in Michael's arms and soaked up what little he could of the man's scent. He kissed Michael's arm, trying to etch the taste and texture of Michael's skin into his mind.

He knew what he wanted, what he couldn't have, what he denied himself because of his pride. He'd risen far, but only by wearing a mask and running from place to place, seeking another company to save or sell. Yet here of all places, for one glorious moment, he'd been wholly himself. Complete.

All thanks to a stranger in khaki shorts and a parrot shirt. Sam found something to say at last. "Thank you."

"The pleasure was all mine." Michael kissed his neck. "You needed that, I think."

"Yes." More than even Sam had realized.

He didn't know how long they sat there on the bed, holding and being held. Eventually, inevitably, Michael stirred against him.

Time to say good-bye.

Sam didn't protest when Michael let him go—what would be the point? He pushed down the hollow feeling in his chest when they both stood. It was just sex after all. A fling. A single night where he could finally be the man he truly was. Sam's heart tightened as if held by a fist.

Michael wrapped the used condom in some tissues and tossed it into the trash. Sam stared at the can until warm fingers lifted his chin and he found himself looking into Michael's gold-flecked eyes. Somewhere along the line, Michael had lost his shirt and taken off his glasses. He looked older and wiser without the frames blocking his face.

"Are you going to be okay?"

He didn't bother lying. "I don't have much choice, so yes."

Michael furrowed his brow. Obviously not the answer he'd been expecting.

Sam held Michael's gaze. "I'll be fine." That wasn't a lie. It would take a bit of time, but he'd manage. He had to. There was a new job waiting for him once he left Curaçao.

A new challenge. A company to rescue and money to be made. He didn't have the time to be an emotional wreck. William and the board would be watching.

Michael's expression softened. "You're an extraordinary man. You'll find someone."

Sam tried to keep the bile from his face. He had found someone. If his life had been different, he'd exchange numbers and try to see if there was more beyond extraordinary sex. But the person he was in this hotel room wasn't the person he'd be once he stepped back onto a plane. "Thanks."

Michael let go, stepped away, and started to dress. Sam didn't have to. Didn't want to—that meant slipping the mask back on. He bent to pick his clothes up off the floor and winced as the skin of his rear pulled and stung.

Right. "How bad is my ass?"

Michael's chuckle sent a shudder through Sam. "No broken skin. I made sure of that. But you'll be sore and quite bruised for a several days."

"So I'll remember you every time I sit." Sam huffed a laugh. "I'll have that, I suppose." The memories.

Flip-flops were the last item Michael donned. Sam had been right about the footwear. Parrots. Shorts. Glasses. Perfect. "I'm glad I met you."

Michael stepped forward and claimed a kiss. "Me too." Then he headed toward the door. When that closed, everything would go back to the way it had been. A sick lurching gripped Sam's heart and he couldn't breathe. There had to be some change. He needed a reminder of this night so it would remain real. "Michael!"

The call halted Michael at the door. He turned.

Sam scooped up one of the cuff links, crossed the room and pressed it into his hand. "Take it. Please."

For a moment, Michael looked as if he might protest. Instead, he nodded. "Good-bye, Sam."

"Good-bye."

Michael turned, opened the door, and left.

Sam stood in the entryway for a long time after the latch clicked, staring at the door handle. Then he shook himself and locked the hotel door.

Enough. His life was what he'd chosen it to be. He had a job to prepare for and a company to pull back from the brink of mismanagement. And one fewer cuff link.

It was the last thing that gave him the most hope.

CHAPTER TWO

MICHAEL TOOK OFF HIS GLASSES AND RUBBED HIS EYES. The numbers and letters on his screen kept blurring into each other. Sleep would have helped, but he hadn't had the time for more than three or four hours a night since he had come back.

The price of a week away from work should not be two weeks of sheer hell. But here he was. He picked up Sam's cuff link and rolled it between his fingers. Some of the stiffness between his shoulders eased. At least he had that night to remember. The taste of Sam's skin, the sound of his abandonment when he came, and the way his tight ass had milked Michael's cock—that memory kept him from going apeshit all over the office.

The problems had started on the plane when he'd turned his computer back on. Damn the in-flight wireless because e-mails had *poured* in. Not even a day after he'd left —and of course he'd been dumb enough to tell his coworkers he'd be out of contact—that asshole Vince had instigated a release of routing software for a cellular backhaul customer. As VP of Engineering, Vince had the authority to fire the guy Michael had left in charge. Frank bent to Vince's will and certified the release as tested.

They *had* tested the release before Michael left, but there had been so many problems with regression, integration, and interoperability, he'd thrown the whole lot back to development with a laundry list of bugs to fix, but Vince only ever saw testing as the bottleneck to release.

Once Michael had left for the tropics, Vince broke the bottle and let the release go out into the wild, with disastrous results. Three customers put the code into production and their networks went down. Support was swamped with angry calls 24-7. Vince blamed test for not doing their jobs and Taylor, the CEO, called a meeting and threatened to fire everyone in test—including Michael—until one of the other test engineers, Jennifer, had shut Vince and Taylor down.

God, part of him wished he had been here to see that. At five foot nothing, she'd climbed up onto a table with a fist full of e-mails and the voice of an opera singer. The truth of Vince's doings came out and that had opened the floodgates. Eventually Steve from development admitted they were still working on the bugs and that the code had huge issues.

By the time Michael had stepped off the plane in Pittsburgh, both Vince and Taylor had been sacked, the angry customers had been downgraded to the last stable release, and the board of directors was ready to hang Michael for having the audacity to go away for a week of vacation, as if the entire episode had been his fault.

He didn't even bother reminding the board if they'd left Michael as VP of Engineering and Test, the whole episode wouldn't have happened in the first place, but no, they'd demoted him after he'd been left high and dry by Rasheed and Susan.

The board had brought on Taylor and Vince over Michael's objections.

Fucking suits.

How long would he pay the price for having trusted his former friends and cofounders—and in Rasheed's case—former lover? He'd stayed, despite them selling the company out from under him. Oh, he still had some shares, but not nearly the portion he should have had as the third founder—hell, he wasn't even considered that. Just employee number three, Susan and Rasheed's first hire.

Bullshit. All of it. He should have left when Susan and Rasheed fled to California to play family, but he couldn't let what he'd worked so hard for shrivel and die and leave his team behind with no continuity, no transition. So here he was, three years later.

Michael set the cuff link down in front of his monitor. He hadn't been this angry since they'd left. *Shit.* The past was unchangeable. Focus on the now.

Wasn't much better. Today, the crappy code Vince had released was decidedly less messy but still not working correctly. Worse, the board was bringing in a new CEO to "fix" things. Like that would happen. Taylor had worked out *so* wonderfully. This time, they hadn't even asked for Michael's opinion.

Probably because the new suit would take all their hard work and turn it into a lovely pile of cash for the board. Sell the company—that's what the board members wanted—get a stable release, get some cash for the intellectual property, and get out. Never mind all the folks who'd lose their jobs and years of hard work for a pittance.

Damn, he sounded bitter. Michael scrubbed a hand over his face and put his glasses back on. Time to think about retiring. Or perhaps changing careers to something that didn't keep him up until four in the morning or give him ulcers. Fly back to Curaçao and find Sam.

Except those people he hired—the ones who trusted him—they'd still be here. And those early designs still bore his name, even if he'd been sanitized out of the official history of Four Rivers.

Sam? Sam was long gone. A memory, like everything else.

Michael's computer chimed at him.

New mail. Another meeting, this one a one-on-one with the new suit later in the afternoon.

Apparently, he was some super-amazing technical snot of a CEO who liked to get his hands dirty. He'd been scheduling meetings all morning with everyone. There was a meet-and-greet at eleven, then meetings, meetings, and more meetings.

"Yes, I'll accept the meeting request from S. Randell Anderson," he muttered at the screen, then clicked send.

He glanced at the time. Fifteen minutes until the meet-and-greet. He probably ought to head to the lunchroom now and get a seat in the back before they were all taken.

He hadn't bothered to search for info about the suit because everyone else on his team had. Undergrad in engineering at MIT, an MBA from Yale. Anderson had bailed out a dozen failing companies and turned them either into thriving businesses or sweet fruit to be plucked and devoured by a larger company. He had a good track record. Some said he was honest and fair. Others that he was ruthless and driven.

Michael snorted at that. He'd never met anyone at the executive level who didn't lie through their teeth, even the few he'd counted as friends. He suspected *ruthless and driven* were closer to the truth.

He pushed himself away from the computer and headed toward the back of the office.

The lunchroom walls and floor were dotted with primary colors like some kid's crayon box, but it was the only space in the office large enough to hold all-hands meetings. People had already claimed most of the seats in the too-bright room. Some folks, mostly marketing, sat in close to the front. Several more employees were scattered at the lunch tables. Michael joined his team against the large windows in the back of the large, echo-prone room, but didn't sit, though folding chairs had been set out from the rack that sat in the back. Instead, he leaned against the windowsill and waited, watching the door.

No sign of the new CEO or of William Vandershoot, the head of the board. They must be holed up somewhere. Maybe nursing jet lag.

Ganesh from development weaved his way through the tables to join Michael. "Hey, when this is done, can you help me with that bug you sent? I can't seem to reproduce it on my environment."

"Sure. We can run it through on my box. I know they were seeing it intermittently in the field, but I can reproduce it fairly easily."

The sounds in the room changed, became more hushed. Mike looked at the door and stopped breathing.

He knew the man following William into the room. The dark hair, the lean face, those pale eyes.

Sam. *Holy fuck.* It was Sam.

Michael leaned against the windowsill, digging the sharp edge of the marble into his back. He needed something to keep him upright because his legs weren't doing a good job.

S. Randell Anderson. Sam. The rat-sucking board had

hired *his* Sam as CEO. The fantasy-fling he'd relived dozens of times so he could forget this mess walked in behind William.

Sam's gaze met his, and for a split second, the lunchroom vanished. Sam's lips parted, as if to speak Michael's name, but he turned and offered William a professional smile, as though Michael didn't exist, as if they hadn't fucked in Curaçao.

This was not good. Michael bit his tongue and forced his heart rate back to something reasonable. He wanted to run—escape the room, find his car keys, and get the hell out of downtown.

Sam could not be his boss, not after Michael had spent a night fucking and spanking the man. No way in hell.

But there Sam was, taking the microphone from William. He tapped the top and spoke. "Good afternoon."

That silenced the rest of the lunchroom. Michael sucked in a breath. His heart still beat a mile a minute, and hearing Sam amplified didn't help. That same voice had begged Michael to take him harder.

This was so so so not good. Michael wanted that voice to beg him again. Wanted that man on his knees and that mouth wrapped around his cock.

Shit. Michael gripped the windowsill. There was nowhere to run. He could only listen.

"As you've probably guessed, my name is S. Randell Anderson. The S is for Sam, by the way." He paused and his gaze skimmed over the crowd, lingering briefly on Michael. "That's the first question everyone asks."

A flutter of laughter.

Sam smiled. "You can call me Randell or Sam or Randy or You Fucking Jerk. I don't particularly care, as long as you're willing to work with me." Another pause, and the smile faded into that same intense smoky look Sam had held in the bar. "And I do mean work, because the next several months are going to consume you and me. I apologize in advance to your families and friends for that, but you all know why I'm here."

No laughter now.

Sam glanced around the room. "Four Rivers Networks is in dire straits. That half-baked release that went out into the field did more to kill your reputation than a string of low sales quarters. If something isn't done, by this time next year, this office won't exist."

The murmurs returned and Sam held up his hand. "I'm not going to lie to you and tell you everything will be okay and if we're all one happy corporate family, sunshine and rainbows will cover the building with gold and money will fart out our asses." He leaned into the microphone and his voice boomed. "Not going to happen."

A deathly silence hung over the lunchroom, broken only by the sound of Sam's shoes as he walked back and forth in front of them. "However, I wouldn't be here if there were no hope, no way of turning things around. The first task I want everyone in this room focused on for the next month is to put out the quality release that should have gone out to our customers. I know you can do it because you've done it before. That will go quite some way toward regaining your reputation as a builder of world-class networking software and equipment."

Michael's brain swam and the garish colors of the room made him nauseous. This couldn't be happening. If Sam were a CEO, then Michael was sure as shit he wasn't openly gay. Someone in his team would have mentioned that, so Sam was another fucking Rasheed.

A woman at one of the tables raised her hand, catching Sam's attention. "And what are you going to do?"

"That's a good question." He pointed to the table. "What's your name?"

"Metap."

Good for Metap. Jennifer sat next to her and together they were a force to be reckoned with. Someone had to challenge Sam. He fucking couldn't at the moment.

"Metap," Sam repeated. "I'm going to smooth over a ton of ruffled customer feathers and try to make sure they don't cancel contracts. I'm going to work with your managers to get you all what you need to get the job done, and I'm going to be the wall between you and the idiot directors who don't know how much effort it takes to put out the highly complex product you do." Sam looked over his shoulder at William. "No offense."

That gained Sam a few chuckles but William looked pained.

Sam worked the room like a pro. Said all the right things. Begrudgingly, Michael had to give the man credit. Sam-the-CEO didn't sound like your average suit—he wasn't coating it with sugar then flinging poo at them. Maybe... this CEO might work out after all. His cynical side scoffed at the thought. The same board had demoted Michael, despite his role in starting the company. They'd hired Taylor and Vince. He couldn't trust anything the board did.

But there was Sam, in the front of the room and a deep part of Michael wanted to trust him.

Because Sam had trusted Michael. Surrendered to him. Had come for him.

There was that light-headedness again. How the hell were they supposed to work together? All Michael wanted to do was pull Sam out of the room, find somewhere private, and kiss the man. Or fuck. Or tan his ass. God, to feel that mouth again, taste his skin, hear him beg for more and more.

He wasn't supposed to like the CEO. He certainly wasn't supposed to lust after the man. And after dating—and hiding that he was dating—Rasheed, he wasn't about to march down that path to disaster again.

Sam took several questions, but Michael didn't hear them over the thumping of blood in his head. He studied the way Sam's lips moved, how his fingers held the mic, the way the curve of his smile crinkled the lines near his eyes. Every time their gazes met, Michael felt the same burn of desire he had felt in Curaçao, to strip the suit off and master the man underneath.

Sam. His brand-new CEO.

***

SAM'S FINGERS SHOOK AS HE TOYED WITH HIS ONE remaining Copernican universe cuff link. He'd bought the pair the first time he'd made enough money to afford something utterly frivolous and expensive, and chosen the design to remind himself that he was not the center of the universe despite his status and success.

So many of his colleagues had succumbed to thinking that the world revolved around them, that they were there to lead the little people and whip them into doing what they should, never realizing that the so-called little people were the ones who inspired and innovated and motivated. Those CEOs acted as if every invention had sprung fully formed from their skulls.

Four Rivers Networks was a fine example of that. The board might have hired Sam, but he worked for the employees. These folks here had been royally screwed over by an incompetent and near-criminal CEO and had suffered under an egomaniacal VP of Engineering. Every one of them deserved better. It was a wonder they hadn't all packed up and moved on to one of the larger high-tech companies in Pittsburgh or left town altogether like the Four Rivers founders had.

When he'd asked the engineers why they hadn't jumped ship, they'd pointed toward the one person they loved working with and for, the man who'd kept those two idiots in check for the last three years, the person who motivated a small team of engineers to create a product that scared the pants off larger routing companies.

Mike Sebastian. Sam stared at his cuff link. Michael.

The same man who'd lovingly bound Sam's hands with his own damn tie, spanked his ass, then fucked him until he couldn't see straight.

Lead Test Engineer at Four Rivers Networks.

According to what Sam had learned from the board, Mike had been the first person the founders of Four Rivers had hired after they'd formed the company, and he'd remained on after those two had abandoned the company for greener pastures. The engineers, hell, even the marketing folks who worked directly with Michael praised his intelligence and tenacity.

The rational part of Sam's mind—the business side—shrugged. It made sense. Michael had willpower and determination, but was also considerate and kind. His résumé was impressive—he'd been the VP of Engineering and Testing early on and several of the patent applications had his name on them. That he hadn't left when the board had restructured him out of power spoke of a loyalty to the people at Four Rivers and to the engineering—something rarely seen in business today. In the same situation, Sam doubted he'd have stayed. It had been a crap move by the board, one to consolidate power with people they trusted.

Idiots. The troubles with Taylor and the failed release wouldn't have happened if they'd left Michael as a VP, Sam was sure of that.

Obviously, the board didn't trust Michael, probably because he had too much power in the early days. But everyone else did. That said quite a bit about Michael.

Had Sam been in a better state, he might have dug deeper into why there was such a discrepancy between the board and the guys in the trenches, but his emotions—well, he'd boxed those up tight and shipped them off to some foreign country the moment he'd spotted Michael. He could not afford to become a blathering idiot in front of a roomful of employees. He hadn't. But it had been a near thing—much closer than he wanted to admit.

Why did *Michael* have to be *here*?

Ever since Curaçao, all of the daydreams he'd jacked off to in what passed for a home these days—they were all of Michael. They varied from simple lovemaking—Michael fucking him slowly in bed—to kinky—Michael in leather, whipping him on a rack. Those fantasies were *safe*. He could indulge in his desires without anyone ever knowing he liked being bent over and claimed.

Michael had done exactly that. Hell, Sam had begged for Michael. Moaned for the man. Tasted his cock.

Sam set down the cuff link, fingers shaking far more than he liked. His body ached and had from the instant he'd seen Michael's shocked face in the crowd. In all his reunion fantasies, he'd imagined Michael's cool exterior slipping away. None of those equaled the impact of seeing it for real. Michael still wanted him.

If only they had met again for any other reason than *this*.

Michael knew Sam was gay—in a carnal and visceral way that both frightened Sam and hardened his cock. Coworker. A direct report. An employee. The *last* person in the world Sam could take to bed. Or beg to be taken to bed.

Not that Sam would take that chance, not with William hanging around. If only he'd go back to California —but no. He'd taken an interest, damn it. These early days were critical—either the employees would trust Sam, or he'd have to raise the asshole-CEO level a notch. He'd rather not do that, but it would take focus and careful maneuvering. The right words paired with the right actions.

He'd never been so unfocused and wrecked on his first day as he was now.

Worse, he had an inkling of why Michael had been so eager to fuck him that night. The desire to control, yes, lots of men had those needs, but how much had been about the desire to screw the boss, at least figuratively? There was no way Michael could have known who Sam was. No last names. No titles. One night.

At least Michael wouldn't be running to the board to scream "gay." Not that they would do anything but fire him. Not even William would stalk a man down a dark alley— the man was all bluster. Sam's secret was safe for the time being.

He exhaled. God, what a mess.

His computer dinged almost at the same time a knock sounded on his door. The rapping stole his breath and increased the beating of his heart.

Punctual. Of course he would be. Sam took three calming breaths that did nothing and spoke. "Come in."

The door opened and Michael walked in. He pushed the door shut and leaned back against it.

He wore khakis, but slacks this time, matched with a sedate dark purple polo. Once more, Sam couldn't see Michael's feet, but he guessed boat shoes, no socks. Same brown eyes, same glasses, and an expression Sam couldn't read because it kept changing.

Heat prickled along Sam's arms and legs and the ache in his bones turned into fire. "Michael."

"Holy fuck, Sam." Michael didn't move.

"I guess you didn't bother to look up anything about your new CEO?" He could play this part. The businessman. The emotionless boss.

Michael pushed himself off the door. "No. They're all the same."

"How so?"

Michael didn't look away. "They're all suits."

A hollow, yawning pit formed in Sam's stomach. He covered by shrugging. "I'm a suit."

Michael crossed to the desk and folded himself into the guest chair. "That's the problem." He leaned forward and gripped the edge of Sam's desk. "Did you know that I worked here?"

"No. When I came back to the States, they told me that the recent problems had started when Mike, the testing guy, went on vacation. But I never thought—never suspected— you were *that* Mike." He would make it through this meeting without cracking the mask. He had to. "It's a fairly common name."

Michael leaned back in the chair, his lips twisted into a smirk that wrenched Sam's stomach into knots even as a tingle traced up his spine. "Well, that's a convenient explanation."

"Believe me, had I known, I wouldn't have let you buy me that drink."

The smirk faded into puzzlement and Sam could breathe again.

"I was going to replace Taylor as CEO before the blowup. There were deeper issues with him." Like Taylor dabbling in shady stock practices that could have dropped the Feds on Four Rivers and sunk the company.

"They didn't tell us that."

"No. There wasn't much point. Critical issues first, everything else can wait." The rest would come out, once a case had been built, if the board decided to pursue.

Michael frowned. "The board met in Florida. The week I was away."

Sam quelled the sudden desire to squirm in his seat. "Yes." He paused. "Yes, I was there. I told you."

Michael's expression shifted—probably remembering—then snapped back into focus. "Why were you in Curaçao?"

He spoke through a very dry mouth. "To celebrate."

A tremor ran through Michael. "You were my boss when we fucked?" His elegant fingers tightened around the arms of the guest chair.

"No. Not officially." Sam leaned back, glad that the leather of his chair was cool against his dress shirt, because his skin certainly wasn't. "Look, neither of us knew. We were strangers in a bar." It was a mere technicality, if anyone ever discovered the truth, but he clung to it as hard as he held on to the image of Michael from Curaçao rather than the half-angry, half-horrified Michael that sat before him now. He hoped he wasn't shaking, because he couldn't tell. His nerves were on fire.

"Ships in the night." Michael shook his head. "Not anymore."

"No, not anymore." Sam glanced at the cuff link still sitting on his desk. The next question might ruin all the memories Sam had of Michael before today. "Can you leave what happened in Curaçao behind?" Because it could never come out. If the board even got a whiff of that, Sam would be out on the street. Hell, Michael too, probably.

Michael's white-knuckled grip on the chair answered the question quite clearly.

Both the cold drip of fear and the warmth of elation ran through Sam. That night *had* meant something to Michael, then. Sam hadn't just been a suit to fuck and leave behind.

Though, Sam really had no place to be smug about it, not when his pulse beat at marathon rate and with his cock semi-hard. That night had been in the forefront of his mind for two weeks. He could not succumb to the emotions Michael had churned up, but it was much too late for that.

Next question. "How much do you care about your colleagues?" Quite a bit, given what Sam knew of Michael's past. Still, he wanted Michael's answer.

Color rose into Michael's face. "What the hell kind of question is that?

"An important one." He spoke the words with the same intensity imbedded in Michael's response. "I've talked to your coworkers and everyone points to you as the person who makes this company tick. Whether you know it or not" —he paused and studied Michael's hard face—"you're the linchpin that holds this mess together."

Michael didn't move for several seconds. Then he sighed and seemed to sink deeper into the chair. "Please don't tell me that."

"Look, I know what you've been through—"

Michael's reply lashed like a whip. "No, you don't. Don't even think that you do."

Sam caught his breath. His arms shook. *Fuck*. Dead silence between them.

Michael spoke again, softer this time. "There's a difference between reading what's on paper and actually living through the time."

"Of course." Sam's cheeks burned. More to the story, obviously. He wasn't about to pry now. "Regardless, you're passionate about all you do."

He'd felt that in Curaçao, long and hard.

A thin smile appeared on Michael's lips before vanishing. "What we've built here. It's good technology. Good code. And the people here—" He straightened. "They're great folks, Sam. Wickedly smart. We've done more with a handful of people than all the big boys have in the same amount of time. They deserve better than what they've had."

"That's a large part of the reason I'm here." He'd seen their equipment at a client site and watched the larger companies try to break it. Rock-solid code... until three weeks ago.

"No." Michael coughed a bitter laugh. "You're here to sell us out. To make some fast cash."

More heat crept up Sam's neck. There was truth to Michael's accusation; the board did want to sell the company. The bonus Sam would get if they managed that was quite nice. But he wasn't here just to make money—that was never the reason he stepped into a company like Four Rivers. He lowered his voice, but not his intensity. "I want to see that the right things are done."

"And what right things would those be?" Michael didn't move, but his dark gaze pinned Sam against the chair and sent a bolt of heat to his balls. "Fire staff? Push us to our limits before handing over our IP?"

Sam resisted the urge to fidget under Michael's scrutiny. He leaned forward, taking control. "Not if I have my way." He let that sink in. "The board wants out. They'd gladly sell the intellectual property and fire everyone if they could, if it wouldn't be such a bad PR move. I'm here to prevent that."

Michael continued his study of Sam. "And what do you want to happen?"

Sam hoped he hid the shudder that ran down his spine. What he wanted was to be stripped of his clothes, Michael's lips on his and Michael inside him again. That wasn't even an option. God. His legs shook. "I want this company—and the people here—to be acquired. Not just Four Rivers' IP, but all the talent as well." He paused. "That's the only route to survival."

"Is that even possible after"—Michael's face twisted— "the debacle we just went through?"

"It's a hell of a lot harder now than it was a month ago. But I think we can still manage it, as long as we can fix the damage done. Show them that we can turn things around, that the people here are as good as you say."

Michael frowned. "Show who?"

Sam froze. Damn, the man was perceptive. "I can't say."

"Can't or won't?" Hard words.

"Does it make a difference?" His response was soft, but equally unyielding. He might be submissive in bed, but the hell he would be in his own office.

Michael sighed, and finally looked away. "Not particularly, I suppose."

"Are you willing to work with me, Michael?"

A genuine smile graced Michael's face, one that sent electricity down every nerve. "Call me Mike. At least at work."

"Mike." There would be no calling him anything after

work, no matter how much Sam wanted the man. One night had to remain just that. Too much to risk losing.

"What about you? Are you willing to listen to me?" Michael scooted to the edge of the chair, inching closer. "Or will you throw me under the bus when things don't go smoothly? When my team finds issues? When I contradict you?"

Sam's chest ached. So, back to being a suit. Fine. "I don't punish people for doing their jobs. What kind of asshole do you think I am?" That came out far stronger than he'd intended.

But the shock on Michael's face was priceless.

Sam softened his voice. "I've an open-door policy. I'm always willing to listen, and I do actually act on what I hear."

"You don't know how many times I've heard about an open-door policy, that the CEO wants straight talk."

"I mean it." Whether Michael believed or not. "I believe in honesty." He ignored the voice in his mind that whispered about hypocrisy.

"I'm sure you do," Michael said, his voice low, almost sensual. He reached across the desk and plucked the cuff link off the surface. "Just like you want me to forget Curaçao."

It was as if all the air in the room vanished. Sam's chest tightened, and he focused entirely on the shining piece of metal Michael rolled between his fingers.

"And I wonder," Michael said, "can you leave that night behind?"

The proof that he couldn't danced between Michael's fingertips. Sam's ass burned for Michael's hand and his cock was full and stiff. He swallowed, though his throat was desert-dry, unlike his back. That was slick with perspiration, enough so that he'd have to wear his jacket to hide the wetness if he left his office anytime soon. Any ground he'd gained in this tête-à-tête, he'd lost in an instant. It must have showed.

"I thought as much." Michael set the cuff link down on the desk. "So how do we navigate around it?"

Sam found his voice, though it cracked like autumn leaves. "Professional decorum." He cleared his throat. "What happened in Curaçao—"

"Stays there?"

"Yes. It has to." The salt of Michael's skin, the velvet touch of his lips, the rough sound of his breath when he came... all that had to remain a memory. It certainly had no place here at the office in Pittsburgh. "Anything else would be breaking more corporate policies than I care to count." And would unveil far too much about Sam to everyone around him.

"I can handle that." Sam couldn't tell if that was conviction in Michael's voice or the knowledge of a lie well told. It too closely mirrored his own voice, his own lies.

Michael stood, and once more, Sam realized just how tall Michael was. "I'm going to hold you to listening, though. And protecting these folks." He waved at the door.

Sam rose, his legs surprisingly steady. "I'd expect nothing less. I'm glad to have you on board."

Michael chuffed a laugh. "Let's see what you say after a couple of manager meetings."

Sam rounded the desk and walked toward the door. "I may surprise you."

"You already have." Michael's voice took on that smoky quality that sank into Sam's ears and straight to his balls. Sam couldn't help looking up into Michael's face and the amusement that danced there.

Sam held out his hand and Michael took it, his grip firm and his hand warm. Every second they touched, Sam wanted to fall to his knees, unzip those khakis, and go to heaven. Or hell. Everything about Michael turned him inside out. Michael knew the true Sam. Everything he tried to hide.

They let go at the same time.

"Well," Michael said. "This is going to be interesting."

Sam croaked a chuckle. He reached for the door handle and opened the door slightly. "We'll make it work." There was no other option.

Michael looked down, but his continued amusement was almost catching. Sam followed his gaze.

Sam had been right. Boat shoes without socks. *And I know you.* His skin tingled.

"Thank you for the straight talk," Michael said.

"Anytime."

Michael glanced up, then turned and left Sam's office.

Sam closed the door with care, then leaned his forehead against the wood. Interesting wasn't even close to the right word. Having Michael near and not touching him—not begging Michael to touch him—would be sheer hell.

Sam pushed himself away from the door and returned to his desk. He'd deal with all of that later. Right now, he had to get ready for another meeting.

If only his hands would stop shaking. He curled them into fists and shoved thoughts of Michael aside. He couldn't let one single fuck, a quick fling, get the best of him.

Even if it had been the best night of his life.

CHAPTER THREE

Michael strode along the North Shore Trail, past PNC Park, and toward the Fort Duquesne Bridge and wiped away the sweat that threatened to trickle into his eyes. The weather was unseasonably warm for early May, but he wasn't about to complain, even if he had to break out shorts for his afternoon walk.

The office building had a gym with showers, but nothing beat being outside, tromping pavement, climbing steps, and crossing bridges. Quite a workout, if you walked at a decent rate, plus sun, city, nature, and a bunch of other office dwellers outside getting healthy. Walkers, runners, bikers—everyone flocked to the trails when the weather turned nice.

A sunny day in Pittsburgh? You savored those like fine wine.

Plus, he needed out of the office and away from Sam, at least for a bit.

Sam had been fine as CEO so far, winning over the engineering staff in the last couple of weeks. His business sense seemed spot-on and he understood much of the technical aspects as well. The man could even code, though Sam admitted he was horribly rusty. Yes, he was hard-nosed and pushing everyone to meet deadlines, but he was also often the first person in the office and one of the last to leave. Sam practiced what he preached.

The office followed Sam's lead, plunging into a working pace Michael hadn't seen since the early days.

Sam wasn't the usual type of CEO, and not simply a suit. Michael reluctantly agreed that the board had done something right for a change. Sam wasn't the board's pawn, and they seemed to be letting him work toward their mutual goal of acquisition.

Michael and Sam had even managed an easy business relationship, on the surface.

Underneath, Michael still undressed Sam in his mind and fantasized about bending that taut body over the executive conference room table and fucking him until they both came. Leave Curaçao behind? Hardly. He relived that night far too many times. Only it wasn't the thrill of undoing a man of power anymore—it was all about the Sam he knew now.

How easy it would be, too. A whisper, a suggestion, he could have Sam on his knees. He'd caught Sam watching him when no one else was looking, the subtle flush and the shifting of his suit coat to hide a larger-than-normal bulge in his trousers.

No, Sam hadn't put aside their time together either. The desire was there, burning as hot as ever.

Michael picked up the pace of his walk, passed under the Fort Duquesne Bridge, and then headed up the stairs to the walking bridge over the Allegheny.

The worst part was that Michael *liked* Sam. The more time he spent with Sam, the more he wanted to spend with him, and not just in a state of undress. Sam liked Marvel flicks, shot pool, enjoyed fishing, and even ate his catch. He'd mentioned wanting to rent a kayak from the place under the Roberto Clemente Bridge and paddle up the Allegheny to see the shore from the water. Sam had even suggested a company-sponsored night at PNC Park in the summer for one of the Pirates' fireworks nights.

Those were all things Michael wanted to do. Heck, they'd even talked about their mutual desire to bike down to DC along the Great Allegheny Passage.

Unfortunately, Michael's lust was also still present and as potent as ever. Certainly they had sexual chemistry, but what that hell did he do with a budding friendship on top of all that? He couldn't *date* his own damn CEO any more than he could bend Sam over a chair and whack his ass in the middle of the office.

He didn't even know whether Sam was openly gay. There was nothing—*nothing*—that Sam did or said that pointed to being out. But there wasn't much that pointed to him being in the closet, either. They didn't discuss family or relationships, which was probably just as well, since Michael had a piss-poor history with other men, anyway. They either wanted Michael to control every aspect of their lives, or they were like Rasheed—deathly afraid of being gay.

Sam was a little too domineering to want the former. The latter—he could see Sam in the closet, easily. After all, the man had flown to Curaçao to be fucked when there were plenty of gay bars in Miami.

Michael crested the short set of stairs to the walking bridge and pushed his pace faster, climbing the slight bow toward the center of the bridge. He wanted to run, stretch his body to the limit to burn off some of his energy, but the brace on his knee reminded him just how foolish that would be.

Even as a friend, he couldn't go out to dinner with Sam. Too much had passed between them that night in the tropics. Michael looked out at the confluence of the Allegheny and Monongahela Rivers and at the huge plume of water from the fountain at the Point. Too much water under a bridge.

The water under this bridge was blue-green, reflecting the clear sky. Cars and trucks whooshed past nearby, separated from the footbridge by a strong wire fence and the coils of yellow-painted steel cable that ran from the deck to the arch above. Bikers, runners, and fellow walkers passed in the other direction, but the noise of the traffic on the main bridge blotted out most of the quieter sounds. Like the footfalls of a runner coming from behind and stopping right next to him.

One moment he was alone; the next, Sam walked beside him, breathing hard through a smile that was as cheerful as the weather. "Great day, huh?"

Michael skittered to the right slightly and glanced over. Then took a second look. God.

Sam wore running shorts and a loose tank that let Michael see far too much of his body. Wet with sweat, Sam's skin glistened in the sunlight. Heat ran down Michael's spine and the pounding of his heart had nothing to do with the quick pace of his walk. Sam looked like a freaking cover model. "Yeah. Unusual for this time of year."

That grin didn't disappear. "Did I startle you?"

"A bit."

"Sorry." The amusement in Sam's voice said the opposite.

Michael couldn't help chuckling.

They walked in silence the rest of the way across the bridge. Once away from the sound of traffic, Michael stole another look at Sam's long body, his powerful legs, and tight ass.

Jesus. Get a grip. Stop checking out your boss.

"Did you injure you knee?" Sam gestured at the brace on Michael's left leg.

"Back in college. Tore it up real bad playing soccer. Surgery and everything." That had been a painful nine months of his life.

"You need it for walking? I don't remember it from... before."

He ignored the second sentence. "Only wear it for strenuous exercise. Walking fast, tennis, biking. Helps keep the knee happy." Michael watched Sam, but with Sam's eyes behind mirrored sunglasses, Michael couldn't tell where he was looking. "I can't run anymore."

Sam frowned. "Well, that sucks. Do you miss it?"

"God, yes. Walking's good. But it doesn't clear the mind quite like a run." Well, there was one other thing that did. But he was *not* going to think about sex while walking next to Sam.

"Now that's the truth," Sam said. "There are very few things that relax me as well as running."

"Is that why you're out here?" Michael said. "To de-stress?" He'd seen William—fresh in from the West Coast and grumpy as all hell—stalking into Sam's office this morning. That man was poison.

Sam's frown deepened. "Please tell me my stress level is not that obvious."

"I don't think so. Not to others."

This time Michael knew Sam regarded him from behind the sunglasses. A warmth that had nothing to do with exercise or the weather settled deep in Michael's core. They walked down the path from the bridge to the river trail in silence.

It was Sam who spoke first, his voice much softer than before. "But it's obvious to you."

Very obvious. The tension in Sam's shoulders, the way he tapped his foot a mile a minute during meetings, clicking the end of his pen against his leg. Little things that few would notice. Unless, of course, they watched Sam closely and frequently. Michael pressed his lips together.

Sam chuckled, but it was bitter. "Of course it is." After they walked a few more feet, he spoke again. "I wish you could do something about that."

Michael focused on the pavement in front of them. It kept him both from tripping on the uneven concrete near the bridge pylons and from seeing Sam's expression. "You want me to stop noticing, or—"

"Or."

That single word unleashed a storm of energy down Michael's arms and legs to his fingers and toes. Other areas, as well. *Keep walking.* It was tricky to ignore his growing erection and hoped it wasn't too apparent to those passing by on the trail. One of the best memories of Curaçao was of Sam relaxing under his hands, his slaps, his cock, the way the tension eased from that beautiful, willing body.

Sam spoke again. "I know. I shouldn't mention it. But running doesn't always cut it, and you—" He broke off and muttered something that sounded like a curse.

They neared the Andy Warhol Bridge. The nook behind the pylon was hidden from the trail. Sure, it was exposed to the 10th Street Bypass, but cars whizzed by so fast, and what were the chances people in them would be coworkers? He could pull Sam back there and—what? Kiss him? Bite him? Cop a feel? No fucking way. "You keep this up, you're going to need to take another run." And Michael would have to spend the rest of the afternoon walking around and around the city.

"Wouldn't work. Not when it comes to you."

Shit, shit, shit. They were not having this conversation. "You're the one who told me to leave Curaçao behind. What the fuck are you doing, Sam?" Every nerve in Michael's body sang.

Sam pushed the sunglasses up into his hair, revealing eyes that were far too harried and a little too wide. "I *asked* you if you could leave it behind. I didn't tell you."

Closeted or not, Sam was nothing like Rasheed—his ex would never have propositioned Michael in the middle of the day. Or any other time, really. Desire threatened to steal all of Michael's breath. This meeting wasn't an accident, he'd lay odds on that. "We agreed on professionalism." He attempted to keep his voice cold and distant. "Anything more would be unethical."

Those proud shoulders straightened. "I'm aware of that."

"Are you even out?"

Sam made a choking sound. "I've been."

And that could mean anything. Either that Sam was out now, or he'd been out before and lurked in the closet now. Michael pulled in air through clenched teeth. Dealing with the fallout from Rasheed had been a nightmare. He kept walking.

"Look, I'm not asking you for anything." Sam's hands were balled into fists and his whole body seemed as tense as a band about ready to snap. It was amazing he could still move.

They passed the tempting nook under the bridge and

continued toward the convention center. Michael lowered his voice. "No. You're begging."

Sam stopped walking. Michael took another stride, then halted as well. He turned—not completely—but enough to see Sam's anger, and beneath that, his hope. They stood for a moment, watching each other before Sam spoke, matching Michael's tone. "I suppose I am."

Fucking hell. Michael's blood might as well have been on fire. They could not remain like this, stretched and fraying like old thread. One of them was going to break, and then where would the company be? Sam, at least, needed a level head if they were to make it through to acquisition. They could always find another person to head up test. Maybe this time, he'd be the one to run away.

Or stay and pick up the pieces again.

Regardless, if they were doomed to fall—and it sure as hell looked like it—he might as well make it a controlled descent. Especially since focusing Sam, beating and fucking away the stress in his trembling body in Curaçao, had gotten Michael off like nothing else. And now he knew what Sam needed. Could be more creative.

Michael's heart lodged itself in his throat. "Follow me." He turned and resumed his walk. He didn't stop when he reached the convention center, but turned up the tunnel walkway that wound through a water feature and away from the river. Sam still hadn't caught up. He might not. That would be for the best for the both of them, in all honesty.

Intellectually, he hoped Sam had made the correct choice. Shredding the rules, their professionalism was fraught with danger. Better to leave each other alone.

Joy ripped through Michael when Sam appeared at his side at the corner of Penn and Tenth. Relief, too—and that told Michael something he didn't want to hear, so he pushed it aside. Sam said nothing and his sunglasses hid his eyes again, but his hands were relaxed and a faint smile graced his lips.

Even when Michael entered the office building and headed to the gym, Sam did not speak. In the empty locker room, a silence full of tension and anticipation pulled a different kind of cord between them.

"Here?" Sam murmured the word. He stopped near a locker but didn't reach for the lock.

Michael unlocked his locker, fished a towel out of his gym bag, threw it over the bench, and peeled his damp t-shirt from his body. "The sound of the showers hides a multitude of sins."

Sam made a noise that was halfway between a grunt and an inhale. "Jesus. You're serious."

Michael kicked off his shoes, removed his socks, then slipped free of his shorts and underwear. He let Sam drink in the view of his erection before wrapping a towel around his hips. "You have a choice. Either get naked and into a shower, or tell me you've changed your mind and never bring this up again."

Sam folded his sunglasses and set them down on the bench.

Michael held Sam's gaze. Last chance. Either push this over the edge or walk away.

They stood on the precipice until Sam kicked his shoes off. His socks followed, and then his shirt. Michael exhaled a breath he hadn't even known he'd been holding.

Sam hooked his fingers around the waistband of his shorts and underwear and pushed them down in a long, slow motion that exposed the smooth skin of his hips and the ever-widening trail of hair to his dick. It took forever for the cloth to travel over the bulge of Sam's erection and fall to the floor.

The little tease. "You do realize a coworker could walk in here, don't you?" Michael said.

A wide and wicked smile answered that question. "Isn't that half the fun?" He turned away and headed—without a towel—toward the showers.

An exhibitionist? Michael slipped his hand between the edges of the towel around his hips and ran his thumb over the head of his cock before stroking it a few times. Oh, the possibilities there. Except Sam—

Sam should have been off-limits. Michael closed his eyes and let the warmth of his arousal and the tug of his hand on his cock wash over him, tighten his skin, and strengthen his resolve. What the hell was he doing? He wasn't this reckless. In the past he'd wanted to be, would have loved to slip in a kiss with Rasheed while at work, but that never happened. This—was a bit much, even for him.

Then again, Michael had never wanted any man more than he wanted Sam. Every part of Michael's body cried out to give Sam what he wanted—and to claim his Sam again.

The gym bag—his work gym bag—lacked condoms and lube. Because you didn't fuck your CEO while at the office. Every inch of his skin tingled as he pulled his belt out of the locker and the bottle of body wash from his bag. Sam enjoyed a bit of pain, and there were other options for pleasure.

Running water echoed in the locker room, creating a blanket of sound over the utter silence of the space. Would it be enough if someone walked in? With any luck, they wouldn't need to find out.

Michael followed the noise to the farthest shower in the

bank and pushed aside the curtain, rattling the rings on the bar. Under a stream of water, surrounded by steam, Sam stood, leisurely tugging at his dick. His eyes were closed but he had a shit-eating grin on his face. Of course he did. He'd won, the master manipulator that he was.

Michael flicked the nonbuckle end of his belt against Sam's thigh with enough force to get his attention.

Sam flinched backward and gasped, his expression a beautiful mix of shock, pain, and lust. He wasn't masturbating anymore. Instead, his hands were pressed against the tile of the wall he leaned back against.

A red mark rose on Sam's thigh. Lovely. "If you want to jack off, you can do that on your own time." Michael stepped into the stall and pulled the curtain closed before unwrapping his towel from his waist. He threw that over the curtain rod.

"Sorry." The focus of Sam's attention slipped down Michael's body, then back up. "Can I suck your dick?" Sam was barely audible underneath the rush of water against tile. "As an apology?" The grin returned.

Like hell Sam would dictate any of this. "No." Michael set down the body wash and looped the belt over his shoulder then crossed to Sam. The scalding water stung Michael's skin as he entered the stream, but he ignored the shock, grasped Sam's arms, and crushed his lips against Sam's.

Sam groaned and opened to Michael, his chest grinding against Michael's. With his tongue, Michael thrust inside, claiming Sam's mouth for his own, roughly exploring every part. He slid his hands down to Sam's waist and pulled their bodies tight until thighs and cocks pressed together.

Sam shuddered against Michael, all sinew and stress, and kissed back as if they were at war.

Maybe they were. This situation was rash. Wrong. Michael broke off and opened up some space between their wet bodies. He tasted Sam with each bitter swallow.

Breathless, his cheeks red from more than the hot water, Sam gripped Michael's arms before he could pull away any farther. "I know what's going through your mind. Boss. Employee. Everything we said we wouldn't do. But I can't *think* right now. The board is breathing down my neck, engineering is whining about timetables, and I have a stack of shit to do, only I— Michael, please, please make the world vanish for a while. I need—" Sam gulped in a breath. "I need you."

Michael's own desire—to calm and focus Sam—voiced from Sam's own mouth. *Shit.* That didn't change who they were—the roles they played outside the shower. "I'm a piss-poor therapist." As Michael loosened his grip, Sam tightened his.

"I don't need to talk. I need a good fuck." He dipped his head and took Michael's nipple in his mouth.

The nip of teeth and the teasing of Sam's tongue on that sensitive nub sent a bolt like lightning straight down Michael's spine. Every inch of his body tingled and his cock tightened. Want coiled tight in his belly and all thoughts of leaving the shower fled. "You need your ass tanned."

Sam chuckled and let up. "That's part of my definition of a good fuck."

Of course it was. Michael hooked a foot around Sam's leg and pulled him off balance enough to spin him and press him up against the wall of the shower. He spoke into Sam's ear. "Hands on the wall. Don't move."

Sam obeyed, his breathing heavy and his body shivering against Michael's despite the warmth of the water.

Michael kissed the nape of Sam's neck and stepped back.

From beyond the shower curtain, a locker slammed closed. Michael's heart ticked up a notch and he took the belt off of his shoulder. His aching balls pulled tighter and desire snaked deeper into Michael's center. To strap Sam with someone else in the room? That was pushing the very edge, for both of them.

He folded the belt in two and let the wet leather dangle down. Sam hadn't moved, hadn't flinched at the sound from the locker room. How much higher would it drive Sam to know someone else might be listening? How much did Sam want to be overheard?

If Sam was in the closet, how much did he want to be shoved out of it?

Michael's skin burned like fire. He lifted the belt and laid a blow against Sam's right ass cheek.

Sam flinched and gasped, and a thick red line appeared on his skin.

Silence from beyond the curtain. Either the person had left... or they hadn't. Blood pounded in Michael's ears as he strained to hear over the water. His fingers and toes tingled from too much need. It wouldn't take much to make him come.

"Green." Sam's breathless whisper. "Please."

So, Sam remembered his colors from Curaçao. Heat raced up Michael's arms and legs and his reply was just as soft. "That's not begging." Before Sam could say anything else, Michael laid the belt three more times against Sam's ass in rapid succession. Left. Right. Left. Wet leather cracked against wet flesh.

Sam writhed against the wall, his breathing labored.

If there were any other sounds coming from the locker

room, Michael couldn't hear them, not over the rushing of his own blood, the sound of the water, and Sam's whispered words. "More, please."

God, yes. The world dropped away to just running water and Sam's shining body sliding against the tile wall trembling with pain and need. Sexy as hell, and all Michael's doing.

This time, Michael started slower and softer, alternating sides of Sam's ass, bringing up the speed and sharpness as Sam tried not to move with each blow. Stripes of red layered over the pale flesh of Sam's cheeks until there was nothing but various shades of red that edged toward purple. Sam arched against the wall, his mouth open in a silent cry.

Michael held back his own moan. The shock up his arm when the belt met Sam's skin, the slap, Sam's breathless noises of agony and delight—it was nearly too much. The desire in Michael's core twisted like Sam's body. It wouldn't take much to come. A few strokes of a hand. Or the velvet touch of Sam's tongue.

That thought alone nearly pushed him over the edge. His balls tightened.

Michael whipped the belt four more times, hard and fast—striking the last blow across both cheeks at once.

Sam's short cry echoed around the shower and his legs buckled.

Michael dropped the belt, caught Sam, and turned his quivering body around. Michael caressed Sam's back and brushed fingers over the abused flesh of his ass. Pressing his lips against Sam's neck kept words from spilling out of Michael. *Let me take you to dinner. I want to hold you all night long. Be mine.* Impossible, wonderful things. He wanted to be this for Sam—master him when he needed it, clear his head, then give him his control back.

God, Sam was everything he'd ever wanted, everything no other lover had been. Rasheed hadn't even been able to stand a nipple pinch, let alone a strapping.

Sam's face was a beautiful mess of lust, pain, and adoration. "God, that was—" His voice was as rough as the rattling of water against the tile. "I can't even begin to describe—"

Michael stopped the rest of Sam's words with his mouth. Maybe Sam wanted the same things he did. Maybe he didn't. But they could not be like this—CEO and employee—for much longer. Michael couldn't quit, not yet. Later, once everyone at Four Rivers was safe—or as safe as they could be in this industry. He owed that to them, owed it to himself to be there at the end.

And if the only thing Sam saw in Michael was a quick fix of endorphins, a fun way to de-stress? Or worse, if he was yet another man who was only gay in private? Fuck, he didn't want to know.

Sam moaned against Michael's mouth and his hands slid down to Michael's thighs then cupped his ass.

Their hard shafts slid together and it was Michael who groaned. He was so damn close. Michael gripped Sam's chin and broke the kiss.

Water slid over Sam's brow, down his nose. His dark hair lay plastered to his head. Pale eyes watched Michael, but Sam didn't speak.

Michael pushed his thumb between the seam of Sam's lips. "Get on your knees."

Sam pressed his hands against Michael's chest and dropped—slowly, so that his body skimmed down Michael's —to kneeling. Sam's lips parted a fraction and he looked up.

Michael caught himself on the wall of the shower when his legs turned to jelly. No wonder Sam got what he wanted in the boardroom. The man had tempting and teasing down to an art form. "Let's see if you can take all of me this time."

It was hard to tell whether it was fear or determination that flickered in Sam's eyes, but his hot mouth engulfed the head of Michael's cock and Michael nearly came right then, his whole body tingling with need for release. Sam found the slit of Michael's cock and licked at it with abandon.

Light danced before Michael's eyes and he fought against the rising tide of his orgasm. Now his muscles trembled, his body shook. He placed his other hand on the wall in front of him and closed his eyes.

Mistake. That only intensified everything, from the water pounding against his side and the drumbeat of his heart to the soft inferno of Sam's mouth as he sucked more of Michael's cock in with every stroke.

Fire rose from the base of Michael's spine straight to his skull. He clawed at the tile grout and bit back the cry that threatened to leave his lips. Not yet. From the burning of his body and the hazing of his vision, he was fighting a losing battle against his impending orgasm. Michael longed to lose to Sam, to spill his seed down his throat. Every part of his body sang for release.

Sam engulfed Michael again, and this time Michael nudged his hips forward and found almost no resistance. He opened his eyes.

Sam's lips stretched wide around the base of Michael's shaft. All of him. Michael moaned and Sam backed off, gasping for air. He glanced up and gave Michael a feral grin before he took Michael deep again.

A whip of desire lashed out from Michael's core, flaying his nerves with pleasure and stealing his sight and breath. He came buried in Sam's throat, shooting more than he thought possible into that willing mouth.

Sam milked him until the tremors subsided, then licked his lips. "Did that meet your expectations?" The devil resided in Sam's rough voice and in the mischief dancing in his eyes.

Michael could only murmur Sam's name. He pushed himself off the wall and held out a hand.

Sam took it and Michael pulled him into his arms. He kissed Sam, tasting himself on the tongue Sam thrust into his mouth. Sam's cock nudged Michael's belly and a zip of awareness—a warmth Michael did not want to name—ran through his blood. This man would be his undoing.

Michael broke the kiss, nipped at Sam's neck, then spoke. "More than met." He stepped out of Sam's arms and retrieved the bottle of shower wash. He thumbed the flap open and drizzled the liquid over Sam's shoulders and down his chest and back, then dropped the bottle, not caring about the noise it made. He ran his hands over Sam's chest, lathering the wash, then moved to his back.

Sam tipped his head and his hard shaft pressed against Michael's stomach again.

He shouldn't leave Sam hanging like that, but he enjoyed seeing him on the edge, the way his body moved, the shudder of his breathing. Michael scrubbed lower, over Sam's striped ass.

Michael dug his fingers into Sam's cheeks, and Sam's rough breathing turned into a cry.

"That hurt?" Of course it did, but he wanted to hear Sam's answer.

"Yes."

"Too much?"

A breathless laugh. "From you? Never."

Michael scraped his fingers across the swollen lines from his whipping and Sam twisted. Time to end this—as much as he enjoyed having Sam at his mercy in this little space they'd carved out—the real world beckoned from beyond the shower. He ran a hand over Sam's chest to gather what lather the shower hadn't washed off and took hold of Sam's cock. With the other hand, he slid a finger between Sam's ass cheeks and teased his hole.

Sam moaned in Michael's embrace and tangled his hands into Michael's hair.

Michael plunged his tongue between Sam's lips. God, Sam tasted so good. And his kiss... the sound of the shower lessened as Michael's blood rushed in his ears. When this was over, then what? He pushed the thought—and the lump in his throat—away and stroked Sam's cock. No gentle teasing, just a hard hand-fucking. He circled Sam's hole with his index finger then pushed inside.

Sam's grip tightened, pulling Michael's hair taut, and he broke the kiss. "Oh fuck!" Sam repeated the curse into Michael's neck.

Michael nipped and licked at Sam's collarbone, tasting tap water, spice, and salt, then he bit Sam's flesh and pushed his finger into Sam's ass as far as it would go.

With a breathless shout, Sam came, his whole body shuddering with the force of his orgasm. After a few moments, Sam sighed and wilted into Michael's embrace. "God, that was so good."

It had been, better than Michael wanted to admit. This little encounter wouldn't be enough to sate his appetite for Sam, which was a huge, huge problem. He kissed the spot he'd bitten that already shaded toward purple. "You're going to be sore tomorrow."

"I'm sore now." Sam pulled away, grinning, and bent to claim the bottle of body wash. "I like that aspect." He squirted wash into his hand then offered the bottle to Michael. "Keeps me sharp."

Michael took it and worked on cleaning himself off. He had no marks on his body, no visible bruises, it was only his heart that hurt like hell. "We can't do this again." He choked out the words. He would drown in Sam's needs—and his own—if they kept this up.

Sam's smile melted. He looked down and rinsed off, a faint crease forming on his brow.

Michael took his turn under the water, then shut the stream off. The silence afterward was absolute. Mike grabbed his towel off the curtain bar, dried himself, wrapped it around his waist, then retrieved his sodden belt. He held up a finger to his lips.

Sam didn't move. His throat worked his Adam's apple up and down, but he said nothing.

Pushing the curtain half open, Michael stepped out into the locker room.

It was empty. Exhaling, Michael opened the curtain the rest of the way. "I'll get you a towel." He didn't wait for a response before returning to his locker to grab his spare towel. He took it back and handed it to Sam.

"Thanks." Neutral tone. Sam's eyes were rimmed with red, probably from the extended shower.

He hoped to God it was from the shower.

They didn't speak as they toweled off and dressed. But when Sam picked up his watch and grunted, Michael couldn't help but look over. Suit pants. Crisp gray shirt. All the evidence of their time together hidden beneath cloth. Sam met Michael's gaze and turned his watch. "It's not as late as I thought."

"What time is it?"

"One forty-seven. Plenty of time before my two-thirty meeting with William."

A long lunch, but not horribly so, given how late they both worked. Michael's pulse still beat like he'd been working out. The warmth in his chest was gone, replaced by a cold knot. "Sam, I—"

Sam waved the words away. "You're right. This shouldn't happen again." Sam paused and put his watch on. He lowered his voice. "It just complicates things."

That was an understatement. Michael stuffed the towels and wet belt into his bag. No one would notice it missing if he left his shirt untucked. "It's not that I don't like it."

Sam's smile was slight. "I know that." He moved to the full-length mirror and set about fixing his tie. "I was out in college—in undergrad. Dated. Marched. All that."

So many things Michael wanted to say. He bit his tongue and finished packing his gym bag.

Sam shrugged into his suit coat and transformed back into a CEO. Except his eyes were still red-rimmed. "But the business world is very different." Tight voice. Clipped words.

Fucking hell. Another one. "I understand." Michael shouldered his bag. "I'll see you upstairs." He almost made it to the door.

"Michael." Sam wielded the name like a whip made of silk.

He stopped and swiveled around, despite himself.

The suit spoke of power, but the raw emotion written on Sam's face twisted the lump of ice in Michael's chest. Complicated? Holy fuck, he didn't want to name what he saw there. Nor what he felt in his own soul. He of all people shouldn't have a thing for his CEO, especially given what had happened the last time he'd dated a coworker.

Sam exhaled. Inhaled. "No one has ever made me fly like you do."

Michael backed into the door. This was worse than Rasheed. He'd been a lover and a friend, but they'd never fit together like *this*. Sam—complemented him, *completed* him. And the fucking man was in the closet because of *business*. Michael's throat tightened so much he could barely breathe. "I have to go." The words came out as cracked and shattered as he felt. Too many thoughts tripped over themselves on the way to twisting into his heart.

He turned and fled the locker room.

SAM'S ASS HURT, BUT NOT IN A GOOD WAY. THE CHAIRS in the conference room must have been designed by someone who hated sitting—they numbed the limbs while driving aches up the spine. Sam didn't shift in his seat— years of meetings like this one had taught him that a board of directors looked for those little hints that their prey was uncomfortable.

And today, Sam was their quarry—the fox running over the hills. The board knew exactly what he was going to say —he'd sent them his presentation three days ago. This meeting, with its expensive catered lunch, was designed to make Sam dance and the rest of the company's sphincters tighten—exactly what the board wanted.

Well, how about that. Sarcasm worthy of Michael. Sam had gone completely native.

He curled his toes in his shoes because the board wouldn't notice that.

Michael.

They still weren't talking. Not since the shower. Just a word or two here and there. Terse e-mails about aspects of work, copied to the group. The lack of true communication hurt, in every way that was bad and far more than he thought possible. He didn't know how to bridge the gulf that had formed between them. He missed Michael, his laugh, his grin, even his freaking parrot shirts. There was no color in Michael these days—only blues and blacks and grays.

William cleared his throat. "You've made good progress, Randell."

He forced himself to relax and smile. "Thank you. The team has been giving it their all." It wasn't false flattery. The development and testing teams had succeeded in cleaning up the most egregious errors in the software they'd released. What remained was a set of new features their prospective buyer wanted in the product. Tricky, cutting-edge development. Hell, the IETF hadn't even hammered out the new protocols yet. Lots of infighting among different companies.

From William's expression, Sam knew there was a shoe dangling somewhere over his head.

"We are, however, concerned about the timeline going forward."

And there it was, in all its hard-soled glory, falling right on schedule.

Sam let his smile fade away, but kept his expression neutral. "Concerned?"

The screen flashed up a slide with the schedule. It was aggressive, with the engineering team completing development of the new features, functional testing, and then regression testing, all in three months.

"We think you should be able to complete coding and testing in two months." William tented his hands. Blond hair and blue eyes spoke of his Dutch ancestry, but there wasn't any warmth at all in the man. There never had been, in all the time Sam had known the venture capitalist.

Two months. That nixed pretty much all of testing. "We can deliver the functionality in two. But unless you want the same debacle as last release, we need four weeks for testing."

The rest of the members of the board shifted in their seats. Sam held himself still, but relaxed. This was not going well. Something else was afoot.

"Mike Sebastian's estimates have always been conservative. He's done the same amount of testing in less time. A week after code freeze should be enough."

"Michael knows his job." Far better than William did. Sam flattened his palm against the hard surface of the table. "A week isn't enough time to find and fix bugs and perform regression testing."

"Mike is known for his volatility. He inflates issues. Always complains about deadlines." William smiled. "He's a drama queen." There was just a hint of emphasis on the last word. "Are you becoming like him, Randell?"

Sam's blood ran cold. Those were loaded words—a hint William didn't approve of Michael's sexuality—and maybe more. Sam ignored the klaxon in the back of his mind. "A week isn't enough, not for the complexity of the new features."

"I'll agree that it's aggressive," William said.

"It's idiotic." Dead silence in the room.

Shit. He hadn't meant to say that out loud, but what was done was done. And anger felt good—and was just as usable as calm. He rose from his chair. "If you want this release rock solid, then you need to give us the time. Maybe we can shave off a week, but four?" He shook his head.

"Two weeks," William said. "No more."

Still not enough time. "When you brought me in, you agreed to trust my judgment."

William smiled and leaned back in his chair, as if he'd already won. "Or buy you out."

Ice seeped deeper into Sam's veins. They could. It was the ultimate threat. Pay him a hunk of cash and he'd be on to "spend more time with his family" or "pursue other opportunities."

Where would Michael be then? Out of a job, along with the rest of the company, because it was obvious that William didn't want a merger, he wanted to ditch the IP, take the cash, and run. But why? That made no business sense. No time to dwell on that mystery, though.

"I suppose you could get rid of me." Sam slipped out from behind his chair and walked toward the front of the room. "Are you a betting man, William?" He knew the answer to that question. They'd been in Vegas together.

Sam's movement forced William and the other board members to twist in their chairs to stay focused on him. It was an edge, a sliver of control.

"What are we wagering?" A mix of caution and excitement.

Hooked.

"Money. What else is there?" Sam stopped at the front of the room, behind William's chair. "You—you all want to cash out of Four Rivers. Move on to new projects." He gripped the back of William's chair and rocked it slightly. "You can either cash out with a failed project—William's preferred method—and get very little on your return, or trust me to deliver to you a product that will have Sundra Networks writing you a blank check."

He pushed off of William's chair and walked toward the back of the room. "So, which bet will you take?"

"What if I told you Sundra wants the release in two and a half months' time?" William's voice betrayed his anger.

An ache flickered against the back of Sam's skull, and he swallowed his fury. He reached the opposite end of the conference table, then leaned over, pressing his fingertips against the surface. "If that's true," he said, his voice low and strong, "then you should have told me that from the beginning, rather than wasting my fucking time playing games."

The board members squirmed in their seats. William's face turned red.

What the hell was William's plan?

Brigitta Holderolff, the sole woman on the board, cleared her throat. "Sundra wants it in two and a half, in time for Routing Forum."

Sam straightened. "Then what are you willing to give up?"

No one spoke for a moment, and then they all did, to him, to each other. Sam reached his chair and took a seat. Now it was just up to negotiations. Ice gripped Sam's spine. He'd have to give something as well, if this were to work.

Michael would not be pleased at all, and that confrontation he dreaded more than a year's worth of board meetings.

Worse, though, was the mix of fury and calm in William's steady gaze. Sam schooled his expression, despite the dread eating up his spine.

Sam found the server room cold and deserted—which was perfect. No one came in here, giving him the privacy he needed to decompress after the board meeting. The whirring of the ventilation system and the fans on the rack-mounted equipment created a shield of white noise, blocking out conversations in the hall and soothing his nerves. No dinging of e-mail or ringing of phone in here. He wasn't sure he even got cell reception huddled among all the electronics. Blessed silence lurked in a blanket of humming.

In the back corner of the room, he sat on a step stool tucked behind one of the equipment racks and nursed the start of what he suspected would become a very bad headache.

After some hard bargaining and quite a bit of raised voices, he and the board had struck a deal. They'd given Sam three weeks for testing, and the more experimental protocols would only be certified as beta released—full testing would not be needed. The rest of the features would be released for general availability.

Michael would not like it. Hell, Sam didn't like it. He had done his best to carve out as much time as he could for the testing team, but there'd still be late hours and working weekends in their future. Sam rubbed his temples. He wasn't ready to face Michael yet, especially the way their interactions had been of late.

Lately, Michael might as well be a ghost. He existed in the office and Sam caught glimpses, but they no longer spoke. Hell, most of the questions from the testing team came from people other than Michael.

That time in the shower had been a damn good fuck, but if he had known it would ruin the blossoming friendship, he'd never have asked. The look on Michael's face in the end—after a slight hint that Sam felt something beyond physical attraction, Michael had run for the hills. Sam's throat tightened. He should have known. Michael had made Sam's place in his life very clear. Just a suit, a captain of industry to be bent over, beaten, and fucked for kicks.

That wasn't entirely fair. Besides, had things continued... then what? A relationship meant stripping off the mask he'd worn since grad school, that of the prudish but probably straight man.

Sam shivered. Maybe that persona was already gone. The look William had given him—that comment...

No. William wasn't that observant. It had more to do with Michael than with Sam—Michael who *was* openly gay.

Sam never thought he'd long for his undergraduate days, but in some ways, he'd been whole then—even though he could never keep a boyfriend and the whole four years had been one long, tumultuous fight with professors and students alike.

Then the night in the alley had happened and he'd done nothing. Sam shivered. Well, he'd made his choices. Paid his price, it seemed, too.

Certainly, the impending news from the board wouldn't improve Michael's opinion of him, even if there were any hope of a relationship.

That shit William. If he had his way, Sam would be the captain of a sinking boat. That slick smile and too-hard handshake at the end of the board meeting did not bode well. The man wanted Sam to fail, that much was obvious, but why? Why bring him here in the first place, if not to raise up Four Rivers like a phoenix from its burning pyre?

Maybe Taylor wasn't the only one with sticky fingers in

the cash jar. Sam sat up. Time to do a little research. See what William was into. Perhaps the way things with Michael had turned out was for the best, as well. Once Four Rivers was sold, he'd be off to a new struggling company. His nomadic life left little room for friendship, let alone anything beyond that—even if he hadn't stuffed himself into the closet.

As Sam stood, the telltale *beep-click* of the security pad sounded from the door and Sam's heart skipped a beat. For a moment, he felt like an errant child, caught hiding where he shouldn't be; then his brain kicked in. He was the CEO and if he wanted to sit in the server room, he damn well could. He coughed and stepped out from behind the equipment rack.

Michael stood in front of the closing door, mouth parted, his glasses glinting in the florescent lights. The door clicked closed with a rattle of wood against metal.

"What are you doing here?" Michael said.

"I work here." Sam deadpanned the words.

Michael exhaled, exasperation overtaking his surprise. "I meant what are you doing in this room? It's not like you know anything about mail servers or routers."

The words and the assumption—that Sam was technically incompetent—pelted like sleet on bare skin in winter. Heat, not the pleasant, enjoyable kind, rose in Sam's chest and he had to force himself not to grit his teeth. "Actually, I started out in IT, managing a room not so different from this one." He let that nugget sink in and enjoyed the coloring of Michael's cheeks. "Why are *you* here?"

The muscle under Michael's left eye twitched.

Sam slid a cool smile into place. "Crashed the router again?" He couldn't help throwing that at Michael.

"I didn't crash it. Development's shitty build did. I'm here to do my job." He moved, brushing past Sam to where one of the zone routers was racked. He pulled a keyboard out from behind a small monitor and banged on it. "God damn, even the console's locked up."

Not good.

As part of testing, they ran different parts of the office network through Four Rivers' equipment—and woe if a zone went down, since Michael heard about it from fellow coworkers. Immediately.

The lights were illuminated on the router, but several of them were red.

"I really don't like doing this." Michael stared at the box for a moment, then pushed the power switch to off.

Sam winced in sympathy. The router would either reboot fine, or not. If not, they'd either managed to fuck up the flash or one of the processors on the line cards. Either way, off to hardware the card would go. Fixing it would cost precious time and money.

They both exhaled as the boot sequence flashed on the console and scrolled through normally. Michael logged in, ran a quick diagnostic. "Core dump." He logged out. "I can do the rest from my desk."

"Glad it came back," Sam said. There weren't many spare line cards around. Too expensive to keep a stockpile—not when customers needed them.

"Me too." Michael shoved the keyboard back behind the monitor and then faced Sam. "I doubt you're here to fix a server, though."

Sam let go of the chip that had lodged itself on his shoulder. "I was recovering from the board meeting."

"Ah, yes. Suit food. I saw the remnants of upper-crust fruit salad in the lunchroom. Someone claimed there had been lobster rolls, but they were gone by the time I got there."

Michael's sneering tone was so blatant, Sam tasted the bitterness on his tongue. "There were three left, I think." He headed for the door, adjusting his tie as he walked. "So sorry you didn't get one, *Mike*."

"Sam."

He stopped, despite himself. *Damn it all to hell.* Michael would always be there, under his skin. It took more effort than Sam expected not to turn around. "Yes?"

"The meeting? How'd it go?"

He didn't want to have this conversation now, not with his head throbbing and heart threatening to beat its way out of his rib cage. "As well as could be expected." He reached for the door handle.

"Did they accept our plan?"

Our plan. As if they'd actually talked these past few weeks, rather than communicated by group e-mail. Sam brushed the smooth, cool, silver finish of the handle with his fingertips. Freedom lay beyond the door. He let his arm fall to his side. "Of course they didn't," he said, turning around. "You know how these things go."

Michael's face was a mask. "What did you agree to?"

"Three weeks."

"God damn it, Sam! Four was barely acceptable. Three?"

Michael's outburst only increased the ache in Sam's head. "Three. Plus the draft protocols will be beta, so you don't have to worry about those."

Michael didn't say anything for a moment, though his jaw worked. "You threw us under the bus. So much for all your promises."

Every muscle in Sam's body tightened. The pounding

in his head matched his heart—too damn fast. Calm snapped like brittle wood and he pulled himself to his full height. "Stop being so fucking melodramatic. I don't have time for this shit."

Sam might as well have slapped Michael. His face reddened and he took a step back.

There was a certain grim satisfaction in that. *Yes, I can be the suit you so hate. Surprise.* "Three weeks," Sam repeated. "Can you accept this?"

"I—don't know."

That was a pity. Sam liked Michael—too much. Missed their budding friendship horribly. The days weren't as bright without Michael's smile. Sam only had himself to blame for that. Had he been able to keep his needs in check, they wouldn't be at this moment. The shower had been a disaster. The tightness in Sam's chest twisted and stabbed, turning his words to gravel. "Then I'll find someone who can."

Michael wavered, then reached out and grabbed the server rack. "Are you firing me?"

"Not yet." Sam didn't look away. "But I will, if you get in the way of me protecting the 'great and wickedly smart' people who work for you."

"You call this protecting them?" Michael let go of the rack and took a step forward. "Undercutting their time? Setting them up for an impossible task?" His voice boomed in the small room.

Sam didn't wince, though the sound sent light flashing across his vision. "Once you're finished being irate and you have two brain cells to rub together again, consider this—I got you three weeks when I knew you needed four. What do you think William wanted?" Sam watched Michael for a long moment, memorizing the play of expressions that passed over his face, then Sam turned and pulled open the server room door. He was most of the way down the hall before it thumped closed.

His lungs barely worked and people stepped out of his way as he passed. Too many. *You're a mess. Slow down. School your expression.* He didn't—couldn't. The utter look of betrayal, of shame, he'd seen on Michael's face bored into his skull with the same efficiency as the migraine.

Once in his office, he closed the door, then leaned his forehead against its cool surface.

He should have known better. No friends. No lovers— especially no lovers. This job precluded all of that because it required ruthlessness and precision. He could be fair and even kind, but attachment led to failure. For the sake of all Four Rivers employees, he had to succeed at this venture— their livelihoods depended on that. If it meant losing Michael? Well, in business, no one was irreplaceable.

No one.

Even the one man he most wanted to keep.

CHAPTER FOUR

An hour later, Sam slipped out of his office and took the long way around to the lunchroom—the route that wouldn't take him anywhere near Michael's cube. Sam didn't want to chance a run-in with Michael, but sulking in his office hadn't improved his dry throat or pounding head. With any luck, there were still a few free cans of soda—or "pop" as Michael called it—in the fridge.

God, Michael. What the hell was he going to do about that?

He still wanted Michael—his companionship, his touch, his smile—all that simmered between them, but neither of them needed the stress of the shattered friendship that lay beneath them. If they were to make it through this release, this—situation—needed to end, one way or another.

If it meant firing Michael? Sam pressed a hand against the refrigerator when his heart tried to gouge its way out of his chest. He would do it. If he had to, he would do it.

He yanked open the door. Inside, Sam found two cans of diet cola and one lone can of ginger ale. He took the latter, grabbed a packet of something called "headache pills" from the generic first aid box on the wall, opened both, then washed the pills down with the "pop."

If only the rest of his life were that easy to solve. He rubbed his forehead and waited for the medicine to kick in.

At least it was damn quiet in the office—that helped his head, though not his anxiety. If Sam hadn't seen the clock, he'd have guessed it was well after five, not a few minutes before three. Not a single soul talking in the hallways—usually three o'clock meant chatter around the coffeepot. Instead, everyone had their heads buried in work at their desks.

This release was getting to them all. The whole place felt constricted, nervous, like a dark sky before a thunderstorm. The rest of the company might have no clue they were being courted by Sundra, but that tension, the worry, the anticipation, hung in the air anyway. Completely understandable, given their CEO kept late hours and the board had an on-site meeting. All that added up, and no one at Four Rivers was stupid.

The rumor mill must be grinding like wild.

Another fire Sam needed to put out: all the incorrect conclusions that were undoubtedly flying around, like the office closing or mass layoffs. Those falsehoods killed productivity.

He really didn't have time for this shit with Michael. They should be a team. Partners.

Partners.

Sam shivered. That word rolled in his brain for far too long.

Wouldn't happen. Not with Michael, not with anyone else, not while he pursued this career—and he'd come too far to just give up now. He was happy enough.

Yeah, and if he kept telling himself that, maybe he'd

believe it. No partner, no lover, no Michael. Perfectly *happy*.

Sam curled his hands to fists.

He'd caused many companies to move on to better things—seen their employees well compensated with better and more challenging work. His presence had changed the environment at several places—better policies for domestic partners, better anti-discrimination rules in hiring.

You're no saint. Too many companies had folded on his watch. People out of jobs. Men and women he'd had fired—because it was just business, after all.

At the heart of it all, Sam was a closeted gay man in a career where sharks and snakes preyed. And he was one of them, no matter what he told himself. A suit. What if he came out? What then? Or stopped running long enough to let himself care about Michael? Except he already cared. There was a laundry list of "what-ifs" that scrolled through his brain whenever he thought of Michael.

Coming out meant switching careers, to one that didn't involve venture capitalists, boards of directors, and CEOs. He would be quite fucked by all of them the moment they knew. He'd seen it happen. *Been there.*

Sam let out a breath. His head hurt more than ever, and he hoped it was the last surge before the meds took the edge off. His whole body shook.

The picked-over remains of the board's catered meal lay spread out over several tables. Nothing left, really. A leaf of lettuce here, some crumbs there. A tub of cocktail sauce. Sam gathered and pitched the empty plates into the trash, savoring the satisfying thump they made. They were the only objects he could throw with any force without breaking something important.

And tossing around chairs and tables wouldn't help anything.

Instead, Sam wiped down the tables and set about straightening them up.

William had been right, in a way. Michael had overreacted, which was unusual. How much of that was job stress and how much was the remains of their friendship? Sam didn't know.

On one of the tables by the wall, several photo albums of Four Rivers' early years had been rifled through and knocked out of their usual neat stacks. Sam straightened the pile, then on a whim took the first one and opened it.

And there Michael was—a younger version beaming back with a grin that tightened Sam's heart.

It was the same smile Sam had seen in Curaçao, one that spoke of excitement and thrill.

Michael stood with a woman and a man holding up a homemade Four Rivers Networks sign. If Sam had to guess, the two other people were Susan and Rasheed, the founders of Four Rivers.

The title under the photo said, "The Three Musketeers."

Sam flipped through the book. Photos of the first office —a tiny converted house up north of the city. Rasheed on a skateboard in the driveway. Susan holding a line card in what looked like someone's garage. A group of ten engineers in front of a hardware bench. That photo read, "First packet passed!"

The younger Michael nearly always wore that smile, the one Sam never saw at the office.

What happened to you?

Sam flipped to a newspaper clipping about the company with the headline FOUR RIVERS MAKES WAVES.

There again was the photo from the front of the album, only this caption read "Four Rivers' Founders: Susan Patterson, Rasheed Esfahani, Michael Sebastian."

The silence of the lunchroom pressed in on Sam's skull until he could barely breathe. He read the caption a second time and stared at the photo, lingering over Michael's bright smile.

Michael Sebastian. *Founder.*

Sam read the article. And there it was again, the combination of Michael's name and that word.

Holy shit.

Sam turned back to the beginning of the album and glanced at the photos. Flipped past the article and studied the pictures there, as well. Michael and Rasheed. Susan and Michael. The three of them together. Shots of a holiday party, the three clinking champagne flutes. Michael resplendent in a tux, his arm over Rasheed's shoulder.

Sam closed the album, his face as warm as a voyeur's.

Michael had been a founder. Only he wasn't now, so *something* had gone horribly wrong. The incorporation of the company hadn't listed Michael, just Rasheed and Susan. Yes, Michael held a decent amount of private shares, but nowhere near the amount a founder should. It was as if his role in forming the company had been completely erased except for a few dozen photos in an album and a faded newspaper article.

If it were true...

Shit. No wonder the man was bitter.

Every snapshot in the album said that Susan and Rasheed had been Michael's friends. Sam's nerves prickled with a combination of excitement and dread. He was still mad as hell at Michael, but there was a puzzle here to be solved, and Sam needed to know now rather than on the cusp of acquisition—they were too close to the end for this to blow up in his face. Sam tucked the album under his arm and picked up the can of ginger ale. He had some web searching to do.

He liked Four Rivers and the people here. What he'd said to Michael had been true; he'd protect the employees. Even if it meant firing Michael.

And if it means unmasking yourself, your past?

He had no answer to that.

At six in the evening, the air-conditioning shut off. Michael winced as the thumping of the warming vents sounded throughout the office. He should have been used to it by now—this was hardly the first time he'd stayed at work this late, but it always sounded like the ceiling was about to fall down.

Today, he almost hoped it would. Put him out of his misery.

He'd lost three hours after finding Sam in the server room. Oh sure, he sat at his desk. Stared at the screen. Plunked on the keyboard. Got no work done. He should have gone home, but it would have looked strange given all that needed to be finished, and he wasn't entirely sure he was functioning well enough to drive, anyway.

Sam was willing to fire him. Toss him out of Four Rivers. Out of Sam's life.

Michael took a deep breath, one of several hundred he'd taken since he'd sat down at his cube, and exhaled. On his screen, the core dump from the zone router sat in a terminal window, but the lines blurred and shook and made no sense and his fucking heart wouldn't stop racing.

Michael couldn't decide whether he was more angry at Sam or himself. Sam shouldn't be *in* his life; he should have never bought Sam that drink. Four Rivers was Michael's life, not Sam's, and Sam—

Sam looked exquisite in the throes of an orgasm. Shivered under Michael's touch. His skin marked so beautifully when hit by Michael's hand or belt. Sam's smile was incomparable and his laugh was something Michael doubted he'd hear again. That was the worst. He could handle not touching Sam in the future, but somehow, they'd gone from lovers to friends to enemies.

Life wasn't supposed to work like that. On the other hand, they were back to employee and CEO—what they should have been from the beginning.

They'd ended up at this point because Michael had broken his own rule and gotten involved with a coworker. A fucking closeted coworker. Who *liked* to be whipped. Craved it. Begged for it. Something Rasheed never needed or wanted.

Sam had threatened to fire him. Something Rasheed would never have done.

"Shit." Michael took off his glasses and rubbed his temples.

E-mail dinged. Michael squinted at the window. A meeting request. From Sam. Michael gripped the edge of his desk as the world spun. No amount of cardio had ever prepared him for the pulse rate he was running now. He steeled himself, put his glasses back on, and read the invite.

Sam had sent it to test and development. *Thank God.* So he wasn't being fired.

Not yet. Sam's voice echoed in Michael's head.

He pushed that memory aside and focused on the message that accompanied the invite.

I want to meet and discuss the release direction that
was decided upon at the BoD meeting. The summary is
that we must have the release completed by Routing
Forum. I know this is a quicker time frame than
originally planned. We'll be releasing a few features as
beta to give test as much time as possible, but it's still a
short window. Here's the proposed timeline. Bring your
questions and solutions to the table. Let's make this
work. -Sam

Michael studied the milestone dates. Routing Forum
was in six weeks, give or take. Three more weeks for dev
and three weeks for test. Big event, too. Sponsored by—

Holy shit.

Sundra Networks sponsored Routing Forum. A
Fortune 500 company and one that always made the "best
to work for" lists. Clarity slammed back into Michael as if
he'd put on a pair of mental glasses as well. He glanced
around his cube because he had to do *something*. Sundra
was wooing them. That had to be it.

Why hadn't Sam told him that they had to have the
release by Forum?

*Because you didn't give him a chance, you fuckhead.
And you've been running from him since—*

Since the shower. Since he'd seen that look on Sam's
face, the one behind every mask, and heard the words Sam
spoke—and those he hadn't voiced as well. Sam needed him,
wanted him, wasn't out. Michael had no idea what to do
about that, didn't want to deal with the twist in his heart.
The breakup with Rasheed and the aftermath had nearly
killed him.

But this? He could fix this.

Michael brought up his instant messenger. The dot by

Sam's name was green. Before he thought too long about it, Michael typed a question.

Are you still here?

One click and the IM was sent. A moment later, the window flashed.

Yes.

Michael pushed himself out of his chair and headed for Sam's office. Movement, that was good. His heart still tried to punch a hole in his rib cage.

Sam must have heard Michael coming, because he swung his chair toward the door as Michael approached. Cold expression, arms crossed. Michael expected that, but seeing Sam closed off only served to increase the tightness in his lungs. He spoke anyway.

"You should have—"

Sam leaned back in his chair. "I should have what?" Each word was clipped.

Michael placed his hand on the doorframe to steady himself against the anger laced in Sam's words. *I'm fucking this up.* "Let me try that again," he said. "I should have listened to you rather than running off at the mouth."

Some of Sam's cold mask melted. "Yes. That might have been better."

"May I?" Michael pointed at one of the chairs in front of Sam's desk.

A nod, nothing more. Sam's arms remained firmly crossed. A spark of irritation rose in Michael, but he swallowed it and sat. He deserved some of this cold shoulder. "If they need the release by Forum, then your plan makes a lot of sense."

"Imagine that." Bitter humor there.

The spark threatened to burst into anger. "I'm trying to apologize here."

Sam's mask cracked. It wasn't ice beneath, but heat. "Well, you're doing a shit-poor job at it." Sam's skin colored, and it was only then Michael noticed how strained every one of Sam's muscles was.

I'm really fucking this up.

Sam must have read some of that in Michael, because his expression shifted to one of exhaustion. "I thought you trusted me, that you saw me as more than just a suit come to make money off your backs."

He opened his mouth to say that he did trust Sam, that he knew he wasn't just here to make money—then snapped his jaw shut. Because it wasn't true. He looked at his hands to avoid Sam's gaze. "You're still a CEO."

"Yes, I am. Your CEO, in fact." There was a long pause before Sam spoke again. "Michael, whose office was this?"

The question threw him completely. "You mean before you? Taylor's."

Sam's voice deepened. "And whose before that?"

Every nerve in Michael's body buzzed. He didn't want to think about the time before Taylor because it included too much Rasheed. Too much joy and hope and most of his shattered dreams, both personal and for the business that wasn't his anymore.

Sam had threatened to *fire* him.

"Mine. It was my office." He spoke the words barely above a whisper because to took so much effort to get them out.

"And Taylor took it from you, along with your title and your position."

Like lemon juice squeezed into a wound. It still hurt way the hell too much. He nodded, unable to speak. It was then he noticed the photo album sitting next to Sam's keyboard. Heat flared in his chest, unlocking his voice. "What the hell are you doing with that?" He lashed the words out.

Sam must have known exactly what Michael meant. He didn't shift, didn't turn to see what Michael stared at. "Research."

Of Michael and of his past, because that's all that could be found in those photos. Glimpses of secrets. Hints of the truth. "You could have asked me, you know."

The noise Sam made was somewhere between a croak and a snort. Dismissive, yes, but full of pain as well. "Really? Today's been the first day you've said more than three words to me since—" He paused. "Are you going to tell me what happened?"

"Three years ago, or that afternoon in the gym?"

Sam tented his hands, elbows on the desk, his fingertips brushing his lips, and said nothing.

The one was the root of the other, in many ways, and Sam wanted both, it seemed. Michael leaned back and pushed Sam's door closed. He was pretty sure they were alone in the office, but sound carried in odd ways. And if he had his way—which he usually did—he wouldn't be the only one answering questions. "Okay. Let's have this out."

Sam didn't move, just keep looking at him over his fingers. For a moment, Michael wished it were his hands close to Sam's lips. He'd force a digit into that hot mouth and Sam would suck because Sam loved to surrender, loved all the things that Rasheed hadn't.

"You've read the article, I take it."

"Yes." Sam spoke against his fingers. "You were one of the founders."

"In name. In practice. But not legally."

"How the hell does that happen?" Fire in Sam's words. Anger. Sam flattened his hands on the desk.

Michael's stomach lurched—Sam's ire wasn't directed at him, but at the unfairness of what had happened. Which was worse, because the last thing he wanted from Sam was *pity*.

He wasn't the one hiding in the damn closet.

"It happened because we were all idealistic, hopeful, stupid, and screwed up." Michael took off his glasses and rubbed his eyes before putting them back on. "I met Susan first, when we were both undergrads. We hit it off as friends and lab partners. After our second cup of coffee to discuss our lab project, I told her I was gay because I saw that look."

Sam nodded. He shifted and leaned back. "I know what look you mean."

Hope mixed with apprehension. Sam had worn it well in Curaçao. "She took it well, and with that off the table, we became best friends. We both stayed at Carnegie Mellon for grad school."

"And you met Rasheed there."

God, Rasheed. That beautiful, fucked-up, intelligent man. "I actually met him before the semester started, in a bar. He was cruising the gay scene, fresh in from Dearborn and away from his family for the first time. All silk and leather and nerves."

That unsettled Sam. A flush crept up his neck and he shifted in his chair. "Did you pick him up that night?"

Michael's turn to nod. Dark hair, neatly trimmed beard, and a wiry build. Rasheed had been just squirmy enough to be irresistible to the younger and less wary version of Michael. Popped Rasheed's cherry, too, but he wasn't about to tell Sam that. Not now. "Two days later, I walked into a lecture hall and there was Rasheed. He turned so white, I thought he might faint."

Sam let out a breath. "I take it he was in the closet?"

"He might as well have been in Narnia. He was so scared that I'd out him. That being in the same room with me would cause a big fat gay label to fall from the sky and hover over his head. That somehow, by standing next to me in Pittsburgh, his folks two hundred fifty miles away would find out he liked men." Michael paused and watched Sam carefully. "You know how that goes."

Sam twisted in his seat again, the flush returning. Served him right. "Yes. I do know."

Those words were an acknowledgement. Well, good.

"So you dated?" Sam's voice was tight.

"I dated him. He fugitively saw me from time to time to fuck. He told his folks he was dating a woman from school."

For a moment, Sam looked dumbstruck. "And you put up with that?"

Michael flinched. He really should have dumped Rasheed then. Mistake one. "I couldn't keep away from him and he couldn't stay away from me."

"Who did he tell his parents—shit. Susan?" Sam looked horrified.

Michael would have laughed if the outcome hadn't been so painful in the end. "Yeah. He said he was dating Susan. It made some twisted kind of sense. We were all close friends and Susan knew we were a couple. Played the part of the girlfriend on the phone because she cared about us both and was willing to keep his secret. After graduation, we all rented a town house together. Got the idea for Four

Rivers in the kitchen. Founded the company a couple months later."

"Did they—was he bi?"

"No, while we dated, he didn't have sex with anyone else. And I'm pretty sure he wasn't bi. Early on, he talked about how he wished he could be attracted to women, because it would have been easier, given his family's expectations."

"Kids." Sam's voice was soft.

"Of course. He was the only son and a second generation Persian. His parents were liberal in many ways, but still very conservative in others. They expected Rasheed to marry. Pass on the family name."

"I've met both men and women like that," Sam said. "They can't deny who they're attracted to, but it pulls them apart from all the expectations their families had—all that had been heaped onto them from a young age."

Michael folded his hands into his lap. "Your family like that?"

Sam shook his head. "My parents are kind of a cross between hippies and Quakers, so a strong sense of being whatever you are runs in the family. They didn't blink when I told them. Plus I have a brother and a sister and they both have kids."

"So it's just corporate culture that keeps you from being gay?"

Sam opened his mouth, then closed it into a thin line. When the words came, they were sharp and full of edges. "I *am* gay. I just don't go out of my way to announce it."

"No." Michael matched his tone. "You go out of your way to keep from showing it."

Several emotions played across Sam's face. Anger, fear,

lust—and shame. "I thought this conversation was about you?"

Michael huffed a laugh. "Is it?"

Sam took a deep breath and settled into his seat. Irritation laced his voice. "So after grad school, you were dating a closeted guy, living with him and the woman he said he was dating, and you all were founding a company?"

Put that way, it sounded more than a little crazy. It also put the conversation back into Michael's court—so like the businessman Sam was. Well, Michael would get his answers from Sam later. "Yes, exactly."

Sam seemed to chew on the idea for a bit, then asked, "How did you end up founding a company and not being a founder?"

Because he'd been too damn trusting. "Since Rasheed and I were a couple, all three of us agreed that splitting the company three ways would be unfair—it left Susan holding only a third and the two of us with the majority."

"That makes a certain amount of sense from her point of view, though..."

"Not from mine?" Michael leaned back in his chair and looked up at the ceiling. "This is where I admit, despite all the warning signs the relationship was doomed, I was stupid in love." He choked on the last word, hot anger following hard on the sharp stab that never—quite—went away when he thought about those years. "So we split it in half. Susan became CEO and took half. The other was in Rasheed's name, as Chief Technology Officer, with the understanding that if we ever sold the company, I'd get half of Rasheed's share. Susan and Rasheed signed all the paperwork. I didn't put my name on any of it."

This time, when Sam parted his lips, it was in shock.

Understanding paled his face. "You—never signed? Anything? Even an agreement with Rasheed?"

An old, familiar ache settled in Michael's chest. "I told you we were stupid and screwed up. I've lived with the consequences of simply trusting someone every day since the board took over." Michael unclenched his hands. "I should have thought of the repercussions of pressing Rasheed."

Sam leaned forward again. "You wanted him to come out." Wariness there, but also a glimmer of something that might have been longing.

Perhaps Sam wasn't so wed to the closet. Maybe he needed a push and then they could—what? Sam was still the boss. Michael swallowed the bile in his throat. "After five years, I figured it was time. We'd been sharing the same bed for ages. I wanted all that went with that—holding hands in public, not having to worry that anyone seeing us out to dinner would get the 'wrong idea,' the constant lies to his family—Susan knew them better than I did. So I threw down an ultimatum."

Sam's tented fingers were back at his lips. "He said no."

"Of course he said no. He loved the sex—but not me. I was a good fuck, but couldn't give him what he wanted. And he wasn't ever coming out, because good sons didn't do that to their parents." Once, remembering Rasheed's words would have torn Michael up inside, but there was nothing left to shred, just the hollowness of knowing that he'd blinded himself with hope.

He'd paid—and Four Rivers had paid—for that mistake. "I made plans to move out and told both Susan and Rasheed I wanted my third of the company."

Sam had a distant look for a moment. "I'm guessing this

all went down right before they sold their shares to the board."

"Bingo," Michael said. "Susan was amenable, as was Rasheed, since it meant a bigger cut for him. Four Rivers was large enough that we needed more venture capital, so it was a good time to switch all of that around. Or so they said. The process was supposed to take a couple of months."

Sam shook his head. Probably because he knew enough to guess what had happened next.

"I believed in both of them—in their integrity and honesty. But in the end William and the board owned the majority of the shares and Susan and Rasheed were on their way to California. I was supposed to get a nice big cut of Four Rivers, but they hadn't made that contingent when they sold their portions."

"William and the board screwed you over."

A searing burn tore through Michael and he dug his nails into his palms. Four Rivers had been his dream. "Yup."

Sam was silent for a moment. "Susan and Rasheed went to California together, didn't they? As a couple."

The anger loosened. "More than anything, Rasheed wanted a normal life—to him that meant a heterosexual life. And Susan loved him in her own way and understood who he was. I suppose she could live with that."

Again Sam fell into silence and Michael let it stretch and fill the room. Finally, Sam stirred. "You stayed. At Four Rivers. After all that, why didn't you walk away?"

Michael found himself swallowing through a very tight throat. "It was all I had left of him. Of them. Of those years of friendship." He took another breath. "I couldn't just leave the people I'd hired to fend for themselves against a board full of vipers and their new hand-picked executives."

"So that's why you hate the board—the suits." Sam leaned back in his chair. "And why you don't trust me."

Sam cut right to the bone. Again. "I thought this was a conversation about me?"

Sam's chuckle was dark and delicious. "Is it?"

He deserved that. "This is why I don't trust the board. *You* aren't the same."

"Bullshit. I'm a suit." Sam twisted the word into something ugly. "Your boss."

His beautiful, masochistic, type-A, closeted boss. Michael shivered, despite himself. He wanted Sam. More now than ever—but Sam was correct. Michael didn't trust him.

"Of all the people in this company," Sam said, "you know me far better than anyone else. Have I ever given you a reason not to believe that I mean what I say?"

Michael raised his gaze. Sam still watched him, but now the lines of hurt etched his face. "No, you haven't." If anything, Sam had given him every reason to believe. Been more open with him than anyone had ever been, including Rasheed.

"I understand where you're coming from now, but please consider where I sit. You have no idea what it's like to balance the wants of that board of vipers—as you call them —with what is right for the company and its employees. I want to see you all rewarded for the years of work you've put in and the shit you've taken. They want to get as much money as they can."

"I know."

"No you don't. Fuck, Michael, if you did, this would have been a very different day."

Those words were like a two-by-four to the shoulder blades. He flinched under the impact.

"I am a suit," Sam said. "You're right about that. I'd like to think that I'm altruistic, but that's not entirely true. I do like helping people—it's a great feeling—but I love the rush of success, the high when everything works out, especially if I've had to cajole the board. The money's nice, but I give a lot of that away. What the hell am I going to spend it on anyway?"

Sam as an adrenaline junky made sense. The running. The desire to be thrashed. "I don't know. Most higher-ups I know seem to like cars."

"I haven't owned a car in years. I move around too much."

A different shock hit Michael. "How do you get to work?" Pittsburgh wasn't an easy town to live in without a car. Sure, there were buses, but they kept cutting the routes. Besides, Sam on PAT Transit?

"I walk. I'm renting a furnished apartment downtown."

"But—how do you get groceries?" There wasn't a store for miles.

Sam laughed and the sound danced through Michael—painful and sweet. "The Strip District? The Public Market? It's not like I can't walk a couple dozen blocks." His grin widened as if he could read Michael's thoughts. "Sometimes I even put on jeans and a T-shirt and take the bus to Squirrel Hill."

Michael attempted to envision Sam in jeans and failed. Tight jeans, maybe? Something that hugged Sam's legs? Even then, it was hard to dispel that body wrapped in a well-tailored suit. Or naked. The desire that had never faded pulled tight around Michael's core. "I'd have to see it to believe it."

Sam chuckled, then his humor faded. "Are you willing

to work with me on this release? It'll be much easier if I have you on board."

The coil loosened. "Would you really fire me?"

Sam lowered his shoulders. "If it was the best thing for the company, yes. I have to balance my own desires with what's best for everyone here."

His desires. Michael suppressed a tremor. Fuck it all. A relationship—or any more sex—with Sam was out of the question, but the man knew business. "I'll do whatever you need me to do to make sure we succeed." If Sundra bought them, they'd all be set for a while. Acquisition and merger, the ultimate goal. Even when they'd founded Four Rivers, that had been one of the stars they'd reached for.

Sam's answering smile felt like a caress and had the same effect. Michael's spine tingled and he shifted in the chair. Sam might be his boss, might be hiding in the closet, but that smile still lit the room—and Michael.

"Let's get to work then," Sam said. "Have you had dinner yet?"

"No."

"Good. We'll grab a burger and a beer and figure out how to do this." Sam pushed himself out of his chair.

They didn't talk much on the trip down the elevator, nor on the short walk over to The Sharp Edge, but everything suddenly felt right in Michael's world again, except the knot of fear that pulled tighter with each step they made together.

He could deny it all he wanted, but this road felt too damn familiar.

And he hadn't gotten the answers he'd wanted from Sam.

MORE THAN ANYTHING, SAM WANTED TO REACH ACROSS the two-seater bistro table and kiss Michael. Hard. Repeatedly. Until the distance between them melted away. Instead, Sam picked up his bowl-shaped glass of Belgian white ale and drank.

He'd not lied about putting the needs of the company ahead of his desires. No more trysts. But it was hard, damn hard, to keep away from Michael. There were so many things *right* about the man. If only Michael could stop having such dipshit moments.

If only he could stop wanting Michael so damn much.

"So," Michael said, studying the paper napkin he'd been writing on, "if we switch over the zones to hubs, we can use those routers for automated testing. Run more scripts concurrently."

"Eliminate bottlenecks to save time. Good thinking." Sam took another sip of beer. With Michael engaged again, there wasn't much doubt they'd meet the deadline. Sundra would sign. Then what? Sam already had a number of inquiries from other companies. He only needed to pick the next place, the next challenge. His throat tightened. The time he most hated was approaching—leaving everyone behind. It would be worse, too, because he could imagine alternatives, if only he had the balls to let go of his career.

Hearing about Michael's past hadn't helped. That had twisted Sam's heart and not only out of sympathy—it also illuminated the dark corners of Sam's own choices. He didn't want to dwell on those, or the reasons behind them. Keep moving forward.

Michael put down the pen. "I don't know why I was so worried. We might even be able to get the draft protocols tested completely." He reached for his own beer.

"I won't tell the board you said that. If we manage, it'll

only be icing on the cake. If not, no loss." Icing. Now that would be interesting to lick off of Michael. That thought left a hollow in Sam's chest, even as a low burn simmered at the base of his spine and his cock twitched. Michael would probably make him kneel. Maybe tie his hands. Sam tapped a finger against his glass. *Oh, stop that.*

The server came and removed the detritus from their dinner of burgers and pommes frites. The napkin, Michael folded and tucked into his back pocket. Lucky little thing.

No use mooning over what you can't have. Even if Michael had promised to do whatever Sam needed him to do. The places that could take Sam, were he a little less ethical.

Less ethical? *You're the one who got him to strap you in the shower.* And look at what had happened after that.

"I'm glad we worked things out," Michael said.

"Me too." Their job interaction and the plan for the release, they'd fixed those. The other—the desire that stretched between them and threatened to strangle the friendship they had eked out—that was far from mended. Didn't matter, though. He'd be gone in three months, at the longest. He didn't buy cars anymore, and he didn't get into relationships. The beer turned bitter in his stomach and the tightness returned to his chest. *Coward.* But he'd seen what this level of business did to the careers of gay men. To the lives of gay men.

He'd miss Michael horribly. Already had, every day since the gym.

"You're very quiet." Michael wrapped his hands around his lager glass full of the four-buck Mystery Beer—something light and summery, but good. Michael had let him taste.

"I'm just pondering the imponderable," Sam said. "It's

been a long day. Meeting with the board always takes it out of me."

"I made it much longer."

True. What he now knew about Michael's past—Rasheed and Susan, the way the board had screwed Michael—that tumbled around in his brain faster than the alcohol in his blood. The headache was gone, though. The anger, as well. "Since it brought us here, to this moment, it was worth it."

Michael stroked the condensation on the wall of the glass. "I'm sorry."

He spoke so quietly, Sam nearly lost the words under the music and the chatter in the bistro. The room swam, but not due to his consumption of beer. Giddiness and apprehension collided, leaving Sam breathless. "For what?"

"For the server room. For being pigheaded." Michael paused and dropped his voice even further. "And for leaving the locker room like I did."

Sam leaned forward so he could hear Michael over the noise. A few more inches and their foreheads might have touched. "I didn't know what to make of you running like that."

"You're my boss. In Curaçao, it was one thing, but here..."

Sam ran his finger around the top of his glass. "Here it's more than a little improper." If they'd been different people, a romp in the shower wouldn't have meant anything... but they were who they were. "Had I known about"—he waved, not wanting to say Rasheed's name aloud—"your past, I wouldn't have pushed."

"I know." Michael paused and a tiny grin lifted the corner of his mouth. "It was the hottest thing I've ever done."

The deep notes in Michael's voice sent sparks down Sam's spine. He tried to hide his own smile. Probably failed. That afternoon would top his favorite memory list, for sure. "Ditto." He sat back to give them both more space. If he hadn't moved away, he'd close the distance and start their problems all over again.

Michael sat back as well. "They don't know. Your colleagues."

That sucked the heat out of the room. "That I'm gay?"

Michael nodded and picked up his beer.

He owed Michael this much, certainly. "No. They think I'm a prude." Because men at his level weren't gay. Or rather, gay men didn't make it to this level. It was bullshit, but that was that. He'd chosen to play the game to get what he wanted—make the tech world a bit better for the people in the trenches, make a pile of cash, and thumb his nose at the establishment. The bitter taste in his throat returned. Except he was the establishment now. "They used to send women up to my room. I'd send them straight back down. Never occurred to them that there might be a reason other than morals."

Michael choked on his beer. "They sent you call girls?"

"Sure. At industry events. They also invited me out to strip joints. It's a thing." The first time a woman had shown up at his door, he'd waffled between wanting to quit and wanting to beat the living shit out of the guy who'd made the call. He had tipped the woman well and sent her on her way.

He would never resort to violence. Ever.

Maybe he should have quit back then. Made different choices. Michael sat an arm's reach away. So close. Too far.

"That's a shitty thing," Michael said.

"I don't disagree with you on that." Sam drank the last

of his beer. Venture capitalists—the ones like William—had more money than soul. After two more attempts to entice Sam, the women had stopped appearing at his door. "They sent me a guy once, as a joke. I sent him back like the others."

An odd look passed over Michael's face, curiosity twined with trepidation. It was an expression Sam had seen on many people, though never during a conversation like this. "What?" He let his irritation seep into his voice.

Michael's face reddened and he finished his beer, placing it decisively on the table. "Was he hot?"

Sam clamped down on the laughter that threatened to pour out. That would only draw attention to them, and he liked this place. A block from his apartment, it was somewhere he could fade into the background. People-watch. Dream. He took a deep breath. "Utterly. You know the statue of David? He looked like that, I swear to God."

"You could tell that from under his clothes?"

"He wasn't wearing anything under his coat."

Michael's mouth worked, but no sound came out for a long moment. Then a deep exhale. "And you sent him away."

"With five Benjamins."

Michael's eyes were wide, his mouth open. The dumbfounded look.

Sam chuckled. How he loved doing that to Michael.

If he stayed, he could keep doing that to Michael.

Their waiter came with the bill and he grabbed the black folder before Michael could. Wasn't hard. "Working dinner."

"I won't argue with that."

Sam pulled out his wallet, put the corporate card in the folder, and handed it back to the waiter. His cheeks hurt from grinning. Lighter heart, full stomach, and Michael was no longer mad at him nor running out the door to get away. There was only one way the night could be better—but he wasn't asking. No sex. No play. Even if the heat in his core kept creeping up his spine every time the skin at the corner of Michael's eyes crinkled just so.

Too many ghosts between them. Rasheed. The closet Sam had stuffed himself into after that one night in grad school.

Sam's stomach dropped. He wasn't going to think about that. Not here, not now. Not the bruises on that student's face or...

"Why'd you let him go?" Michael's voice pulled Sam back into the present conversation.

"Hmm?"

"The David-for-hire."

"I prefer choosing, not having someone chosen for me." He'd nearly asked the Adonis to stay. "Besides, my colleagues would have hung that over my head—not only sleeping with a prostitute, but a male one. It's—" Sam paused, then sighed. "It's not good to be out in this profession."

The check came back. Sam added the tip and signed. He'd not hesitate to send that perfect chest back today. He'd much rather have a tall, dark-haired man who had the balls to order him to his knees. Even if he did regularly wear shirts with palm trees and parrots.

When the waiter left, Michael spoke. "Is everything business to you?"

"No." He held eye contact with Michael. "It probably should be. But no."

Michael didn't move.

The heat Sam had felt under his skin flared to life. He

could take Michael home. He knew what words to say, how to get under Michael's defenses, which buttons to push. The desire was there—he saw it in the tick of Michael's pulse point at his neck, the way he swallowed, the sweet look of indecision that flitted across his face.

Sam could chase those ghosts away. Have Michael one more time.

No. Rasheed. The job. The student kneeling in tears in the alley—God, tonight of all nights, why did he have to think about that?

Michael was only an itch. He'd jack off later, alone. "It's late. We should call it a night." He pushed himself away from the table and rose.

Michael stood, but more slowly, his breathing shallow. "Do you ever make mistakes?"

Fuck. "Yes, of course I do." All the damn time. Every day he denied who he was. That day he hadn't reported what had happened. Sam waited a moment, but Michael said nothing more, so he headed for the door. Michael followed.

Once outside into the cooler night air, Sam spoke again. "Accepting a drink from you was not one of them."

Even in the dimmer light, Michael's relief was evident. The relaxing of his shoulders, and unclenching of his hands.

"I've had businesses fail. Sometimes the miracle doesn't happen."

"You can just leave when that happens."

The sour taste of bile rose in Sam's throat. Someday, Michael would learn to think before he spoke edged words. "I could, yes. I never have. I stay until the end and try to get as many people jobs elsewhere as I can. I figure it's the least I can do."

Michael seemed to chew on those words. "Sometimes it's hard to believe someone like you exists as a CEO."

Man, what Taylor must have done to Michael and Four Rivers when he took over. "We're human. Some are good, some are bad, like in everything else." Some remained silent for all the wrong reasons. Sam stuffed his hands in his pockets. "I'm down a block and across the street."

Michael looked toward their office tower, even though it was obscured by many other buildings. "Short commute."

"It is exceedingly convenient." They walked the block and crossed the street. And lonely. No community. It would take a handful of words to convince Michael to come up. Goosebumps rose on Sam's arms, hidden by his shirt and jacket. Would Michael use his hand or his belt? Or find something in the apartment? The man had a creative streak.

"Do you ever worry that someone will out you?"

There was that cold trickle again. Haunted eyes staring back at him. "Yes." He paused and considered. "I'd like to think that my track record is more important than who I prefer to bang, but I've seen guys like me come out. No one calls them anymore. No company needs their help. The well dries up. It's... I haven't given away *all* my money. Just in case." Sam looked up at the white brick building that was his home at the moment.

"You hate it," Michael murmured, a little too close to Sam's ear.

Sam exhaled. "We all have something we dislike about our jobs." He didn't give Michael time to respond. "What about you? People at work know you're gay now?" If they were going to have this conversation in the middle of the street, he wasn't the only one who was going to be grilled.

"There's a rainbow flag in my cube and I've mentioned going to Pride, so yes, they all know. I haven't dated anyone since Rasheed—and no one knew about that—so there's been no boyfriend at the holiday party or anything like that."

"Do you want to date someone?" The question slipped out before he could pull it back. Damn the beer and late hour. The memories. Sam faced Michael, because you didn't turn away after asking that.

"Well, I'd like to try. But circumstances..." He shrugged. "Plus, he's in the closet."

Yeah, he was. Firmly, too. Sam closed the distance between them and pulled Michael into a kiss. Folly. Pure folly. But damn, those lips, that heartbroken expression. He broke away and stepped back. "The circumstances are shit. The closet is shit."

Michael stared at him, face ruddy, lips wet. "What do you—" He swallowed and then straightened.

The sudden craving in Michael's expression spiked desire straight to the bottom of Sam's spine. Every nerve tingled and his cock filled.

"Do you want me to come up?" Michael spoke low, his voice like silk over skin.

"Desperately." That, too, slipped out without thought. But Sam followed it with more words. "But you're not going to."

Michael froze again and in the dim cast of twilight and streetlights, confusion replaced desire.

"We can't fuck this up. The job. Four Rivers. We nearly did." Because it wasn't just sex—it had never been just sex for Sam. Yes, he wanted more. Dates. Ice cream in the park. Long walks. Stupid stuff. Things you didn't ever do with your employee.

Things you did with a boyfriend. A partner. And he couldn't be that for Michael. Not when he moved so often.

Not when he hid his sexuality. Not after what Rasheed had put Michael through—because Sam would put him through the same damn thing.

Michael's stance changed, shifted. "You're right, of course."

The longing to kiss him again was overwhelming. Instead, he forced his lips into something he hoped resembled a smile. "Good night, Michael."

Michael's expression didn't change. "See you tomorrow."

They turned almost at the same time, away from each other. Sam pulled open the door to the lobby of the building and entered. He didn't look back. He could never look back. Not in this career.

***

SAM TOSSED THE PEN AT HIS CLOSED—AND LOCKED— office door. It clattered against the wood, then dropped silently onto the office carpet. Documents covered his desk —financials, the incorporation papers, board minutes, the little folder that contained Taylor's dirty deeds—every piece of information he'd been able to find that might contain some hint of William's motivations. Because you didn't try to kill then sell a company for negative return on investment. That was insane—the very last resort. Actively working against your best hope for creating a company of value, ripe for acquisition? Sam shook his head.

He'd spent a good part of Sunday combing though the pages in front of him—and there the clues were. Tiny little hints that meant nothing to someone not horribly suspicious. A note about William's presence at some key dealings. The fact that he'd been instrumental in hiring

Taylor—and had overridden several internal checks and balances in the hiring process to make sure they "got the best person." During the churn-up after Susan and Rasheed had left, William had set himself up as the continuity guy— though Michael would have been the obvious choice.

William had *never* been that hands-on before.

Then there were William's little bonuses, the ones that *seemed* to be based on sales—but the timing and the amounts didn't add up—at least not to Sam.

He ran a hand through his hair. A forensic accountant would probably have a field day with the papers strewn on top of his desk. Especially the inexplicable fluctuation in the petty cash account. Sometimes it had perhaps one hundred dollars, other times, nearly three thousand. But no one paid much attention to petty cash. Pennies, when some of the equipment in the labs cost as much as a luxury car. Or more. Problem was, in the end, none of it was concrete proof of anything other than bad bookkeeping.

William wasn't on any other boards at the moment and had no record of any current dealings with any other companies. Just Four Rivers.

That only fueled Sam's suspicions. He'd never know William not to be sleazing up at least three companies at once.

What a way to spend a weekend. Sam rubbed his forehead. He should have been sleeping in. Reading. Being bent over a table by Michael and fucked senseless.

Sam let out a breath through clenched teeth. That last thought came complete with the memory of being filled by Michael's cock, the sharp pain of leather against his back. The dark scent of Michael and leather, the tang of Michael's semen on his tongue.

He adjusted his hardening dick, then pulled another

pen from the holder on his desk and lobbed it at the door. A third followed, for good measure.

Damn good thing Michael wasn't in the office today—most of the company had been here yesterday, working on the release, but today it had been just him and a handful of folks—and everyone else had left after lunch.

Fuck. He should write some of this down, but the last thing he needed was to be sued if those notes wound up in William's hands. Which could happen, given how much access William had to the office. Sam tapped a finger against his lips. Now that was something else he should look into—badge records. The system recorded whenever anyone carded themselves into the office.

Sam stood. Server room, then.

He kicked the fallen pens out of the way and unlocked his door. Relocked it, too—paranoia wasn't healthy, but the records in there? Some of them he'd pulled from the CFO's office—not exactly innocent paperwork. Better under lock and key, especially if William was making unexpected visits. Though, for all he knew, the man had access to the master key for all the offices.

He didn't really want to think about that.

Sam used his card to unlock the server room and pushed the door open. Being back here only reminded him of Michael—the length of that body, the way those lips turned either to a smile or a frown, the intensity of Michael's commands. Sam swallowed the thoughts and headed to the right, slid the keyboard for the security system out, and typed in his user ID and password.

Denied.

Sam stared at the screen. Now that was damn odd. He should have had the same access as the IT manager. He'd asked for that when he'd joined—made it contingent, in fact, on his hiring. Too many old IT habits. He liked unfettered access. He'd also cajoled IT into giving him the root passwords they weren't supposed to give to anyone—it paid to speak the language of the tribe.

Sam took out his phone, looked up what he needed, and logged in.

Yes, William had been visiting the office. Quite a bit on weekends. A chill ran down Sam's spine. *Like you're doing right now.* Granted, ostensibly he was here because of the release.

Sam looked over his own records—and hovered over the entries for today. One to enter the office, the other to enter the server room. Oh the temptation, to delete that one line, to cover up his tracks, except that would make him as bad as William. Having root access to the system he could explain —but altering the records? No. He switched back to William's page, printed off a copy, and logged out.

List in hand, Sam slipped back to his office and studied the pile of records on his desk. Time to get to work correlating some of this with when William had been physically present at Four Rivers.

An hour later, a fourth pen joined the other three on the floor.

Some intriguing patterns had emerged—William tended to be in on weekends when the petty cash count swung wildly. Some of the dates also corresponded to known times Taylor had moved money around—but it still wasn't enough because there was no proof that Taylor had been in the office at the same time. Only William. Sam already had Taylor's list of visits in the dirty deeds folder.

Security camera footage might have proved they visited together, but those records were stored off-site in a secure facility built into an old limestone mine. Not like he could waltz in and ask for them. The language of the tribe wouldn't take him *that* far.

Besides, none of the cash they'd found Taylor with had ended up in William's hands. Sure, William's response to the Taylor crisis had seemed a bit over the top, especially since they'd been thick as thieves at one point. But that wasn't motive.

There wasn't any motive for William screwing around with Four Rivers.

A sudden longing for Michael nearly overwhelmed Sam —he could help sift through this mess. He'd been at Four Rivers the entire time—knew what wasn't written down.

And he wanted Michael again. Inside his mouth, inside his body, in his mind, making him fly. Every day. Desire so strong it hurt his heart, stole his breath, and pained his soul. This unquenchable need had to end, and soon, before it broke them both—and everything else—to pieces.

He'd run out of pens to throw, which left only one option. Call in a favor.

Sam picked up his cell phone, flipped through his contacts, found the name he wanted—Fabian Miles—and tapped to connect.

Fabian answered after three rings, his dusty voice barking out his name.

"Hey, it's Randell Anderson. Sorry for calling on a Sunday. I hope I haven't interrupted anything."

"Randy? No, no. I was just"—something thumped on the other end—"cleaning the garage. Wife's been after me for weeks. How are you doing?"

They shot the shit for a few minutes—Fabian recounting the health of his family, his companies—"You're not looking for a new position, are you?"

Sam's spine tingled. "Not at the moment."

"Shame. I'm on the board of a start-up that could really use someone like you. Boston area. Large data storage devices—better tech for the cloud and all that. Good stuff, but their management—" Sam could picture the older, silver-haired man shaking his head. "Crying shame. Sure I couldn't tease you away?"

Sam looked at the calendar on his wall. If the release went off as planned, he might very well be out of Four Rivers soon. His heart hollowed. A new job would solve this issue with Michael, give them both the distance they needed. Sam's lungs tightened, but he spoke anyway. "I may be freeing up in a couple of weeks."

"I'll send you the info."

"Thanks."

Another bang, then a scrape from Fabian's end. "I'm sure me snapping you up to fix a mess and make me money isn't the reason you called."

Sam had to laugh, even though his heart hurt like hell. Leave Michael? But yes. Yes, that would fix many things, including Fabian's company. "I'm trying to dig up some information on William Vandershoot."

"Oh, don't tell me you're working with that asshole again." A pause. "*You're* the guy they got for Four Rivers? After the Taylor thing?"

"That would be me, yes. William wasn't pleased."

"No, I bet he wasn't."

Now that was an interesting comment. Sam considered his next question. "Fabian, are there things I should know?"

A grunt. "Maybe. What *do* you want to know about William?"

Everything wasn't a good reply. "What's he got his fingers into? Where else is he working? Officially—"

"Randy, you've been around the block enough times to know William doesn't do everything officially."

"That's why I'm asking. If he's got something else going on, I sure as shit don't know. Not like he's going to tell me."

Fabian coughed a laugh. "Oh yes. You, who show him up. The younger, better-looking, more successful man. And you're ethical."

Sam winced. *Ethical.* Except for the part where he was bending over and begging his employee to fuck him hard up the ass. If Fabian knew, this phone call wouldn't be happening. Church-going, devout, and kind Fabian had twisted his face into knots the one time they'd both been at a tech conference in Chicago during the same weekend as Pride.

But Randell Anderson wasn't gay. Just *ethical.* Sam chewed on his own hypocrisy. "I figured if anyone knew, you would."

A chuckle from the other side. "Because I like keeping my enemies closer?"

His turn to laugh. "Pretty much."

And then Fabian told him. Within a minute Sam sprang up to retrieve one of his pens from the floor and started taking notes. He'd filled a page with writing by the time Fabian finished.

"That enough?"

Holy hell was it ever. "Yup. That's great. I owe you one."

"Come to Boston and I'll owe you twenty."

Boston. How apropos. The place where he'd climbed into the closet all those years ago. Bile burnt his throat and he coughed. "I'll look over the information. Get back to you."

"Great." More clattering, then the laughter of children.

"Look, I've got to go. I'll forward you the job details tonight."

"Thanks, Fabian."

"It's nothing. Talk to you soon."

Fabian hung up.

Sam set the phone down on a file of financial records, then dropped his head to his hands. Between William and the thought of returning to Boston, the sick, sharp taste of bile threatened to overwhelm Sam.

Apparently William had quite a bit going on off the books. Fingers in dealings with several other companies—including some of the same ones Taylor had been officially a part of when their money had gone missing.

Then there was the investment scheme William had on the side.

There'd been rumors about one with Taylor, but no hard evidence. Sam closed his eyes. What William had his hand in sounded close to a Ponzi scheme. People plunking money in and getting great returns. Unheard-of returns for this point in the market.

If that were the case, then Four Rivers would have been in deep shit if Sam hadn't been brought on board. Every last employee—including Michael—would have been out of a job by now. Sell the assets, make a bit of money, shove it out as interest and lure more people in.

Did someone else on the board know what the hell was going on? Or had they just been sick enough of William's mishandling of Taylor to hire Sam and screw it all up by accident?

Shit. This was over his head. He should do a bit more digging to verify what Fabian had told him—but if any of this were true, he needed to hand it over to Sundra's legal folks. He ripped the sheet off the notepad and folded it into a tight rectangle. Research, he could do from his apartment.

Sam sat back, then stared at his cell phone.

That left Boston and the ache in his chest where his heart should have been.

When Four Rivers was safe—when Michael was safe—he needed to leave. Keep moving. Unless the Boston gig was a complete waste of time—and if Fabian wanted him to come, then it wasn't—he'd say yes and return to being Randell Anderson.

Michael—well, the man deserved someone not mired in the muck and stench of *business*.

Sam grabbed the financial records he'd borrowed. Those files needed to be returned and the rest of the papers needed to be cleaned up; then he could start thinking about exit strategies.

He glanced at the calendar. A week left until Forum. Another city—another hotel. One last time for Sam to be himself—if Michael agreed to go.

Sam exhaled. Getting Michael to attend Forum? Easy. Sundra wanted to meet him—the man who'd been there from the beginning. Michael would jump at the chance. Enticing Michael into one last fling? Sam shivered. Easy as well. All those buttons to push.

It was the *code* that needed to work, or they were all finished.

CHAPTER FIVE

Michael put the pen down for the millionth time. The end was already chewed to bits. Too many final tests had turned his bad habit into a near compulsion. His screen flickered with terminal windows running scripts; the scrolling text jangled his nerves as scripts executed command after command.

Forum started in four days. These were the last tests he needed to run to stamp the release ready to be shipped. If they passed. *Please, please pass.*

They'd spent the past three weeks in high gear. Everyone who could worked long hours in the office, and those who couldn't put in time from home. Even Sam had stayed, rolling up his sleeves and helping with installation testing. He also pulled out the company credit card and ordered dinner for the office every night.

And they'd done it. Michael eyed his screen. Maybe.

Shoes scuffed the carpet near his cube and he turned to see Sam in the aisle. No jacket, loose tie. His hair was even a touch unruly. "How's it coming?"

Michael gestured at the screen. "Still running. Shouldn't be long now."

Sam stepped inside the cube and touched the guest chair. "May I?"

Michael nodded. Sam pulled the chair up next to Michael's and sat.

Sam's presence was not exactly soothing, but it was welcome. They'd found a rhythm again as coworkers, as boss and lead, and that eased the tension in everyone around them.

They made a good team, really. He ignored the sudden hollowness in his chest and picked up a pen, a different one than before. It too, was chewed on the end. He tossed it back. "Fuck." It was only a murmur, just a curse under his breath. He doubted Sam heard. He bounced his leg until the cube walls vibrated and Sam put a hand on his thigh.

"Stop."

The touch, the command, ripped through Michael and stilled everything, even his breathing. The warmth of Sam's hand blazed through Michael's shorts and straight to the back of his skull. He shuddered and took a deep breath. The room seemed both dimmer and brighter. Was this what Sam felt when Michael took control? *Jesus.*

"The tests will pass." Sam didn't remove his hand.

They hadn't touched, not in any intimate sense, since dinner at the Sharp Edge. Probably a good thing, since Sam's hand on his thigh was making it very hard to think.

"How do you know?" Somehow Michael's voice didn't falter, didn't sound unnatural. He stared at the scrolling text, even as his cock hardened.

A deep chuckle, one Michael felt in his bones. "Because it's you." Sam tapped his fingers and Michael fought to contain a moan. "Your attention to detail has been the bane of everyone's existence for weeks. I doubt we missed anything."

"We always miss something." It was the nature of software. Hardware, too. None of it was perfect.

"I'm not talking about weird corner cases or the box not working when submerged in water or set on fire. I mean normal functionality. A product as rock solid as you've released before."

Only if the tests passed. Michael hazarded a look at Sam to find the other man watching him.

The desire to kiss Sam was overwhelming. He nearly did, twisting slightly in his chair. The things he wanted to say. *I want you. I need you.* Every nerve felt like a live wire. Rock solid didn't just describe the release...

Get a grip. He's your goddamn boss. Beyond Sam, a little rainbow flag sat, stuck in a mug of pens. A reminder. Never again. Michael cleared his throat. "I certainly hope so."

They turned back to the screens at the same time. Three of the five windows no longer had scrolling text. All three read "pass." Sam gripped Michael's thigh, but this time the breathlessness Michael felt wasn't from that touch, but from watching one of the test scripts cleaning up and resetting the hardware.

"Here we go," Sam said.

The script finished. Pass.

Together they sat and watched the last script run, both leaning forward toward the screen. When the script entered the cleanup phase, Sam hissed.

"Come on, come on," Michael muttered. This job would give him an aneurysm one of these days.

Pass.

Neither of them moved. "Holy shit," Michael whispered.

"Told you." Sam leaned back, his voice low as well. "You're the best." Finally, he took his hand from Michael.

The loss of the warmth, the pressure, the knowledge of Sam's presence sent a bolt of sadness straight through the joy and relief coursing through Michael. Unsettled, he stood. "I guess we should tell the team."

Sam rose as well, and pushed the guest chair back to its place. "You should let them know. It's your victory. You've been working toward this for so long."

Sam didn't mean the release. "Thanks." Michael needed to calm down. Good God, they were done. Everything passed. "Mind if I send everyone home?"

"God, no. Kick 'em out." Sam's grin was huge. "They deserve the rest." He turned to leave, then paused. "Michael?"

"Yeah?"

"Good job." Then Sam was gone.

Michael grabbed the back of his chair. The words had been professional. The tone, however, had been a caress, like silk on skin, as if Sam had spoken entirely different words, as if he had said—

Michael shook himself and walked out of the cube. Enough with fantasies. Time to spread the good news.

IN THE END, THEY SENT EVERYONE HOME, EVEN HR and support. Michael finished his rounds and found himself in front of Sam's office. Inside Sam tapped away at his keyboard, seemingly oblivious to Michael's presence.

"You should go home, too," Michael said.

Sam started and whipped around in his chair. "God. Don't do that!"

"Sorry." He leaned against the doorframe and tried to keep the smile from his lips.

Sam snorted. "The fuck you are."

Seeing Sam breathless and reddening? He'd never grow tired of that. Michael shrugged. "Didn't think I was being all that quiet. And you should go home." So damn good to be able to banter again, if nothing else.

Sam waved his words away. "Can't. I have presentations for Forum to work on." He cleared his throat. "Actually, I've been meaning to ask you something about that."

"I'm an idiot with PowerPoint." Michael pushed himself off the doorframe and took a seat in one of the guest chairs. "So, I can't help you there."

"Not about the presentations. About Forum."

That was interesting, as was the ruddy hue of Sam's face. "What about Forum?"

"They would like to meet one of the engineering staff. Someone from the technical side of things."

They? "The board?" That didn't make sense. The board knew Michael, all too well.

Sam shook his head.

A little flutter, like a micro bolt of electricity ran through Michael's chest. If not the board, then Sundra Networks. Still, he had to ask. "Why?"

"Why do you think?" Sam leaned back in his chair. "Sundra wants to see if we really know our shit."

"No, Sam, why me?"

Sam didn't speak for several moments, though his lips parted. Eventually, words came out. "Because you founded this place, Michael, official paperwork or not."

The photo album still sat on Sam's desk, reminder of his past, both good and bad.

"You know Four Rivers' tech better than anyone else

and from end to end. And experience has shown me that
you can think on your feet." Sam paused, then added.
"When you're not being an ass."

He couldn't deny the last bit. "I promise not to be an
ass."

"You'll have to give a presentation on the technology."
Sam waved over his shoulder. "I have the slides created, but
it'll sound better coming from you."

The energy he felt earlier flagged a bit. Public speaking
wasn't his thing. Oh he could do it, he just hated it. But to
miss a chance to meet folks at Sundra? Be a part of selling
his company, even if it wasn't *his* anymore? "I'll do it." He
ran his fingers through his hair. "Anything else?"

Sam tented his hands, a trace of a smile flickering on his
face. "You'll have to wear a suit."

Michael quashed his own desire to smile, and winced
instead. "I can do that, too." A dark joy warmed Michael's
core. Sam would see how well he could clean up. Another
chance to fluster Sam, to leave him breathless. If it couldn't
be from sex or a beating, Michael would make do with other
ways.

"Good." Sam spun back to his computer, brought up a
screen that looked suspiciously like travel arrangements,
and pressed a button. "We leave on Sunday." When he
rotated back to Michael, he held something silver in his left
hand.

The cuff link. The lust was nearly instant and almost
painful. Sam must have read his expression, because he
grinned.

You little bastard. It wasn't an invitation, but it was close
to one. All their talks must have worn off. Damn it all.

Well, if Sam wanted it, he was going to get it. Enough

fooling around. He'd show Sam what being out could be like.

Michael rose, completely aware of just how hard he'd become in those few seconds. "I guess I'd better go home and think about packing."

There'd be a bit more than a suit going into his luggage.

CHAPTER SIX

Sam poured himself a coffee from the self-serve kiosk in the hotel lobby, and then joined William at a seating arrangement within view of the elevators. Eight forty-one in the morning at a hotel in New Orleans that bordered the French Quarter. Not that they'd see any more of the local area than on the whirlwind tour William had insisted they take last night. Sam took a sip of his coffee.

There'd been no time to double-check any of Fabian's information, so he opted for doing as Fabian did—keeping William close—at least at Forum.

"Sebastian better be on time," William said.

"He will be." Michael was a poster boy for punctuality. He had four more minutes before their appointed meeting time.

William grunted. He looked jet-lagged and cranky and clutched a coffee of his own. Not surprising, given he'd arrived from the West Coast. In New Orleans, life happened two hours earlier for William and an hour later for Sam and Michael.

If only Sam had been able to enjoy that extra hour with

Michael. But no, William had kept them out late, forgetting that morning came much earlier than in Palo Alto. Besides, there had been no good way to negotiate a possible rendezvous with Michael.

When they'd returned to the hotel, predictably, William had tried to get both of them to head with him to a strip club.

"But then, you don't do women, do you Mike?" The animosity in William's words had set Sam's hackles up.

Michael had laughed. "Nope." Then he'd stood and towered over William and said good night before retreating to the elevators.

Sam had pointed to his watch. "You'll hate tomorrow if you go." Then he'd paid his tab and fled, too.

By the time Sam reached the bank of cars, Michael was gone. Then again, Sam wasn't even sure Michael would agree to another tryst. He'd kept his distance at the airport, slept part of the way on the plane, and his conversations with Sam had been more about work than pleasure. The glint Sam had seen in Michael's eyes when he'd told him about Forum and shown him the cuff link was gone.

Sam took a swig of coffee and winced at the awful taste. Perhaps that was for the best. In three weeks, Sundra would hopefully acquire Four Rivers, and Sam would be packing his bags and moving to Boston to take the job Fabian had offered. He'd been right—the data store company was a perfect gig and it gave him a chance to return to a city he'd fled once before. The contract should be at his apartment by now. A sudden tightness caught Sam in his chest and he checked his watch, then the bank of elevators. Eight forty-three.

There wasn't much time left for them.

"Ah, here he is." William looked behind Sam, toward

the doors to the street just as Michael stepped past Sam's chair.

Coal-gray fabric draped elegantly down Michael's very long legs, and black leather suspenders peeked from beneath a perfectly tailored jacket. When Michael raised his hand to check the time, a silver hint of a cuff link caught Sam's attention. Michael dropped his arm too fast to make out the design of the link, but nothing glinted from Michael's other cuff. He held a takeaway coffee cup that smelled of good beans and chicory.

The hair on the back of Sam's neck rose. Was Michael wearing the Copernican link? A sign of... something?

"I'm not late, am I?" Michael's strong voice rattled the marrow of Sam's bones.

"No, right on time." William answered, which was good, because Sam doubted he could put two words together. He had to find his center really fucking soon because he could not be seen like this. Sam took a slow breath and fought to normalize his heart rate.

Michael wore a suit as if he'd been born into power, as if he lived in one. So very different from the way he looked in khakis, tropical prints, and Birkenstocks. His tie was a swirl of blue and black, with hints of blood red, and even when Sam rose, Michael seemed to tower over him, tall and lean, with impossibly broad shoulders.

Commanding.

William must have felt that too, because he stood straighter, with an air of alertness, and had put out his hand. "Nice to see you again, Mike." Gone was the hostility of the previous evening.

Michael took the offered hand and shook. "William." He turned. "Sam."

Instinct overrode sense, and Sam reached out to shake

in greeting. Michael's hand was electrifying and warm, his grip strong and confident. The silver at Michael's wrist was, in fact, the link Sam had given him. Holy shit.

"Michael." Somehow, Sam managed to say the name without sounding as breathless as he felt. His cock threatened to harden, a serious problem, given that he would be speaking to an audience in a half an hour. It was a damn good thing Michael never dressed this way in the office.

"I noticed a beignet café on our adventure last night. Stopped in this morning for nonbland coffee." He held up his cup. "Highly recommended if you want a local taste."

"Have to remember that for tomorrow," Sam said.

William snorted. "Not me. Mornings come too early here."

Michael smiled. "Better here than New York City? Three hours might kill you, William."

William snorted again.

Michael gestured toward the conference area. Other suited men and women headed that way. "Shall we?"

William took the lead, with Sam and Michael falling into step behind. They entered the main conference area, where the opening keynote would be given. William surged forward to clasp hands with Vijay Malik, the CEO of Sundra Networks, but Sam lingered behind. Off-kilter and more than a little aroused by the man standing next to him, he needed some space to get his head on straight. He had to give his speech after the keynote, and Michael—wanted him. He was certain.

The hotel brew did nothing but cause Sam's taste buds to shrivel, especially after the smell of Louisiana coffee wafting from Michael's cup. He dropped his coffee into the nearest trash can. "Awful doesn't begin to describe that."

Without a word, Michael handed his cup to Sam. It was full, practically untouched.

He shouldn't have, but he gave in and took a sip, then allowed himself a sigh at the rich flavor and sharp taste. He looked at the coffee. "Damn. If I had known this was close by, I'd have asked you to wake me."

"You'll be awake tomorrow."

Sam nearly coughed out his next sip at the assuredness of that statement. "You know what they say about assumptions."

A flash of teeth before Michael's expression settled into a very professional mask. "I'm not assuming."

A bolt of lust flew straight to Sam's cock. That they were playing this game here, of all places, minutes before Sam had to climb on a stage and give his talk made the whole experience surreal, tantalizing, and terrifying. Especially when they'd pretty much told each other they wouldn't do this anymore.

Except, of course, he'd started this round by brandishing the cuff link, because he couldn't keep away from Michael. He'd known what Michael would do, how he'd respond. *You're playing with fire.*

He took another draw of Michael's coffee. "Do you mind if I finish this?"

"Not at all. I bought it for you."

For him? Warmth, but not from lust, settled into Sam's center. He didn't say anything because he couldn't, for the second time that morning. *This man will undo me.* Hell, he already had. Repeatedly. It's why he kept sticking his foot outside the security and safety of being the straight, but prudish, CEO.

The closet was suffocating him. Slowly. Michael was a lifeline. And maybe Sam's doom.

"We should sit. They'll start soon," Michael said.

Sam could only nod. He followed Michael to the front of the room and they took seats near the steps up to the right side of the stage.

Michael spoke again. "Every morning, you walk seventeen blocks to 21st Street Coffee, past several corporate coffee houses. I knew you'd appreciate a fine cup." He stretched out his legs.

Michael knew him. The revelation spread like a flush all over his body. These past weeks, the scant months they'd spent working together, even when they weren't speaking to each other, even though the past—and the present—came between them, Michael had paid attention. Boston seemed entirely too far from Pittsburgh, all of a sudden. Just as sitting inches away from Michael seemed too great a distance to span.

He was leaving because staying meant surrender to the strictures of corporate culture that looked down on gay as weak. Again, one word echoed in his head. *Coward.*

"Thank you." Sam spoke low. "I—" He swallowed words that were entirely too personal. "That was kind."

If Michael said anything, it was lost in the sudden stirring of the room as Vijay Malik walked onto the stage. Lights dimmed.

Sam pushed the mix of thoughts and emotions aside, focusing on the taste of coffee in his mouth, the affection of the man next to him, and the Sundra CEO.

Showtime.

Michael knew he'd unsettled Sam, but he doubted anyone else noticed. Payback for the cuff link in the office and for expecting him to drop everything and be at Forum. Never mind that it stiffened Michael's cock to see Sam off-kilter. When Vijay Malik launched into his keynote, Michael shifted in his seat so that his thigh pressed against Sam's in the darkened room. Sam's hitched breath was music to Michael's ears. Every so often, Michael shifted, to remind Sam he was there, next to him.

Sam sipped his coffee and focused intently on the Sundra CEO. After a few minutes he smiled and pressed back against Michael.

When Malik wrapped up his keynote touting the best year for Sundra yet, Michael moved his body away from Sam's. Best to let Sam catch his breath and compose himself. A few minutes later, strong applause signaled the end of Malik's speech. When it died back, Malik introduced the next speaker—S. Randell Anderson.

Sam rose and strode onstage with an air of confidence that had most of the room leaning forward. He launched right into his introduction to Four Rivers' latest release and his experience as CEO.

Michael relaxed his shoulders a bit. Everything he'd done today, he'd done with this result in mind—get Sam onto that stage with as much energy and power as he could. The future of Four Rivers depended on that, whether or not his secondary plan of coaxing the man into his bed came to fruition. He could be a manipulative bastard when he wanted. The suit helped—which is why he didn't wear one often. That dominant role he liked a little too much, but it wasn't one he desired full-time.

Which was why, in so many ways, Sam was perfect. Submissive at times, but not always. They fit. Except for the boss and not-out part.

On the stage, Sam rarely kept still. He paced to the side

of the screen that displayed his presentation, so close to careering over the edge of the platform that the tension in the room was palatable.

Pure Sam. Intelligent, beautiful. In command.

Well, for the moment. Michael resisted the urge to smile. Sam still wanted Michael. His expression when Michael had arrived in the lobby had been priceless, and one Michael planned to remember. The curve of those lips and the startled, yet hungry, look. Oh yes, Michael cleaned up well, and Sam, for all his type-A control, needed to surrender to power now and then. An image of a very different Sam than the one on stage—naked and on his knees, hands tied behind his back, mouth open in silent pleading—flashed through Michael's mind and stiffened his dick.

Tonight, with any luck.

It would have to be Sam's choice, though. Michael wasn't going to chase after him—just entice. Play. Sam certainly was no Rasheed, but he still had a closetful of issues—and unless he did something about those, there was no hope beyond New Orleans.

Michael's heart ached for a moment and he took a breath. A quick glance at his fellow conference goers told Michael that the room listened intently as Sam spoke of leading from within, of being a part of a team not the head of it, of trusting your employees rather than lording over them.

He doubted it was a speech those in leadership roles expected, especially when Sam stopped and challenged them to walk the talk.

Sam's adherence to his own code was one of the things Michael lov—

Michael pulled his legs in and stared at Sam, as

enwrapped as everyone else, but for an entirely different reason. His entire body numbed then blazed with heat. *Oh, shit.*

Admiration. Desire. Lust.

Love?

Shit. But there it was. Of course it was there, or at least the start of love. Why else was he still here, after swearing up and down to himself he wouldn't be?

Sam was his boss. They could play their power games around the rules, in the corners of life, but this... there wasn't really any way around love.

He couldn't date his CEO. He'd known that from the beginning. He wouldn't date a man in the closet. He'd learned that mistake with Rasheed.

Yet he wore Sam's cuff link, the one Sam had pressed into Michael's hand after he'd slapped and fucked Sam into bliss. He'd brought Sam coffee. Dreamt about him.

Of course it was love.

On the stage, Sam wrapped up his speech. "If you want your employees to work hard, you have to work harder. If you want them to give up their nights and weekends, you better as well, and make it worthwhile. It's not a privilege to sit at the top—it's a responsibility." Sam's voice boomed over the crowd. "So take up the true mantle of leadership, the true cost. Risk your hide, and the reward will be all the greater."

Every transgression carried risk. Michael shifted in his seat. This time, he wouldn't run, no matter what passed between Sam and him. There were other options, other ways they could solve the tangled mess they'd fallen into—if Sam felt similarly. If Sam cared enough to stop hiding who he was.

Rasheed hadn't been willing to change for Michael—

he'd been willing to change for his family, for society—let go of who he was and be someone he wasn't. Sam might be hiding from his colleagues, but unlike Rasheed, he accepted his sexuality. Embraced and reveled in it.

Rasheed wouldn't even fuck with the lights on.

Why, then, was Sam so hung up? He needed to know. Needed Sam.

First things first. Four Rivers had to be safe, and there had to be a secure future for the employees—or as secure as one could be in the corporate world.

Then, Michael would take the leap he swore he wouldn't again.

It was just a matter of figuring out which cliff to jump from.

AFTER HIS SPEECH SAM COULDN'T FIND MICHAEL at all. He'd vanished from the front of the room during the scant minutes Sam spent talking to Dr. Malik. When he made his way back to where he and Michael had been sitting, only the chairs and Sam's coffee remained. Given that William was also nowhere to be found, Michael might have been dragged off to some meet-and-greet.

He hoped that was the reason. Had his speech pissed off Michael somehow? No. Their philosophy of leadership wasn't that different. But there was no way for Sam to slip free of the crowd of people working their way forward to speak to him. No chance to find Michael and ask him what he thought.

How many of the folks anxiously working their way forward had actually listened to the content of his speech? He had no idea. Even if he reached one person, that might change corporate culture for the better—and that would be worth all the energy. That was part of the reason he'd worked so hard to get where he was despite all the costs. He pushed the desire to find Michael aside and walked forward to greet those waiting for him.

Much to Sam's delight, the questions and conversations were thoughtful and heartening—proof that his way of leadership wasn't unknown or unappreciated. As he spoke to the attendees, other sessions started. Eventually, the crowd about him thinned and cleared. Twenty-five minutes later, Sam exited the conference hall. Time well spent.

Sadly, the coffee from Michael had gone cold, but like all good roasts, it held its flavor. Sam drank the rest of it, then tossed the cup. He might have a chance for another warm brew tomorrow. Pinpricks ran up his spine. Had Michael asked for a night together? It wasn't a question he could ask Michael in the middle of a tech conference. Sam still felt the heat from Michael's leg pressed against his and he wanted more. So much more. Had Michael done such things with Rasheed? Probably not, from what Michael had said. *Good.*

How would those people he'd just spoken to have reacted if they had known Sam was gay? That he longed for the touch of another man? Hell, he probably wouldn't have been asked to make a speech. He wasn't nearly at the level where gay no longer mattered and could be celebrated. You had to be head of Apple or American Eagle for that—not someone like him.

And certainly not someone like that grad student in the alley. Sam rubbed his head. He had grown up sheltered, protected. He'd never experienced anyone hurt like that before—not at someone else's hands. Worse than the movies. The smell of blood, fear, anger, and hopelessness.

Sam stared at his hands. Nothing he could do about that now. The past was past. He exhaled and stuffed the memories back into the corners of his mind, where they belonged.

A quick check of his watch told him there was time to kill before Michael gave his technical presentation.

Sam could spend it with his head in the clouds, or make himself useful.

The latter was the better option. Time to see what the competition was up to. He wouldn't be leading Four Rivers—or Sundra—into the future, but he would leave a sheaf of advice for the next person. If Sam had his way, it would be Michael who would run the Pittsburgh office—take the position that should have been his from the beginning.

Sam browsed the exhibitors' hall, making mental notes of the protocols touted, the research explained, the hardware advances on display. Of most interest were the snippets of conversations. He cataloged it all, then found a quiet spot to type several quick notes into his smart phone.

Ten minutes before Michael's talk, Sam found the listed room and took a seat. At the front, Michael was deep in a conversation with Miles Breck, the VP of Engineering at Sundra. William hovered near by, looking like a nervous hen—or a shark waiting for a kill, Sam couldn't decide which. William's presence infuriated—the man had done just about everything to fuck over Four Rivers and Michael and for what? To fuel a scam? *Damn*. Maybe he should just drop all the information he knew on the legal department at Sundra and be done with it.

William likely guessed who Sam wanted in the head role in Pittsburgh, but it shouldn't matter—the directors would cash out and William remained on the board of several other companies. It made no sense to linger after that.

William had screwed Michael once before. Was this somehow personal? A different set of pinpricks tracked down Sam's limbs. William's comments from the previous night sounded in Sam's mind. *You don't do women, do you Mike?* Shit. This better not be about that.

Sam made another note on his smart phone. He had a few more favors he could call in, folks who could verify what Fabian had said. Most of all, he wanted William away from Michael. There'd been enough pain in Michael's life from that man.

A name and a voice reached out from Sam's past. "Randy?"

Next to him stood a familiar—if somewhat older— woman. "Greta?" Indeed, the woman was the spitting image of one of his undergrad partners-in-crime, Greta Bachman. Still all legs and brown curls, though now she wore a sedate gray pants suit. Her leather shoes had flames on them, like a motorcycle.

Some things never changed.

She sat down. "All grown up and a superstar CEO. How the hell are you?"

He snorted. "Not very starlike. But I'm doing well."

"I'll say. I was at your keynote. Same old passionate Randy, making waves."

Waves? Maybe. He brushed the words away. "What about you? Last I'd heard, you were off getting a PhD. Is it Dr. Bachman these days?"

"That was years ago. But yes." She studied the front of the room. "I hear you're bringing Four Rivers to us."

Us? "You're with Sundra?" He hadn't known.

"Director of Quality Assurance."

Sam shifted in his seat and warmth touched his cheeks. He should have been aware of that. And Greta... she knew a whole host of his secrets. Thankfully, most were inconsequential—stupid college stuff. But he'd been vibrantly out as an undergrad. "You're here to watch Michael."

"I've heard he's level-headed, smart, and passionate. Plus he knows his shit." She crossed her legs. "Kind of like you."

Time might not have passed at all. All the old rhythms were so easy to resume. "I'm not level-headed."

She chuckled and dropped her voice to a discrete level. "That's what all your boyfriends said."

He didn't know whether to laugh or wince, and ended up coughing. "Shit, I didn't know any of them talked to you."

"All the damn time." Her smile was infectious. "Is it still Randy? I see you're S. Randell on the schedule."

"I still answer to anything." He paused. "But it's Sam lately. At Four Rivers, it's Sam."

"Sam." She nodded up to the front of the room. "And your test guy? What's he like, really?"

Perfect. Hot. Demanding in every right way. Sam folded his arms and eyed Michael. "Passionate, as you said. An expert. He's what makes the whole damn thing work."

"The router?"

"The company. He's been there since day one." Sam felt Greta's attention shift and looked over to meet her stare. "He can be an ass, but can't we all? He's good, G. You'll like him."

She studied Michael again. "That's what I'm here to find out."

They settled in to watch the presentation. He and

Michael had spent the last day in the office going over the slides. Michael had insisted they strip out anything remotely marketing-esque. Sam balked, but in the end, if this were to be Michael's talk, it had to contain what he wanted, not what Sam thought sounded good.

The resulting presentation—lecture, in reality—was deeply technical. Within the first ten minutes, all the marketing folks slinked out of the room, but Greta leaned forward. She kept nodding her head as Michael talked.

Good. A flood of calm eased Sam's muscles. Greta would be an excellent ally for Michael, and like-minded when it came to technology. Sam suspected they also had similar thoughts on how to run a team, if his memory of her organizing labs was anything to go by.

Michael would be in fine hands and have a fantastic advocate within Sundra, which is just what he needed. He would be safe and have the room he needed to grow into the leader he could be—that he was—and given a title to match.

Sam's serenity shattered. He was saying good-bye. To the job. To Michael. Handing him over to Sundra. The realization punched him in the stomach. He nearly bent over and did suck in a bit of air. Not yet. He didn't want to leave Michael yet.

He couldn't stay. That was the nature of what he did. He never stayed. Never made attachments to a place. A company. A man.

Staying would mean... quitting. Failing. Leaving his career behind. He might as well come out at that point, the result would be the same. Would that be so bad, though? Sam shivered. For him? Maybe, maybe not. He doubted anyone would take a swipe at him now. And he was so screwed in the head lately, he wasn't sure he cared.

But for Michael? It might be disastrous. Sleeping with

the boss? No one would respect Michael, whether they
cared about his sexuality or not.

Michael moved in front of the slide about one of the
draft protocols and explained why one implementation was
preferable to another. Hands went up—questions. Answers.
Small arguments. Michael handled it beautifully. Every so
often, his jacket opened to reveal the long black braces Sam
wanted to grasp and use to pull their bodies together. A
flash of silver glinted at Michael's wrist when he gestured at
a slide.

An exceptional man.

Sam had been lucky their paths had crossed, but if he
lingered, if he continued to twist his own rules, he'd break to
pieces what they were trying to build at Four Rivers.

Employees shouldn't get fucked by their CEOs. And
that's what everyone would see if he stayed, even if the
reality were the opposite.

He had to let Michael go. There'd be no coffee in the
morning because there'd be no tonight. The best thing—the
level-headed course of action—would be to stay apart.

Not just a blow to the gut, but a series of them, each
worse than before.

Sam leaned back, forced himself to relax, and schooled
his expression. He caught Greta's glance from the corner of
his eye, but didn't turn. Instead, he followed Michael's
movements, the dance of his hands, the flow of his pants as
he walked, the expanse of his shoulders. Sam memorized
the sound of Michael's voice, the depth of it, the cadence,
like water flowing down a street of cobblestones.

The person most dangerous to the future of Four Rivers
now was Sam. Time to fire himself from Michael's life.

CHAPTER SEVEN

Michael had expected dinner out. Much like the previous night, William insisted they hit the French Quarter, though this time William invited several others, including Michael's likely new boss, Greta Bachman. Over seafood gumbo, she grilled Michael on testing standards, his methodology, how they used Four Rivers hardware in the office network—everything.

It was a damn fine conversation.

She sat back and picked up her wine glass. "Randy said you were good."

"Randy?" Michael's brain caught up with his mouth. "You mean Sam."

"Randy—Sam." She lifted her glass in salute to Sam, who sat two down from Michael. "Whatever the man's going by these days. We were classmates, way back when we were too young."

Interesting. Greta's tone, her smile, seemed to indicate no animosity. Good. Michael watched Sam speak to some VP of Marketing or some-such department.

They hadn't talked since Michael had handed Sam

coffee in the morning. A flicker of dread chased through Michael. He pushed it away. There hadn't really been any time to talk.

Michael returned his attention to Greta. "Was he always so driven?"

She nodded. "Got him into a ton of trouble with the department. He was a trailblazer in the true sense... he tended to set fire to everything he left behind. Mind you, it usually needed to be set aflame. Lots of old thinking in the hallowed halls."

"Different school, but I remember."

"I'm not surprised he ended up where he did, jumping from company to company and fixing them. Even in engineering, he saw what that needed to be improved on the business side of the world. A way to make space for people to do their jobs."

"Well, he certainly did that at Four Rivers."

"Sounds like you did, too, from what he said."

Michael fished a shrimp out of his gumbo and digested her words. Since the board had taken over he had tried to insulate his people from upper management, give them room to perform and grow without the worry of looking over their shoulders. But his way was to push back at the suits— at the executives. Sam *was* the chief executive, and certainly more than just a suit.

So was Greta.

By dessert, Michael realized Greta was sussing out his opinions on more than just testing—she touched on software development, hardware, even manufacturing and purchasing.

"You guys should know all these things." He spoke softly, over the edge of his coffee cup.

Her smile was as enigmatic as Sam's could be. "From William, yes."

Shit. He'd answered truthfully. With any luck, he hadn't just sunk the acquisition. Who knows what the hell William had said.

They took the long way back to the hotel after dinner. Sam strode ahead with William and the other VP. There was no damn way to get anywhere near him without being exceedingly obvious. Michael wasn't about to pull Sam aside in front of Sundra folks, especially not Greta— someone who had known Sam in college.

He stole another glance at her. Sam had been out once. Did Greta know? If she did... it was one more hole in the closet Sam had built.

How the hell was he going to break that down? Nothing had worked with Rasheed. Sam's reasoning might be different, but the result was the same.

Back at the hotel, William and the VP headed for the bar. Sam paused, but it wasn't Michael he addressed.

"Interested in a drink, G?" The familiarity in Sam's voice and smile made Michael's chest ache. Greta and Sam had formed a friendship over years. Would Michael ever hear such warmth from Sam in public?

Or *would* this be Rasheed all over again? Fuck.

Greta waved Sam to the bar. "I'm presenting tomorrow. I'll be a wreck if I don't sleep. Have one on me." She offered her hand to Michael. "A pleasure. If you're free, let's meet here again at nine. I'd like to talk further."

"I'm free," Michael said.

Greta nodded. After she headed to the elevator, Sam finally addressed him. "You coming to the bar?"

Flat words, nervousness, but not the kind Sam had

displayed in Curaçao. This spoke of walls and restraints, and not the fun kind. Same kind of look. Different guy.

"No," Michael said, then felt his guts fall when Sam looked relieved. "I think I'll turn in."

"Good night, Mike."

Ouch. That was a kick in the teeth. He tried to smile and failed. "Good night." But Sam was already turning away.

Halfway to the elevators, Michael stopped.

What the fuck? He rubbed his temples.

The morning's overtures had been promising and the coffee well received. Every signal Sam had given had been positive. Every one now was negative. Was Michael really going to walk away from Sam again? Every time he'd done that in the past, it had been disastrous for the two of them and Four Rivers.

Sam was not Rasheed.

Still. Michael couldn't march over to the bar and ask Sam what the hell was going on. What he could do, however, was give Sam the option of telling him.

No chasing, but one last chance for Sam to decide what he wanted.

Michael fished in the little folder with the keys to his room, pulled one out and stuffed it into his coat pocket. He headed toward the laughter and clinking of glasses and slipped next to Sam at the bar. "Hey, you dropped your key." Michael placed the folder on the counter.

Sam started and for an instant, he was the man Michael had seen enter a very different bar in a very different place. Hope, the reddening of his cheeks, but then a flash of fear.

He's not going to take it. The ache started at the back of Michael's head and spread down into his heart. So, just like that, it was over?

Sam picked the folder up and tucked it into his pocket. "Thanks. I owe you."

It took every ounce of discipline Michael had not to react, even as euphoria lightened his head more than any drink ever could. "Good night, Sam."

He didn't wait for a reply before he strode to the elevator. The only question now was would Sam use the card?

———

Sam might as well have had a hot coal in his pocket from the way the key to Michael's room made him burn. Two fingers of whiskey on the rocks, downed quickly, hadn't calmed him or numbed his need to follow Michael upstairs. He managed to sit through forty-five minutes of drinks and chat before the pressure in his lungs, head, and dick grew to great to ignore.

The conversation—or rather William's monologue—lulled enough that he could excuse himself.

William snorted. "Night's still young, Randell. I was thinking we should hit a place with a bit more... entertainment."

William meant a bar with barely clothed women. Not at all the scene Sam wanted. Keeping an eye on William didn't mean Sam had to put up with his shit. "Wish I could. The day took more out of me than I expected. I'd only put a damper on the night." He tossed down some bills for a bar tip and gave the men a nod. "But do enjoy yourselves."

As Sam headed toward the lobby he distinctly heard William call him a prude.

If only that were true, life would be much easier at the moment. He pulled out the folder that held Michael's keycard and turned it over. Room 823. Such a simple thing it would be to go up there and indulge in one last fling.

No one down here would know. Michael's hands, mouth, and breath on Sam's skin. The security. The trust.

After punching the elevator up button, Sam turned the folder over again. Despite the desire twining in his belly and the hardness of his cock, he knew better than to give in. Both were conditions he could alleviate with his hand and a cold shower. The tightness in his heart—that was something else entirely. Nothing would fix that but time and distance.

A roll with Michael would only worsen the situation.

The elevator doors opened to an empty car. Sam strode in and pressed the button for six—his floor. The doors closed and the car rose.

He was moving to Boston. He didn't do relationships. This was for the best. If he repeated those things enough times, maybe they would sink in. He couldn't have sex with Michael now—not so close to Sundra choosing Michael as a site manager. It would look like favoritism. If anyone found out, Michael would be out of a job.

Choosing the path Sam's heart wanted would out them as lovers. That would fuck over Michael and the other Four Rivers employees.

It would also pretty much tank Sam's career. He was good at what he did. Really fucking good. He loved the challenge, the freedom, and the excitement. It wouldn't be anything like the situation in grad school—he'd not let that happen again. But it would mean stares and comments and a distinct lack of income. *Yeah, it's not all altruism, is it?*

It was one thing to screw himself, but his wants were not worth the careers of others, especially not Michael's. Desire for money had nearly ruined Four Rivers. Rasheed's need to play straight guy had nearly destroyed Michael.

How were Sam's needs any different? His lust would ruin everything.

Sam tapped the keycard folder against his palm. Michael would be waiting in his room. Naked? Dressed in that delicious suit? Sam exhaled a ragged breath as the elevator slowed and the doors opened onto the sixth floor.

If he did go, what would Michael do? Fuck him of course. But what else? Spank him? Use a belt again? Something else?

The doors closed, and it sounded like his heartbeat played from the speakers above his head rather than up-tempo jazz. The gleaming brass accents of the car interior swam before his eyes. He reached for the buttons and paused over the open door symbol.

He'd miss a good cup of coffee in the morning. Big deal. That was his life. No Michael.

Fire replaced his blood and burned his lungs. He couldn't make his finger press the damn open button.

What would it be like to wake in Michael's bed, in his arms? Sam stared at the panel. He could have that tonight. A good-bye in the morning. Something normal just this once, even if it were an ending.

Another voice from his past, this one akin to his own, whispered in his head. You going to let one bad night a decade ago dictate the rest of your life? You're an idiot, Sam Anderson.

Sam punched the button for floor eight and backed up against the wall of the car as it rose, swallowing air in gulps. It took effort to force his arms to stop shaking.

How much of this bad idea was the whiskey, he didn't know. Probably less than he'd like. Recklessness was becoming a habit—first sex in the shower and now this.

The elevator stopped and the doors opened to reveal the

hallway of the eighth floor. He should press the six button and end this madness before it destroyed Michael. Instead, he stepped out of the car. The hallway blurred as Sam strode to the door of Room 823. He slid the key out of the folder.

Last chance to turn around, but then he never turned back. Sam took a breath and pushed the card into the slot. A whir, a green light, and then he was inside the room. The door closed behind him with an audible thump. After that, the only sound was the humming of the air conditioner and the rush of blood in Sam's ears.

Michael sat on a couch, still dressed in his suit pants, shirt, and suspenders, but sans tie and jacket. No shoes, but dress socks. He set down the e-reader he'd been holding and stood.

Damn, the man was tall. Sam knew that, but the clothes Michael wore accentuated his height. No longer unassuming in Jimmy Buffet shirts and shorts, Michael was every stitch a man of power. That impression only grew as he closed the distance.

Sam couldn't move. Hell, he couldn't breathe.

"I wasn't sure you'd come." Michael stopped close enough that the buttons on his shirt shimmered as he spoke.

Sam followed the line of white circles up to Michael's face. "Until I did, I wasn't sure I would either." He held out the keycard to Michael, who took it.

"Why?"

"Why did I come, or why wasn't I sure?"

"I know why you're here." Michael brushed a finger along Sam's jaw.

The feeling of his stubble moved by Michael's touch sang down Sam's every nerve. Heat and desire flooded his senses and he swayed forward. Michael caught him and tilted his chin up so that Sam had no choice but to look into Michael's dark eyes.

"Tell me why you weren't going to." The faint scent of leather mixed with the earthy smell of Michael's skin.

"We shouldn't be doing this and I want—" He swallowed air. "I want more. More than I should have. More than is safe."

"More?" Michael whispered in Sam's ear before taking the lobe into his mouth.

Sam's nerves exploded as heat traced down his spine. He wrapped his hands around Michael's suspenders and closed his eyes against the onslaught of light that flashed before his vision. He clung to Michael because he wasn't sure his legs would hold.

"More?" Michael spoke a second time, the heat of his breath warming Sam's neck.

"More of you. More time. More of us."

"A relationship?"

And there it was. Everything Sam had been dancing around since Curaçao. The one thing he could not have, not with his career, not with his nomadic life. "Yes."

"And here I thought you only wanted me for my sense of style." Amusement in Michael's voice and a touch of something else, too. Approval?

Sam shivered. "What style? Parrots? Please." Did Michael want what he did?

"You like the suit well enough." Michael nipped Sam's earlobe before whispering into his ear. "Is it the sex, then?"

"Not just the sex." He paused. "Though at the moment, a good fuck would be just fine." He was so damn hard it hurt.

Michael's laugh rippled through Sam's body, turning the desire twisting in his core into fire. Michael slid his hands down to Sam's ass and pulled their bodies together. There was no mistaking the hard length of Michael's shaft pressed against Sam's belly.

"You'll get more than that," Michael said, right before he devoured Sam's mouth.

Sam yielded to the deep kiss, opening to the thrust of Michael's tongue before turning the tables and kissing back just as hard. Michael tasted of spice and wine. So close, the smell of the leather suspenders and linen sent Sam reeling into fantasies of different kinds of leather and cloth.

Michael pulled Sam up until their cocks slid against each other through their clothes. Sam didn't register that Michael had picked him up until his back met the wall and he wrapped his legs around Michael. Braced against unforgiving plaster, Sam thrust, bulge to bulge, all while Michael explored Sam's mouth.

Sam couldn't even moan under the onslaught of pleasure spinning through his body. Dry humping would get him off at this rate.

Michael broke the kiss. "I need you naked."

Sam didn't hide the shudder that ran through him. "Good."

Back on his feet, Sam stripped without care or thought. He kicked his Italian hand-tailored suit away, followed by his shirt, shoes, socks, and underwear. Michael remained dressed, which was just fine. "I do like the suit. You should wear one more often."

Michael stood out of reach, his arms crossed and the outline of his hard-on visible in his slacks. He chuckled.

Oh to wrap his lips around that. "Although it would be distracting to see you like this every day."

"It would be interesting"—Michael uncrossed his arms and removed the distance between them—"to see your reaction at work." Michael ran his hands over Sam's chest, sending chills down his arms and up into his brain. Goosebumps rose when Michael circled Sam's right nipple, then brushed his thumb over it. When Michael gripped the nub hard, a sharp shock of pain went straight to Sam's balls. Chill turned to fire.

He did moan this time.

"I thought you might like that." Michael found Sam's other nipple and applied the same pressure.

It was as if the world became both darker and brighter at the same time. Electrifying. Michael's devilish smile wavered in Sam's vision and his mouth turned dry. He gasped for air, suspended between wanting to pull away and wanting to beg for more.

Michael's voice brought him back to earth. "Kiss me."

Sam went up on his toes, thrust his tongue into Michael's willing mouth and was rewarded with more pressure on his nipples. The sweetness of the pain almost drove him to his knees. That would have been fine by him.

Michael broke the kiss and loosened his hold. "I have something I'd like you to try."

The words themselves were innocent enough, but in Michael's gravelly voice they took on a tone that made Sam tremble, part from desire and part from fear. He followed Michael to the foot of the bed and sat where Michael pointed.

From a duffel bag on the coffee table, Michael pulled out a thin, silver-colored chain with heavier ends—clamps. Sam sucked in air and sparks danced across his skin from his ass to his toes.

Michael's wicked expression was half a smile and half the look of a hungry predator. "You know how to stop me."

Sam did. He resisted the temptation to strain toward

Michael, beg for the pain, the desire, the security, and the calm in his mind that came when his senses were overwhelmed.

Michael applied a clamp and it was all Sam could do to remain sitting upright. The pressure turned to a thousand needles piercing his skin, insistent and hot like a burn. Lightning flashed up his spine to his head, hazing his vision and tightening his balls. "Oh fuck." It took several breaths to get a hold on the pain—and then the bastard placed the other clamp. Sam wanted to double over, but Michael pulled him up and took his mouth again.

Sam answered by digging his fingers into Michael's arms and pushing his tongue into the heat of Michael's mouth. The moan from Michael sweetened the agony radiating through Sam's body and turned it into a silky pleasure.

When Michael wrapped his hand around Sam's cock and stroked, desire twined at the base of Sam's spine. Too much, too fast. Sam broke the kiss. "I'm going to come."

"Don't." Michael kept stroking, slowly. Firmly.

Sam fought against the rising pressure in his belly, the tightening in his balls. The clamps might as well have been two mouths sucking hard on his nipples. Michael pressed his thumb against the slit in the crown of Sam's dick.

His whole body shook with the need for release—from the clamps, from Michael's hand, from the growing fullness of his heart. He would never, ever get enough of Michael. He needed this man in his life. "Please."

"No." Michael took on a cheerful tone. "Put that type-A personality to some use."

He didn't know whether to laugh or curse. He moaned instead and used every ounce of self-control to keep from teetering over the edge into bliss. After several more strokes, Michael finally relented and released Sam's cock.

In turn, Sam let go of Michael's arms and slumped back to sitting on the bed. The clamps still stung and ached, especially when the chain swung between them, but the pain was down to a manageable level—if trembling were considered managing.

Michael loomed over him with the same wolfish grin as before.

"You like seeing your CEO like this?" Sam's words were dusty to go along with the dryness of his throat.

Michael gripped Sam's chin. "I love seeing you like this. I don't give a rat's ass that you're my boss." He trailed his fingers down along Sam's throat, then took hold of the chain and pulled, ever so gently. "I don't think you do, either."

The dull sting turned sharp and drove away Sam's retort. He tried not to twist and failed, turning his nipples into points of agony. Every moment of pain transformed into a sweet dagger of pleasure. It was hard, very hard, not to cry out.

Too many neighbors.

"Lovely." Michael backed away and returned to his bag. Out came a bottle of lube and a strip of condoms, which he placed at the foot of the bed before rooting in the bag again. Sam couldn't help the soft groan when he considered the foil packets.

"Since you've done beautifully with the clamps, come here and pick which of these I'm going to flog you with."

All breath left Sam. A trickle of sweat ran down his back, cooling his overheated skin. Yes, he wanted to be thrashed, but to have it so plainly spoken of... it froze him even as the thought burned.

"Sam."

He rose to his feet at Michael's call, legs shaking, and crossed to the table with the black bag. Each step shook the chain suspended between his nipples. The added sharpness cleared his head and steadied his steps. When he reached Michael's side, he could breathe again. Michael pulled him close and kissed the back of his neck.

On the table lay a flogger and a riding crop. Sam had never been hit with either but knew the effects well enough from the porn he watched. He was about to live his fantasy. Again. The decision was easy. Sharp, hard swats. "The crop."

"Thought that might be your choice." Michael nuzzled his neck, a gentle touch, odd in contrast to the dull burn of the clamps. Sam leaned against Michael, soaking in his warmth and strength.

A slip of a thought flickered through Sam's head that he really should not be in Michael's arms—and he shoved it away. Michael was right. He didn't care. Navigating the consequences of this night could come later. "You didn't pick these... toys up because of me, did you?"

"No." Michael traced a hand down Sam's belly to his thigh, skimming achingly close to Sam's cock—but not touching it. "In college, I was pretty involved in the Scene. But Rasheed... wasn't. I drifted away."

"You didn't do this with him." Joy ripped through Sam. This was *theirs*.

"No. Never with him."

"He missed out. You obviously enjoy being a Dom."

Michael huffed a laugh. "I love whipping people, giving them the pain they want and need. I love topping. I love the joy of a scene well played. I hated being a Dom."

That—didn't make sense. "I don't understand. You and me—"

Michael turned him around. "I adore you. If we weren't stuck in this job together, if you were openly gay, I'd ask you out. I don't want to run your life. I don't want to tell you what to do—not all the time. I just want to make you fly."

"You left." Sam's throat tightened and he swallowed. "In the gym, you ran when I said that." He'd seen the fear in Michael.

"I know. I'm sorry. I'm not running now." He paused. "Whether I stay is up to you."

Sam should have been running for the door. He hadn't expected—hadn't anticipated—Michael might feel the same way. That wasn't part of his plan. He was taking a job in Boston and leaving. Going back to Beantown to exorcise some of his demons.

Except he was standing in a hotel room, wearing nothing but clamps on his nipples, and the man he was falling in love with was about to beat him with a riding crop. "There's too much in my head right now."

Michael tapped the crop against his hand. "I can fix that for you."

"Please. Yes."

Michael pointed to the wall. "Back to me, legs apart, and use your arms to brace yourself."

Sam moved into position. Beneath his palms, the subtle wallpaper dug into his skin, but the abrasion was comforting. "Arms high?"

"Ideally, you'd be cuffed onto a rack or a cross, but since we can't do that here, whatever position is most comfortable and you're least likely to break," Michael said.

A rack. A cross? The controlled heat in Sam's balls threatened to spill out of confinement. He took a breath and concentrated. Arms down. He did push-ups regularly; it would be easy to hold the position under pain. Or pleasure.

Michael tapped Sam's left leg with what felt to be the crop. "Wider."

Sam obliged. Then waited, and waited more, his pulse ticking up with each second that passed. After a moment, he relaxed and opened his mouth to speak.

The crack of the riding crop against his right ass cheek echoed in the room before the pain registered in Sam's brain. A shower of gold sparks exploded in his vision and the sting radiated to his fingertips. The next blow came, on the left cheek. Then another. This one on his shoulder blade. Sam pressed into the wall, scraping the clamps against the hard surface. The agony nearly buckled his legs. He closed his eyes and moaned.

Michael chuckled. "The clamps are a treat, aren't they?"

Another blow from Michael stole Sam's answer. Spots— gold, white, red—danced in his vision as sparks of desire, pain, and delight flooded his body and set his skin aflame. Each time the crop landed, his cock and balls tightened. He laid his head against the wall and fought the urge to twist under the blows. God, he wanted more. He arched his back and rose onto his toes. "Please."

Another crack of leather against flesh, then another. Too many to count. Sweet torment sang in his veins and made his dick throb. Sam trembled, the pounding blood in his ears blocking all but the noise of the slap of the crop.

How long Michael continued Sam couldn't tell, only that every blow sent light into his vision and lifted him higher, away from the world, closer to Michael. Closer to heaven.

This pain was so different from a true beating. Sweeter. Calming. He didn't want it to end. But he was losing his grip on the wall and his legs felt like twisting rubber. Sam slid and the blows stopped.

Strong arms caught him before he fell to the ground. "Jesus, Sam. You need to tell me when you've had enough. That's the whole point of safewords."

"Haven't had enough." The word came out slurred. Sam peeled open his eyes to a world too bright. But it contained Michael, so that was fine. "Keep going."

He couldn't tell if the sound Michael made was a laugh or a moan. "No. Not if you're like this." Steady arms lifted Sam up and pulled him toward the bed. Even when Sam's ass hit the comforter, Michael didn't let go. "You want more than you can take."

"Always." The bedcover pricked against his aching skin and the pain sent a wave of pleasure up his spine. He shivered in Michael's arms. "Teach me how to take more."

"Not tonight." He drew his fingers across Sam's cheek, under the chin, and tipped Sam's head back. When Michael's mouth closed on Sam's, the kiss wasn't consumed by the ferocity of desire. Instead, Michael gave Sam a sweet, slow kiss that made all the soreness in Sam's body blaze. He collapsed into Michael's arms.

"Tonight, I'm going to teach you what comes after pain." Michael tugged on the chain between Sam's nipples before taking off the clamps one at a time.

The relief sent sparks down Sam's spine and he groaned into Michael's shoulder, grazing his teeth against shirt linen. Michael's warm fingers massaged Sam's abused flesh and he kissed Sam's neck, then chin, before reclaiming Sam's mouth.

Desire, like a rush of embers over dry tinder, kindled into flame. Sam responded, consuming Michael's lips and tongue. Sam sought the hard line of Michael's cock, still trapped inside suit pants, needing it to be free.

It was Michael's turn to moan.

Sam knew what came next. "Pleasure comes after pain."

"That wasn't a question, you know." Michael pushed Sam backward onto the bed and rose to his feet. "But is that what you think?" Still fully clothed, he looked nearly perfect, though his cheeks were red and a sheen of sweat wet the edges of his hairline. "Pleasure is what comes after?"

During pain, too. "What else is there?"

Michael said nothing, just loosened the cuff link—Sam's cuff link—from his shirt and removed it.

That simple act spiked Sam's heart rate. "So, will there be a quiz after this lesson?"

Michael chuckled. "Perhaps." He placed the link and his glasses on the table.

Dark hair and eyes. Enigmatic smile. "God, you're beautiful." The words spilled from Sam's mouth without care, without thought.

Michael slipped his suspenders off his arms and worked the buttons of his shirt open. "You're glorious yourself. You have that well-fucked look, and I haven't even been inside you." Michael's pants followed his shirt to the floor, then the rest until he stood naked at the foot of the bed, stroking his erect cock. He reached for a condom. "Can't wait to see what you look like after we're done."

Michael ripped open the foil packet and another shiver twisted down Sam's spine. His back itched and stung like mad just lying against the bedspread. Being fucked against the scratchy surface would be—intense. "You going to tell me what comes after pain. Or do I have to guess?"

Michael snorted. "If you don't behave, you'll never find

out." Michael pushed Sam's legs up and wide. "Hold yourself open."

Sam grabbed his ankles.

"Wider, Sam."

The command forced a moan from Sam and he pulled his feet wider until his thighs ached from the stretch.

"Better." Michael curved his mouth into a grin that held a great deal of lust—with hints of joy. Sam's smoldering want burned in his belly when Michael reached for the lube.

"You should see yourself. So open. So needy." Michael climbed onto the bed, his weight shifting the mattress and the cover under Sam's back. "I love seeing you like this."

The fabric stretched and scratched across what Sam guessed were bruises and raised flesh. The sensation electrified every inch of his skin, even the parts that hadn't been caressed by Michael's crop. The loud snap of Michael opening the bottle of lube tightened the need in Sam's belly. A hollowness in Sam ached to be filled, not just by Michael's cock, but by the taste of Michael's skin, the smell of his sweat. His weight. His love.

Sam's heart pounded against his ribs. *Love.*

"Please."

Michael loomed, bottle in hand. "Please what?"

Sam's whole body burned. Embarrassment fought with lust. He surrendered to the latter. "Fuck me." It came out as a whisper.

"Hmm?" Michael stood still, obviously waiting for Sam.

"Fuck me." Louder this time. "Use me." Sam needed an answer. He spread his feet wider and arched his back, needing Michael's touch. He didn't know which hurt and pleased more, the crop or Michael not touching him. "Teach me. What am I supposed to learn?"

Cold liquid ran between Sam's ass cheeks, swiftly followed by Michael's finger. "Patience. Surrender. Learn to feel, Sam." Gentle pressure teased the ring of his entrance and Michael coaxed him open, then pressed a digit inside. Fire snaked into Sam's head and balls and he moaned as his emptiness filled. Michael thrust in hard but pulled out agonizingly slow, pressing all around, slicking Sam's channel, occasionally lingering over Sam's prostate, teasing the spot with tiny strokes.

Sam twisted on the bedspread. Feel was all he could do. The urge to jack off, to spend himself as Michael finger-fucked him was high, but he kept hold of his ankles and held himself wide for Michael.

Only for Michael. He'd never do this for anyone else.

"Do you trust me?" Michael's question was as sensuous as the touch of the fingers inside Sam's channel.

"Yes." The answer sprang from his heart, because he did.

"Good." When Michael withdrew, the loss of his touch ached more than the crop, but before Sam could utter a plea, Michael set the head of his cock against Sam's hole and pushed inside. The sharp sweet burn of being stretched had Sam gasping for air. Light flashed in Sam's vision and the longing inside Sam disappeared. Michael was there, inside him, above him, murmuring nonsense into his ear. Sam trembled, the honey taste of ache from his back, from being full with Michael, tightened his cock and balls. Every second ticked away in a tangle of hurt and joy and pleasure so close to perfection it was hard to breathe.

Sam couldn't touch himself, not without letting go of his ankles, and he loved the tight fire in his thighs and arms, sweetening the mist of agony already surrounding him.

Only Michael mattered, his rhythm flinging Sam higher, away from his thoughts. *Feel*.

Michael hammered into Sam and gripped Sam's shoulders, digging fingers into flesh. His thighs slapped against Sam's abused ass and the echo of those blows filled Sam's ears. The room brightened with each stinging contact, until Sam was lost in the dizzying heights near release.

The bedspread grated Sam's welts and bruises, those pinpricks of pain mixing with the spike of heaven every time Michael rocked against Sam's prostate. Agony and bliss twisted together and whipped about in Sam's heart and mind. He'd been on edge all night, desire swimming in his veins since Michael handed him the keycard. Sam needed the sweet release from the world only Michael gave to him.

Sam's soul sang and his balls drew up. He twisted, trying to find relief for his cock. "Harder. Fuck me harder."

"Of course." Michael feasted on Sam's mouth and pistoned into him so hard, Sam lost the grip on his ankles. His back turned into a sheet of agony. Sam returned Michael's kiss for all that he was worth, tangling his hands into Michael's hair and wrapping his legs around Michael's torso.

Soaring over the edge of pain and the ecstasy of release, Sam broke the kiss. "I need—"

Michael wrapped his hand around Sam's cock and fisted it with the same staccato tempo as his fucking.

Breath left Sam's lungs. The cord of his desire cracked like Michael's riding crop, sending a bolt of pleasure that seared into his balls. His vision turned white and he emptied his seed over Michael's hand and onto his own chest. He couldn't even voice his relief. That moment of abandonment, the clash between torment and rapture lasted forever and not long enough.

Through it, Michael kept fucking him and Sam rode the sweetness and sting of those strokes back down. When Sam's vision cleared, the utter brightness of Michael's smile, the crinkle at the edge of his eyes and the shimmer of dampness there cracked his heart open.

Open joy in Michael at Sam's pleasure. Delight in fulfilling Sam's needs.

I can't leave him. He didn't want to. Right now, he wanted to give back all that Michael had given him. Sam gripped Michael's ass and pulled him in deeper. "Don't stop. Keep going."

"Fuck." Michael sucked in air and his movements became erratic.

Each thrust sent shocks of sweetness up Sam's spine. Warmth grew at the thought of Michael undone, of the man who took such command losing all control. Sam met Michael's every thrust, twisting his hips and tightening down.

Michael shuddered, and drove into Sam, crying out his own release. His movements slowed and he fell into Sam's arms.

For a moment, only their combined harsh breathing broke the stillness. Then Sam kissed Michael's cheek. "That was phenomenal." He stroked Michael's damp and trembling back.

Michael stirred enough to pull out of Sam. "Holy shit. I saw stars. That's never happened before."

"Fun, isn't it?"

Sam couldn't place Michael's look. It bordered on envy or awe. "That happens to you? Every time?"

He pushed damp curls from Michael's eyes. "Only with you."

"Give me a moment." Michael pressed his lips to Sam's, and Sam opened for a quick taste of a sweet kiss.

When Michael climbed off the bed, the air of the hotel room cooled the sweat and semen on Sam's chest and he shivered. *I want him back. I need him back.* Not just now, but again and again. Thoughts of the future, the promises he'd made about Boston, what being with Michael would open Sam up to, those thoughts lurked in the back of his mind. He pushed them away. Later. He'd deal with that later. *Feel*, Michael had said. Sam did, drifting into the trembling afterglow of release, noting all the aches, the little stings from the welts on his back as he breathed.

Michael returned with a warm, wet washcloth and a towel. With care, he cleaned Sam's chest, then tossed the cloths off the side of the bed. Pulling at the covers beneath Sam, he motioned for Sam to shimmy up the bed. "Let's get under."

They did, and Sam slid into the warmth of Michael's arms as the soft sheets enveloped them. Breathing in Michael's scent, listening to the sound of his heart—it was a perfect a moment. His back stung, as did his ass, but softly. A reminder, not a burden. For the first time in ages, a stillness took hold of Sam, not one born of fear, but a calm sprung from contentment.

"Sam," Michael whispered into his ear.

"Hmm?"

"Did you find the answer?"

The question startled Sam. He said nothing and Michael didn't pry. He rolled slightly to turn off the lamp on the side table.

In the darkened room, Sam traced the lines of Michael's

face in the faint glow from the windows. Trust. Security. Completion.

This was what came after pain, after pleasure, this was what Michael gave him.

He spoke his answer against Michael's collarbone. "You give me peace."

Michael didn't speak, just held him tighter.

Which was exactly perfect.

CHAPTER EIGHT

Michael woke to an empty bed. The mattress beneath his fingers still radiated heat but ice touched his heart. "Sam?"

The sound of running water from the bathroom eased the pressure in his chest. He sat up when Sam stepped into the room. Though sweet to behold, Sam was blurry in Michael's vision.

"Could you get me my glasses?"

"Of course." Sam's voice was heavy and soft with the dredges of sleep. He yawned before grabbing Michael's glasses. Sam sat on the edge of the bed close to Michael.

Michael took the offered glasses and put them on and Sam sprang into sharp view, all curled messy dark hair and slumber-drenched eyes. Sam's back was a mottle of red and purple. No broken skin, but a good bit of bruising and some welts. Beautiful. Michael's cock stirred at the sight.

A glance at the alarm clock told Michael they still had a while before they needed to be up, even if they were to go fetch good coffee. He pulled back the covers a bit. "Come back to bed."

Sam's expression was akin to the rest of him, messy around the edges. He shook his head. "Need to think."

The ice that had melted away returned to grip Michael's heart harder. "About what?" He already knew the answer.

Sam didn't frown, not quite, but his posture, the whole of his body seemed to twist, then still, but not into relaxation. "This," he said. "Us."

Michael hadn't realized he'd been holding his breath until he let it out. He rubbed his face with his hands and tried to calm his pulse. "I'd tell you to stop thinking, but I doubt that would work."

Sam chuckled. "No, it wouldn't." He took Michael's hand and entwined his fingers. "I'm moving to Boston."

A chasm opened up beneath Michael and he fell, hard and fast, tumbling into the unknown. The bed remained. Sam remained. Everything was where it had been before those words had been spoken. Michael tried to yank his hand away but Sam held him tight. His head hammered, ringing from the inside out. "Boston? Why?"

"I'm taking a job there." Sam crawled onto the bed and knelt in front of Michael, never breaking his grip. "At least that had been my plan before I came here." He took Michael's other hand.

Michael's arms shook. Hell, his whole body shook. They'd come this far and now he would lose Sam? After last night? "And now?"

"I don't know." Sam pulled Michael forward into his arms until they held each other. "I had it all planned out. It would be the best thing for both of us. Then I walked into this room last night. And this is... what we have..." He seemed to search around for a word. "Shit." Sam kissed Michael's shoulder. After a moment, he continued. "When we're together, when we're like this, everything is simple and right. When I step outside the room, into the rest of the world, it's all so fucking complicated."

Sam trembled, whether from the cold of the room or from the conversation, Michael couldn't tell. He pulled the covers up around them.

Fear was as potent as ice. He didn't want to be having this conversation. But he'd promised he wouldn't run again, and Sam *was* here talking with him. "I thought you had to stay until Sundra buys Four Rivers or the company folds."

"Sundra's buying. It's a done deal. They'll announce on Friday." That pronouncement should have been joyful, but there was no emotion in Sam's voice. "There will be three weeks or so until the acquisition. End of July."

Three weeks. The tightness and frost in Michael's heart crept into his lungs. "And you're gone once they come in."

"Of course. That's the way these things work."

Off to another company to become someone else's corporate savior, leaving Michael and Four Rivers behind. Just like that. "Do you want to go?"

Sam sat back a little, and peered at Michael. "Are you asking me if I want to leave you?" A hint of annoyance creased his brow, entered his tone.

A spark of hope leapt into Michael's soul and he tried not to cling to it. "If I weren't in the picture, would you want to go to Boston?"

Sam got the distant look that meant he was thinking. Considering. "Their technology is interesting and something that should be doing well in the marketplace. Their leadership has let the company down. I know I can make a difference. If this were six months ago, I'd jump at the chance. It's the kind of opportunity I live for, what I do best."

Michael caressed Sam's face. "Do you want to stay?"

Sam closed his eyes. "I can't. For your sake, I can't."

For a moment, those words stilled Michael and his heart contracted so hard, he thought blood would stop pumping. But leaving him wasn't Sam's entire answer—the love that lurked behind that statement kept him breathing. He stroked Sam's cheek. "That's not the question I asked."

Sam opened his eyes. They were still brilliant, even when they conveyed exasperation and pain. "I know what you asked. God, yes. Yes, I want to be with you. It's just not possible."

The response tied knots in Michael. Sam wanted to stay, wanted to be with Michael. "Why isn't it possible?"

Sam lifted Michael's hand from his cheek, his face a mix of fear, hope, and sorrow. Sunlight filtered in around the edges of the curtains, gilding lines across the bed. "They're going to make you site manager."

Those were the last words Michael had expected to hear. He spat out two of his own. "*What?* Why?"

Sam shrugged. "Pittsburgh will become an R&D lab for the next generation of Sundra's routing products. They won't need a CEO, maybe not even a VP, but the office will need someone to oversee and manage the team there. You're the obvious choice for that role."

What did it have to do with them? How did *that* chase Sam away? "How the hell did I become the obvious choice?" Michael reeled. Too many pieces and not enough *sense.*

Sam coughed a laugh. "By doing your job well. You're the person everyone at the office respects." He paused and added, "Plus you impressed Greta quite a bit with your knowledge."

Well, shit. "I hate management."

Sam waved those words away. "You were a fucking Founder. You've been management the entire time, despite what you or anyone else says. You hired most of the office. You should be a VP. This corrects all that." Sam lips twisted into a grin, the one Michael loved to nip and pinch and beat away. "Technically, you'll be a suit, and I know how much you abhor suits."

"I like them. On other people." On Sam, especially, right before he stripped it off. He exhaled. A suit. A promotion. It was a good thing. Suddenly, the reasoning behind Sam's earlier statements made sense. "If you stayed in Pittsburgh, dated me—"

"Everyone will know we're lovers." Sam finished the thought. "I doubt you'd be willing to hide a relationship again."

"Fuck no. I got enough of that with Rasheed. I'm not going to hide who I am and who I love ever again." He had been doing too much of that these past few months, anyway.

Sam nodded. "Except everyone at the office, and probably quite a few people at Sundra, will think you got the job because I'm screwing you."

"Other way around." Something else occurred to Michael. He watched Sam carefully when he spoke his suspicion. "If you were to stay, everyone in your executive social circle would know the real reason you don't like titty bars."

There it was. Sam colored and looked down. "That's not the reason." But his manner belied his words.

Silence for a good, long minute. Michael broke it. "Damn it, Sam. You shouldn't care what they think."

"I don't!" Sam sighed and scrubbed his face. "Okay,

maybe I do. A bit. It'll be a change and I don't know how they'll react. But that's not why I can't stay."

Michael didn't say anything. He stroked Sam's arm, then took his hand.

"I don't want to ruin your career. Your future," Sam said.

"I can't see any way in which being with you would ruin my future." He squeezed Sam's hand. "I mean, what more could you do to my career than what's already been done?"

"But—"

"Sam, Pittsburgh high-tech is close-knit. Everyone knows I'm gay. Hell, I'm sure there are folks who remember me from my days in the Scene. It's not an issue. No one's going to think I slept my way to the top. They know how I work."

"Sundra isn't Pittsburgh."

Now that was true. Michael twisted his mouth and looked down at their hands. Chances were there would be folks in Sundra who would think he got his position by bending over and taking it, even if the reverse were true. He looked up.

Sam's smile held nothing but pain. "This is why I have a rule not to get involved with people at the office."

"Except we were already involved." One intense night in Curaçao. A single cuff link. Michael let Sam go.

"Yeah, I never expected that. Hadn't planned for it." He traced his fingers over Michael's thigh. "I'm so sorry."

Michael shook his head. There were other options. "I'll quit. Go with you to Boston."

Sam pulled back, shock loosening his features for a moment before they hardened again. "No. You can't. Don't do that for me."

Michael gripped Sam's ankle. "And why not?" More and more, Sam's actions, his statements pointed to a truth that wasn't one Michael liked—he was good enough for Sam to play with, but not to stay with in the long term.

Sam stilled.

Michael's heart hurt. "Is it all a lie? I'd rather you just tell me you don't want me—at least not as a partner. This fucking around with my head—"

Sam tugged his foot out of Michael's grasp. "That's not it at all. Damn it, Michael. I want to be with you. More than anyone I've ever met. That's why I'm in your fucking hotel room!" He paused for a moment. "But you're not mine to keep."

"I'm not asking you to keep me." Michael ran both hands through his hair. "Shit. I'm asking for a date. A night out. I already went through this bullshit with Rasheed. If you're not willing to be seen with me, then there's no point to any of this. You prefer the closet to me." The words were out before he could bite them back.

Sam swayed for a moment. "Now that's fucking unfair." Color drained from his face. "You have no idea what it's like for me. I'd fucking shout from the rooftops that we're together if it made you happy. But I don't want you destroying your life for me. I care about you too much, and I've seen what happens... Shit. Just forget it." Sam shimmied backward and slipped off the bed. "You won't listen." He took two steps then stopped. "Look. What Sundra is offering, it is everything you've worked for at Four Rivers, everything you deserve. It's what you should have had from day one, what you were cheated out of. Don't abandon your career, your dreams, just for a chance to date me."

"I can get another job. Anywhere." Hell, headhunters called him every other week as it was.

Sam drew himself up to his full height. Even naked, that sense of power held. "Do you give a damn about all the folks who trusted in you? You're willing to leave them to navigate this merger all by themselves so you can follow a man you've known for a couple months? Is that loyalty?"

Those words were a knife between Michael's ribs. To leave the team behind without any warning—God, that would be just as shitty as what Sam was doing to him. He'd stayed three years ago to prevent that. "You're going away."

"I don't have anything to leave behind. You've spent nearly two decades building a life in Pittsburgh." Sam scooped up his underwear and pants. "There's quite a difference."

Michael shifted to the edge of the bed and stood. "So I'm nothing, then? This"—he gestured at the bed, the scattered clothing, the crop and the clamps—"isn't anything?"

Sam reached for his shirt. "That's not what I said but if it makes you hate me, if it makes you let me go, then yes. It's nothing. It doesn't mean anything." The gravel in Sam's voice betrayed the lies in his words.

Fuck this shit. It took only a long step to reach Sam. Michael pulled him upright and claimed Sam's mouth, attacking with lips, tongue, and every hurt in his heart and soul. If talking didn't work, he'd fall back on what always had.

Sam stiffened every muscle in his body at the first onslaught, but an instant later, he yielded, folding fast and hard. He opened himself to Michael, moaning deep in his throat. Clothes hit the floor and Sam wrapped his arms around Michael, kissing back with a passion and intensity that rivaled Michael's own. This was real and true, not the words Sam had said.

Michael broke the kiss and Sam grunted his disappointment, his cock hard against Michael's thigh.

"You can't tell me you don't want me," he said into Sam's ear.

"If you think I don't want you, you haven't been listening." Sam nipped Michael's shoulder, then untangled from Michael's grasp. "You're everything I've ever wanted in a friend. A lover."

"Then why the hell are we fighting?"

Sam ran a hand through his hair. "I'm not fight— Look, my life isn't anything I'd wish for another. I go from job to job, city to city. No friends. No home." He looked around the room. "I don't know whether to grab my stuff and go or beg you to fuck me until this all vanishes." A touch of panic entered Sam's voice.

"What are you running from?" Michael hadn't seen Sam's fear before, but should have, given Sam's need to be removed from the world. His mistake.

Sam's bark of laughter was too high pitched. "Me."

Well, yes. "Why?"

Sam stared at him.

"Why?" Michael repeated the word. He removed the distance between them and walked Sam back to the bed. A small push made Sam sit before Michael.

"There's always another job," Sam said. "So I go."

Michael shook his head. "That's not an answer."

"You're not my fucking therapist."

"No, I'm not." He curled his palm around Sam's chin and tilted his head back. "I'm your lover. And your friend, like it or not."

Sam's hands bunched up the sheets and his breath hitched. "I'm the closeted gay guy who is too damn afraid that coming out will sink his career. I'm a coward and a hypocrite. I'm everything you hate, Michael."

Michael let go. Now they were getting somewhere. "Except I don't hate you."

Sam looked at his feet. "You should."

Anger in Sam's slumped shoulders. If Michael had to guess, Sam aimed his fury inward.

"What happened?"

Sam opened his mouth, then closed it. Slowly, the tension in his body slackened. "I met a guy in grad school. He was out and proud—a lot like me at the time. First week of classes, he was jumped in an alley and had the shit beaten out of him. For being a fag. I never—I didn't do anything. I should have done something."

"You saw it happen?"

Sam tensed again. "Yeah. I mean, it was dark, but yeah. I saw it." Sam shuddered. "I was there."

The lines of anguish in Sam, the way he stared at the ground, it spoke so much more than Sam's words—a physical knowledge of the event.

Shit. Oh, shit. Suddenly everything made sense.

"Sam," Michael spoke the question as neutrally as he could. "That student? Who was he?"

MICHAEL'S QUESTION REBOUNDED IN SAM'S SKULL. So many ways he could answer that. When he looked up, all options but one fell away. The line of Michael's mouth, the compassion in his eyes, they reflected back what Michael already knew. Sam's bones ached to voice the truth.

"Me." He breathed the word.

Michael exhaled and took a seat next to Sam on the bed. "Do you want to talk about it?"

No. Yes. He could taste the blood in his mouth, smell the stale dampness of unwashed tarmac and brick. "I didn't start at Yale. I started at Harvard."

"You transferred to Yale after…"

"After I was beat up, yes." Sam balled his hands and waited for the pity, the pithy statements of compassion that didn't mean a damn thing.

He didn't get either. Michael was silent for a time, his brow creased in worry. It smoothed over. "It's okay if you don't want to—"

"I want to." Needed to. "Hell, it wasn't even that bad, in the grand scheme of things. They punched me a few times in the face and gut. Dropped me to the ground and kicked me, then they ran." He'd been sore for days. That pain—had been so unlike anything else. Nausea-inducing, gut-wrenching. He'd been so damn scared he'd pissed himself. "They didn't even break anything. A cut lip, a bloody nose, and a bunch of bruises. That's all I had. I got off light."

Michael fidgeted, his breathing shallow. Probably reacting to what Sam *wasn't* saying. He hadn't been raped. He hadn't been killed—unlike so many others. He'd only thought he was going to die. *Hey fag, where you going?* He shook away the memory and continued. "It was my first week there. I'd found a nice apartment close to campus. Met my professors and some classmates. Everything was great. Loved campus, enjoyed my classes—so different from computer science. I adored Boston. And then…" He shrugged.

"What happened?"

"I went to a meeting for the LGBT student association.

Got jumped on my way home. That's pretty much the story."

"No, not if you transferred to a different school." There wasn't any recrimination in Michael—and no pity. Just curiosity.

I don't deserve this man. Not his care. Not his understanding. "I should have gone to the police. Reported it. Given them my clothes or something. For DNA. I didn't. I ran home, took a long, scalding shower and tossed everything I'd been wearing into a dumpster."

"Understandable. You were probably in shock."

"I was furious. At myself for not fighting back. At them for being ignorant fucks. At the world and everyone in it." Sam swallowed. "The next day, I went to classes and got stared at. Pitied. I was seen as weak." Sam looked at his hands and lowered his voice. "The worst thing was that I kept hearing those voices, that laughter. Everywhere. Half the men around me sounded like the shitheads who jumped me."

Michael held out his hand, palm up. An invitation. Sam took it, twining his fingers between Michael's.

"They probably weren't even students, but I couldn't shake the uncertainty, the anxiety, so I transferred halfway through the term." That had been rough, playing catch-up on coursework. But he'd also impressed his new professors when he maintained high marks. "I decided to wait a bit before coming out at Yale. Check the waters before jumping in."

"Makes sense, considering."

That had been eye-opening. On the other side of the table, he'd heard what people said when they thought you were one of them. "I discovered a subtle, more pernicious kind of discrimination. It wasn't out there in the open, but gay men and women didn't make the same kinds of connections. They weren't invited to the same parties. They weren't hired by the same caliber of company."

Michael squeezed his hand. "Yeah, I know. That was part of the appeal of founding our own company."

Sam hadn't even considered that. He looked at Michael.

"No one ever picked a fight with me," Michael said. "That's an advantage of being six four. Doesn't mean I didn't notice the other things—wasn't subject to them. The comments under the breath. Being excluded from dinners. Off-campus parties. All the other shit."

"I never thought—" But in a way he had. Assumed Michael's life had been easier—despite the shit with Rasheed and Susan. So turned-in on himself, Sam had never considered anyone else's pain. He let his hand slip from Michael's. He really didn't deserve this guy. "I wanted to beat them all at their game. Make it big. Prove that a gay man could do it. But in order to do that—"

"You had to not be gay." Michael leaned back on his hands. "Are you happy with your choice?"

A few months ago, he might have believed the lie enough to say yes. Now? "You know I'm not."

"Then do something about it." Michael pushed himself off the bed. "Stay here. Date me. Start your own company. Times have changed. DOMA's dead—hell, look at all the states that allow same-sex marriages. I bet you'd have people knocking on your door even if you named the place Sam Anderson's Big Gay Consulting Firm."

Sam didn't know whether to choke on laughter or anger. "It's not that easy!"

"It's exactly that easy," Michael said. "You take risks all the damn time. Am I not—is what we have—not worth the gamble?"

A different kind of ice pricked through Sam's veins. What Michael suggested... almost made sense. He'd be willing to try it, if only he knew Michael would be fine, if this would work. But that wasn't a guarantee. Hell, he didn't even know if he could date again—or if Michael would want him when the glow wore off. "I don't gamble."

"The hell you don't." Fire in Michael's words, in the way he crossed his arms. He looked down at Sam. "You take a gamble with other people's lives, their careers, every time you walk into a company. It's not like you risk your own hide, no matter what you said in that speech."

Words caught in Sam's throat, along with his own anger. He pushed them out. "I know I'm an asshole. I'm a corporate money-taking jerk of a suit. If I fail and a company tanks, I get to walk away with a wad cash and I don't have to think about anyone I leave behind." He swallowed. "I'm not that all the time. I wasn't that person this time. But yes, I am when I need to be. Is that really the person you want to be with? Because that's who I am on the other side of that door."

God knew what Michael was thinking now. He'd gone from concerned to angry to unreadable. He had relaxed a bit, though. "Do you like being that person?"

Sam didn't look away. "On occasion. I'm not... I'm far from perfect. I can be quite an ass."

"Yeah, I remember. You *did* threaten to fire me if I got in your way." Pain in Michael, and wariness.

That was exactly what Sam wanted to avoid. But he supposed he deserved it in this case. "If I had known your history, I wouldn't have."

"Doesn't matter now, does it?" Michael ran a hand through his hair and looked around the room. "Look, maybe you should go."

Sam's heart froze. He couldn't move. "What?"

Michael bent down and started collecting the pieces of the suit he'd been wearing. "All I wanted was a couple of normal dates, some time to figure out all of this, see if it would work beyond the office. A movie. A bike ride. Something other than fucking you in a shower at the office." He picked up the riding crop and tossed it into his duffel bag. "But if I'm not worth the risk to you, if you're not willing to put anything on the line, then that's that. You can say anything you'd like, but it's actions that count."

Cold fear punched a hole in Sam's stomach. Every damn thing Michael said was correct. "I'm trying to protect you." The words sound feeble, even to him.

"Oh, bullshit." Michael flung the nipple clamps into his duffel bag. "You tell me how you'd move the stars if you could, except you can if you want to." He turned to face Sam. "Which means you don't want to and I was just a fun diversion for you while you were here."

"That's—that's not how it is." God, he was going to lose him. Probably had.

"Then how is it?"

He couldn't answer, couldn't fit the words around the memory of bruises and whispers and those fucking nights they'd sent hookers to his room.

Michael turned away. "I told myself I wouldn't do this again. At least with Rasheed, I understood."

The pain in Sam's gut folded him over. "I'm terrified," he whispered.

Michael's feet came into view, then his knees. Then his strong, warm hands tilted Sam's head until they were eye to eye. Michael knelt on the floor in front of Sam. Amazingly, there was still no sign of pity in the long lines of concern in Michael's face. "Of what?"

"That there isn't anything beyond the CEO anymore. If I stop running, it'll all crumble away—not just the career, but me too. Because there isn't anything else there to find." He shook. It might have been from the cool air in the hotel room. Probably not. He hated this—the wrenching in his heart, the memories. All of it.

It needed to stop.

Michael brushed a thumb over Sam's cheek. "Sam, did you ever talk to anyone about that night?"

"Oh, hell, no." Sam choked a laugh. "Just ran. Kept running. Nothing to tie me down." Sam uncurled and looked up. "Know any good therapists?"

Michael's deft fingers caressed the back of Sam's neck. "Several." His smile was thin, but real. He gave a halfhearted shrug. "I was a wreck after Rasheed and Susan left. It was either a good therapist or a lot of alcohol." He paused. "And I don't like being that out of control."

Neither did Sam. But here he was, spiraling into the unknown. Might as well keep going. He exhaled a long, shuddering breath. "I haven't signed the contract yet. For Boston."

Hope lit Michael's face for a moment. "Will you?"

After all this, Michael still wanted him? "I don't know. I need you so badly. I broke every single rule I have to be with you. Hell, I shouldn't have even said yes in Curaçao. Should have sent back the drink."

"I have no regrets." Michael's smile and tone confirmed that.

"Neither do I. And I should. That's part of what terrifies me."

Michael let go and sat back. But his expression was thoughtful, so Sam pressed down the slight panic at the loss of his touch.

After a moment, Michael spoke. "Maybe it's time to find out who you are when you stop running. Make a stand. Not for me. Not for Sundra, but for yourself." The corner of Michael's mouth lifted into a smirk. "Lead by example, you could say."

Sam couldn't help the choke of laughter. His words, thrown back at him. Maybe there was something under Randell Anderson after all. "Jerk." He didn't put an ounce of malice behind the word.

"Don't forget pigheaded and stubborn." Michael took Sam's hands in his. "And if we're talking flaws—I get a kick out of flogging people, then fucking them."

Warmth ran up Sam's spine. "That's a flaw?"

Michael grinned. "Only to some."

But not to Sam. Calm settled into him, chasing away the remaining wisps of terror. What he'd said the night before was true. Michael brought peace, and into that space, that freedom, Sam let the sparks of excitement catch fire. A gamble? Oh yes. For both of them.

"Let's try." He pulled Michael closer. "Once I'm not your boss, once this merger is behind us, let's give this a shot. I'll stay in Pittsburgh. Start something new." He was shaking. "It's nuts, but you're right. Everything I said, everything I say"—Sam reached up, removed Michael's glasses, and set them on the bed—"means nothing if I'm not with you." He cupped his hand around the back of Michael's head and tugged him into a kiss.

And this time, he was in charge, probing, thrusting, demanding. In response, Michael wrapped his arms around Sam and pressed fingers against the welts on his back.

Sam moaned, and deepened the kiss. His cock stirred.

Michael broke the kiss. "Are you sure?"

He pressed his forehead against Michael's collarbone. "I want to be. Help me be. Teach me to be."

"I can do that." Michael pushed him back onto the bed, and crawled on top. They touched and explored and kissed —not in frantic need, but slowly, tenderly, until they were both hard and panting. Sam's back sang, his nerves reminding him of the night before. If only there were time for a repeat. He glanced at the clock and stilled.

Michael followed suit, squinting. "What?"

"There's still time for the coffee you promised."

Michael found his glasses and looked again. "More than enough."

Sam pulled him close and nibbled his ear. "And I also need you inside me again. Figured we can multitask on sex and cleanup." He felt Michael tremble for a second, before Michael pulled their hips together, his shaft answering Sam's need.

"Practical." Michael rocked his hips, his cock brushing against Sam's. "And this time we have condoms and lube."

Perfect. They pulled each other off the bed and stumbled toward the bathroom.

The world could wait for now. Everything else, Sam would figure out later.

————

MICHAEL HAD EXPECTED SAM TO BE ASSERTIVE AFTER the heart-to-heart, but not quite this aggressive. Sam rammed Michael against the door to the hotel bathroom, locked his fingers in Michael's hair and pulled him down into a kiss that curled Michael's toes and very nearly had Michael on *his* knees at Sam's feet.

Someday, he'd do that—just to see Sam's reaction—but not today.

Sam broke the kiss. "I hope you have condoms and lube in the bathroom already." He nipped at Michael's collarbone. "Because I don't want to let you go."

Fuck. "They're in the duffel." Well, the condoms, anyway. The bottle of lube was probably somewhere on the floor from last night.

Sam's nip turned painful. "Then, go get them."

An order? Michael tangled his fingers into Sam's hair and yanked his head back, not too hard, but enough to serve as a reminder of who was in charge—at least in the bedroom.

Sam gasped, moaned, and melted against Michael.

"Care to rephrase that?" He smiled down into Sam's lust-filled face.

Oh, the wicked light in those blue eyes. "Please go and get the condoms and lube?"

"Why?"

Sam rocked his cock against Michael's. "So you can fuck me until I can't see straight?"

"With pleasure." He pressed a kiss to Sam's exposed neck, then let him straighten up. "Wait here."

He found the lube under a shirt and pulled a strip of condoms out of the duffel on the table. Sam still stood by the bathroom door, a picture of need and desire—so very different from a scant few minutes before.

Sam was still *here*, had chosen to be with Michael. For a moment, it seemed as if the floor dipped. Michael caught himself on the table and fought for breath, heart full of all the words, the endearments he wanted to blurt out before it was too late. There was time, now, to say those things. More than one night. A future. A chance.

He pushed off the table and made his way back to the bathroom. "Inside." He gestured for Sam to lead, then admired the welts that covered the long line of Sam's back— the marks he'd left, the pain and pleasure and peace he'd given Sam. There was that dizziness again. He put the condoms and lube on the counter. "Sam."

Sam turned, all teeth and brilliance, and dropped to his knees.

"If you—" The rest of Michael words, even what he'd planned to say disappeared when Sam wrapped his lips and hand around Michael's cock. Michael groaned and barely had enough time to grab edge of the bathroom counter before his legs crumpled.

God, that hot, tight, wet mouth. Sam pumped Michael's shaft with one hand, gripped Michael's hip with the other, and his tongue—that fucking tongue of his—slid back and forth against the underside of the head. Lightning danced down every one of Michael's nerves, setting his skin on fire.

Bracing himself against the counter, Michael tightened his fingers in Sam's hair and took back some of the control he'd lost to that talented mouth, slowing Sam's bobbing— but not his damn tongue. He thrust forward, deeper each time—inviting Sam to surrender.

As before, Sam relaxed and opened, taking Michael's stroke down to the root. Again and again. All the time, Sam never missed an instant to tease Michael with tongue or hand—that is, when Michael let him.

That slick heat, Sam's low moans around his shaft, the fire racing down his nerves with every thrust—it all felt too damn good. The sight of his cock sliding in and out of Sam's stretched lips, Sam's deep gasps for air mixing with Michael's own harsh breathing. Every sensation enflamed, ached his balls, need like a cord binding him to Sam. The musk and sweat and sex in the air, in his mouth. The pounding of blood, the fire winding tighter and tighter in his core. In his soul.

Sam looked up and met Michael's gaze—his pale eyes full of desire and surrender—and something far deeper. Hope. Love. Michael closed his eyes against the blinding light of his orgasm and spilled himself down Sam's throat.

When Michael could see again, when the trembling stopped and he didn't need the counter to keep his legs under him, he looked down and found Sam still sitting at his feet.

"You're stunning when you come, did you know?"

The warmth in Michael now had nothing to do with his fading orgasm. "No one's ever told me that, no."

Sam rose, somehow graceful in his motions, despite his breathlessness. "Pity." He closed the distance and kissed Michael. As an equal. A lover.

Yes, they played games, took on roles, but this—this was heaven, too. And God, he loved tasting himself in Sam's mouth. Michael broke the kiss. "And here I thought you wanted me to fuck you."

"I do." Sam turned and eyed the glass-enclosed shower. "Looks big enough for all kinds of fun."

Maybe it was just from the exertion, the sweat, but the lines on Sam's back looked redder and more tender. Michael traced his fingers down Sam's skin, over the angry, raised flesh. "When we're clean, I have some lotion for these."

Sam shivered under Michael's touch. "I don't mind."

Michael chuckled. "You will later. Trust me." He drew Sam back and wrapped his arms across his chest. Sam hissed and arched against the contact, no doubt feeling every stripe the crop had left.

"Really, really don't mind." His voice, deep and gravelly, dripped with need.

Michael slid his hand down Sam's chest and abs, then gripped Sam's erection. "If you want another flogging, you'll need to heal."

"If you say so." Disappointment in that whisper.

He kissed Sam's neck. "I do."

That Sam wanted more didn't surprise Michael. Sam pushed every limit—both his own and Michael's. Just how much pain could Sam take? How much did he want? How much could Michael give him and still feel comfortable? He'd made Sam fly each time, but had not even come near the space where Sam would ask him to back down.

And Sam had been beaten—truly beaten. Ice chased down Michael's spine and he let Sam's cock go. "I need to know something."

Sam must have heard the change in Michael's voice, felt the tension in his body. "Anything."

"Why this, Sam? Why, after all you've—"

Sam rotated in Michael's loosened grip and swallowed the rest of Michael's words with a breathtaking—literally —kiss.

Michael sucked in a gasp of air when Sam freed him.

"That's why." He grinned in a way that should have been illegal in most states.

"I don't understand." And he wanted to—needed to— before this went further.

Sam sobered. "I want this, Michael. Crave it. What you do—it's so far away from a punch in the face or a kick to the ribs or having your leg stomped on"—his breath caught—"it might as well be another planet." Sam ran a hand over Michael's shoulder, down his pecs, as if mapping the contours with his hand. "You're loving.

Careful." He looked up. "And I can stop you with a word."

Sam could. Michael pressed his lips into Sam's hair, tasting the silky strands, the lingering scent of shampoo, sweat, and sleep. "It's just a bit weird when I stop and think about it."

"Then don't." Sam spoke against Michael's throat. "I trust you. Hell, you won't even take me as far as I want to go because it's not safe."

"Not yet, anyway," Michael murmured against his hair. "We'll get there." God, he wanted to go there, too, see Sam writhing in as much pain and pleasure as Michael could tease out of his beautiful body. The thought of it flamed every one of Michael's nerves, reawakening desire. "But if we go too fast—"

"You'll hurt me?"

Michael had to laugh at that. "Yes. But in the wrong way."

"See? There is a difference."

There was. He'd been there with other subs, that moment when something went wrong and the pain went from *fuck me* to *fucking stop right now*.

Sam opened space between them and met Michael's gaze. "You need to trust that I'll say if I need you to stop."

It was, of course, the heart of every bit of play. Trust. Surrender, on both sides, to some extent. "I know this," Michael said, more to himself than Sam.

"Then start doing it."

There went that mouth again. Michael raked his fingernails down Sam's back in one hard, quick stroke.

An instant later, Sam arched up on his toes in a silent cry, his hands clenching Michael's arms and a mixture of surprise, pain, and lust painted onto his face.

Just that nearly undid Michael—that vision of pain and bliss, Sam caught in what only Michael could give.

Then Sam slumped against Michael and groaned so deeply it rattled bone and marrow—and Michael's cock. Sam might get his wish after all.

"Like that?" Michael grazed his lips over Sam's ear.

"Yes." Sam slurred the word.

"Want more?"

Sam tilted his head back and grinned. "Always."

"Then get in the shower." He let Sam go, and damned if the man didn't strut to the glass enclosure like he owned the place. Michael scooped up a condom and the lube and followed, dropping the items on a high shelf. He'd need them soon enough, but not *quite* yet.

Sam turned on the water and adjusted the temperature, and the water sluiced over his shoulders and down his beautifully marred back. Thin parallel lines rose where Michael had scratched him. Michael pressed up against Sam's back, savoring the shudder and the soft moan that rumbled through Sam.

The temperature Sam had chosen was warm, but not overly so. Michael nudged Sam out of the way and turned it a notch hotter, then switch the head of the shower from a gentle steady stream to a hard, pulsating massage. Michael put his back into the stream, letting the abrasive thump of steamy water ease the tension from his muscles.

It was going to sting like hell on Sam's welt-covered back. *Perfect.*

Seemed Sam knew as well. He eyed the showerhead with a mix of trepidation and desire. "Shit."

Michael chuckled, then pulled Sam close and took his mouth. This time, Sam surrendered to the kiss, letting Michael explore and lead. He groaned low in his throat when Michael pressed nails against the inflamed skin of his back, then thrust his hard cock against Michael's thigh.

The friction rekindled the desire to be surrounded by Sam, to hear his cries and witness the pain—and pleasure. He spun them both around, moving Sam into the stream of water, deepening the kiss.

Sam's whole body stiffened when the water pounded against his back; then Sam was the one kissing Michael, taking Michael's mouth for his own—and Michael surrendered to the onslaught. Today wasn't about last night —it was about tomorrow and the next day, and the one after that.

Sam wanted Michael. Needed him. Chose to be with him, even over a lifetime of fears. Michael had no issues switching roles, on occasion. Besides, having Sam kiss like that while rocking his cock against Michael? Hotter than hell. Knowing Sam was in pain and loving every second of it? Even better.

Sam broke their kiss and sucked in breath after breath. "God."

"How's the back?"

"Hurts like fuck." Sam coughed a laugh and smiled. "I love it."

Michael pushed wet curls out of Sam's eyes. "Still want me inside you?"

"Yes, please." Sam nipped Michael's shoulder. "Until I can't think."

With pleasure. He pulled Sam out of the stream, rotated him once more, then pressed his front against the wall of the shower. "You know, it's going to take a while for me to come."

Sam arched back. "Really? I hadn't considered that *at all* when I went down on you."

Of *course* he had. Michael bit Sam's neck, hard enough to evoke a flinch, then spoke in his ear. "Yes, but how long can you keep from coming?"

"As long as you want me to." Sam turned his head to the side and there was the edge of that sly smile. "Until you say I can."

"A fine answer." Michael kissed the spot he'd bitten, then stepped back and retrieved the condom and the lube, and sheathed himself before spreading lube on his cock. Then he worked a slick finger into Sam.

Sam hissed. "Don't... need to be gentle."

"Maybe I do." Michael eased the head of his cock inside Sam and groaned against the tight heat of his ass, then worked himself deeper with slow, easy strokes.

Sam's breathing hitched with every movement, half moan, half gasp, entirely unrestrained. When there wasn't any space left between them, Michael held himself deep in Sam and enjoyed the way Sam trembled against—and all around—him. "Maybe I should just—" Michael kissed the drops of water on Sam's back. "Just fuck you like this."

He withdrew and thrust in again at the same languid rate, as far into Sam as he could. "You feel so damn good."

Again and again, he slid into Sam, savoring Sam's every groan and shudder, his wordless sounds of pleasure, the slow slap and grind as flesh met flesh. The ever-present pulse of the shower, like a heartbeat.

Sam shuddered and his hands slipped down the wall. He rocked back as Michael slid forward, taking every inch of Michael's cock. Michael wrapped his arms around Sam and pulled him up, holding him—them both—still. Together.

Sam lolled his head back in a silent cry.

"Do you like this?" Michael whispered into Sam's ear.

"Yes." The word was a tiny thing, all air and quiver.

Michael moved again, gentle thrusts that rocked them against each other. "And this?"

"Yes. Don't—" Sam lost himself in a groan when Michael pushed in deep. "Don't stop."

Michael didn't, lost in Sam's heat, the rush of Sam's lungs, his groans, and the taste of Sam's water-splashed skin. The shower thrummed until the very air seemed to hum with the pulse. Sam shuddered and slid against him, wet and warm, his fingers splayed on Michael's hips. What felt like eternity might have been minutes—so hard to tell this far into the trance that was Sam, but a sharp need prickled over Michael's skin, quickened his blood.

He thrust faster, with more force, and Sam threw back his head and gasped. That was all the invitation Michael needed to pick up the pace.

"Fuck." Sam bent his head down, hands once more braced against the tile in front of him. Flesh against stone, muscular arms full of strength. He matched Michael's rhythms and force, milking Michael's cock with each stroke, singeing Michael's nerves with fire.

Michael's vision grayed, a sudden spike of pleasure cascading lightning down his veins. He hissed against Sam's back, fighting against the need to bury himself deep and repeatedly in Sam's lithe body until they both shattered. After a moment, Michael slowed down and caught his breath against the knife's edge of want.

Seemed that same blade had found Sam as well. Short puffs of breath shuddered Sam's back and his arms were locked against the shower wall, nails biting into the grout. When Michael wrapped a hand around Sam's cock, Sam's whole body quaked.

"Close?" Michael stroked Sam's cock and thrust deep.

Sam grunted low, then answered. "Fuck, yes."

He sped up. "How close?"

This time the only answer Sam gave was a laugh that sounded more like a sob that only intensified the headiness, the buzzing in Michael's blood.

He kissed behind Sam's ear. "Good."

Sam hissed and rammed back with each thrust. Any control Michael thought he had disappeared, along with everything else in the world but Sam. Need gripped him tight, flaying skin and bone. He plowed into Sam, jerking him off at the same rapid rate.

From Sam's guttural cries and unintelligible cursing, he was barely staving off orgasm.

Just for Michael.

Fire engulfed Michael. His balls tightened and he let out a harsh cry of his own, and then leaned over Sam and spoke one word. "Come."

Sam did, with a shout that echoed against stone and glass and he tightened around Michael's cock.

The shower hazed out and burst into a sea of stars and Michael spilled over into his own orgasm and he emptied himself deep inside Sam. Every movement seared into Michael's skin until couldn't move anymore, could barely stand.

He wasn't sure if he was shaking or if the quaking was Sam—probably both of them. Sam clung to the shower wall while Michael held Sam, breathless and panting, the aftershocks rolling down Michael's limbs.

Sam shifted. "Please do that to me again, sometime."

"Anytime you'd like." Michael eased himself out of Sam.

A groan from Sam. "Not anytime, or we'll never get anything done."

Wasn't that the truth. "Give me a sec." Michael slipped out of the shower long enough to ditch the condom, then was back in Sam's arms. He kissed Sam on the forehead, then the mouth, then brushed a thumb over his cheek. "Still need coffee?"

Sam tilted his head back. "I will always need coffee." His smile was brilliant. "You?"

"Yes." He could take or leave coffee, to be honest. But that wasn't the question he answered.

It was Sam that he'd always need.

CHAPTER NINE

Morning in the streets of New Orleans in July was like walking inside a humid oven. Sam folded his suit jacket over one arm and quelled his desire to take Michael's hand as they strolled down Canal Street back toward their hotel. Michael had slung his jacket over one shoulder. His suspenders stood out against his white shirt.

It was only the intensity of the sex they'd had in the shower that morning that kept Sam from getting hard. Still, he admired the view, along with the thought of leather on flesh. His, preferably. He drew in a mouthful of wet air and grinned.

The morning hadn't turned out so bad after all. A good hard fuck and then coffee with his lover. Couldn't complain about that, even if the conversation from earlier still lurked in the back of his mind.

Sam took a sip from his takeaway cup. He could do this. He wanted Michael. Wanted to be out. Wanted—a normal life.

They both held their second coffees—the first they had

consumed over fresh beignets and laughter in a French Quarter café. That had been a welcome respite, a glimpse at the kind of life possible. But as they neared the hotel, Sam's doubts crept forward, the ones that told him this wouldn't work, that he was foolish to try. He'd never held a successful relationship before grad school and he'd been playing the straight man for too long. But for Michael? Damned if he'd let go now. Time to throw everything on the line. Go get help and get his head screwed on the right way around. Kick the past into... well, the past.

The hotel rose above them. Those who knew Sam as a CEO, as the man who saved companies, they would be inside the doors. He was supposed to have lunch with William and Vijay Malik. While William acted happy about the deal with Sundra, his interest in Four Rivers at this juncture set entirely different nerves jangling. Especially given the information Fabian had offered. William was a venture capitalist, not a technologist—the only thing that should interest him about the deal was the buyout, even if he were running some sort of investment scam.

Perhaps he should have gone to the strip bar with them last night... to suss out William's mind. Then there was the question of what William had known about Michael's original role at Four Rivers—surely the board must have been aware of the news articles, the photos?

Yet they hadn't given Michael his due. William also knew Michael was gay—had that come before or after the board had taken over?

"Stop that," Michael said. He grinned in that way men do when they've gotten everything they've wanted.

Sam had likely worn a similar expression earlier, after Michael had come down his throat. "Stop what?"

"Thinking. You have that look." The grin faded. "Whatever you're worried about, it will be okay."

They paused at the corner and waited for the light. "I know. It's not about us. I'm enjoying this, being with you. I'm just worried about the merger and what could go wrong. Three weeks is a long time."

Michael chuckled. "It wasn't when it came to finishing the release."

Now that was true. Remarkable things could happen in three weeks. Or horrible ones.

The light changed. "You going to be able to behave yourself?" Sam couldn't help teasing. What he said earlier was true. He'd be happy to shout from the rooftops that he was Michael Sebastian's lover. But they'd have to be careful for the time being.

"I'm the very soul of discretion," Michael said. "Most of the time."

Sam snorted and took another sip of his coffee.

"You going to be okay?" From Michael's tone of voice, Sam knew he meant coming out. Dealing with the past.

"Yeah. I'll find someone to talk to. Get my shit together. About time I did, really."

"Good." Michael grinned before he put on a more professional smile.

They entered the rotating door of the hotel, and Sam slipped back into the role of CEO. "I believe Greta has some people she'd like you to meet."

Michael nodded. "She said she'd join me here at nine to fill me in on the day."

The lobby bustled with conference attendees. Sam glanced at his watch. Quarter 'til. They weren't even late.

They weren't, however, the first ones. William stood near the self-service coffee bar, stirring too many packs of sugar into his coffee. He looked up and his attention flicked between Sam and Michael, his expression unreadable.

Shit. Sam smoothed over his own features and took another draw on his coffee. The niggling voice in his brain screamed at him to step away from Michael.

You're overreacting. William was an idiot with a big wallet and a knack for surrounding himself with people who had financial and business sense. There's no way he'd have guessed there was anything between Sam and Michael other than work camaraderie. The worst accusation William had leveled at Sam was that he acted like a programmer.

Sam nodded to William.

William tossed his stirrer and joined them. "Should have come with us last night, Randell. You missed an amazing set of tits."

William spoke loudly, turning a few heads. Sam tried not to wince. He didn't dare look at Michael. "One more drink, and I'd have been asleep in the back of the joint. Glad you and the others had fun."

William snorted. "You wouldn't know fun if she bit you."

Sam gave William his best banal smile before setting down his coffee and donning his suit coat.

William turned to Michael. "What about you, Mike? Want to see what real men like?"

Sam's blood turned to ice. *Holy shit.* He hazarded a look to his left. Michael still had his coat tossed over his arm. He looked down at William and the difference between their heights was breathtakingly apparent. Michael's expression was completely neutral. "I'm not going to answer that." He shifted his attention and looked over William's head. "Good morning, Dr. Bachman."

"Good morning, Michael, Sam." Greta stood behind William, with an expression that was only half as blank as Michael's. The other half was disgust.

Sam saluted her with his coffee. Thank God that was over. Fucking William. He owed Greta, even if she didn't know it. Like old times.

She cleared her throat. "Are you ready, Michael?"

"Yes." He finished the last of his coffee, tossed the cup, and put on his jacket. Another gray suit, but this one lighter than the previous day's. The tie had the bright color of the tropics, but without feathers and beaks.

Pity. He was growing fond of tacky parrots.

Michael gave a nod before following Greta toward the main conference rooms.

William stayed, an angry flush creeping up his neck.

"Well, that wasn't most graceful conversation to have first thing in the morning," Sam said. "What the hell is wrong with you? Need more of that coffee to clear your head?"

William took a sip and twisted his face. "You weren't drunk last night, or tired. You're not interested in women, are you? Are you like him?" He thumbed in the direction Michael had walked.

Sam's heart thudded hard, but he shrugged, mimicking nonchalance and ignoring the last part. "It's not a secret I'm not interested in strip bars."

"Coffee with your employee in the morning? You into that?"

Oh damn it. This better not be going where he thought it might. "We met to talk about Sundra and his potential role there." He gestured in the direction Michael and Greta had gone. "They're obviously interested in him, and the self-serve coffee over there is terrible."

"All the right answers, huh?" William was smiling in a way that turned Sam's blood cold.

What the hell did William know? And how? Sam racked his brain. "What are you talking about?"

William set his cup down on the table before replying. "On one of my visits to Four Rivers, I checked out the gym."

Fucking hell. Sam forced himself to breathe normally, to remain relaxed. He hoped to God it worked because showing panic now would do no good. "And?"

"And I heard you. With him."

William knew. He had known for more than a month. Sam's fear—all the voices from his past—yelled and screamed, then twisted, cracked, and melted away. He couldn't afford that emotion, not with William. "And?" He spoke softer than before, but that single word made William step back.

Sam smiled. This role—the asshole CEO—he could do. "Are you trying to blackmail me?" William might be ignorant of technology, but he played politics as well as anyone at his level.

"That depends on whether you actually care about Mike Sebastian."

"Perhaps I do. Perhaps I don't." Sam spoke through the dizzying panic that dwelt in the back of his mind. "How much are you willing to risk your reputation to find out?"

"My reputation? I'm not the one fucking my employee."

Sam chuckled and swirled the coffee in his cup before taking a drink. "If he were a woman, you'd be patting me on the back and asking for details."

William face reddened. "That's different."

"No, it really isn't." And it wasn't. Like it or not, Sam's relationship with Michael wasn't proper or ethical, even if he had fallen for him. "And knowing you, you'd congratulate me, then stab me in the back with it, just like now. What is it that you want?"

"Four Rivers."

Sam nearly choked on his coffee. "Sundra has Four Rivers. I saw you sign the paperwork myself. I can't deliver something you gave away."

"I mean I want the office. To manage."

The position that was Michael's to take. That should have been Michael's from day one. *Shit.* "You don't know the first thing about routing. Or engineering."

"I don't need to. All I need to know is how to get people to work. I've done that. This deal is proof."

And how to syphon funds. Sam didn't crush the paper cup in his hand. For one, it still contained good coffee. He drank the remains. "I'm not so sure Sundra sees it that way." Hell, if Four Rivers had followed William's plan, only the intellectual property would be on the market, not the talent. Sundra wouldn't have bought.

"That's where you come in. You're going to recommend me."

Like hell. More like drop enough paperwork at Sundra legal to bury William. "Why would I do that?"

"Because if you don't I'll let everyone know what kind of man Sebastian is. How the upstanding, well-loved Mike bent over to get ahead in his career."

Sam's heart stuttered and the cold edge of fear surged in. All thoughts of handing William over to Sundra faded. *Shit.*

Michael didn't deserve to have his name dragged through the mud because Sam had lost discretion. Even if Michael were right about Pittsburgh and how well the community knew him, companies would notice. The scandal would limit his career choices. And Sundra was larger than just Pittsburgh.

There was something worse than being gay in business —cocksucking your way up the ladder. That it was Sam who ended up with a dick in his mouth didn't matter. Everyone would assume the other way around.

It would destroy Michael.

"What happens if you get what you want?" It was a sign that Sam had caved, but he had to know.

William grinned, his teeth too white. "Your friend Mike keeps his job. You leave town. Everyone's happy."

Not acceptable. Nor was punching William in the face. Sam chewed on his tongue and said words that tasted of bitter, bitter defeat. "Let me have some time to consider."

All fang and gloat, William had the aura of a predator with his muzzle in a kill. "You had better make up your mind by lunch, because you're going to give a glowing recommendation to Dr. Malik then." William picked up his coffee and walked toward the conference area. "See you later, Randell."

Sam remained, planted on the spot of carpet, ice running in his veins. That gave him less than three hours to figure out some way out of this mess. All he wanted to do was run out the door.

What the hell do I do now?

Every answer he came up with was a bad choice that led to a broken career or broken heart.

Or both.

Michael shook Greta's hand and some of the
tension he'd carried since following her into the small
conference room slipped away. "Thank you very much. I
hope I meet your expectations."

The talk—interview in reality—had gone well, though
Greta had caught him somewhat off-guard with years'
worth of his goals and evaluations and project notes. Sundra
had been busy and taken an unusual interest in the folks at
Four Rivers. That was good—better than he had expected.
It meant what Sam had implied was true—Sundra wanted
more than just the software and hardware. They wanted
the brains behind those as well.

"If the work you've done over the past seven years is any
indicator, you'll exceed them." Greta gathered the spread of
papers she'd laid out over the conference room table. "We're
glad to have you on board."

What they wanted from him was straightforward—and
essentially what he had done back when Susan had been
CEO. Oversee all the projects at the office, coordinate the
different teams. Be the person who orchestrated
development. It would mean handing over the management
of testing to someone else—he would miss that—he'd built a
good team in the past four years. But to be involved from the
ground up again? He wanted that—had for years. It's what
the board—and Rasheed and Susan—had taken from him.

And yes, technically he'd be a suit. He'd also have the
title that should have been his ages ago—Vice President of
Routing Development—but Sundra had a very lax dress
code. The actual suit was optional; he could still dress like it
was five o'clock somewhere.

There was one thing he had to ask, though. "How much
of this was Sam's idea?"

Greta stacked her papers and slipped them into an

attaché case. A small smile curled the edge of her lips, then vanished. "Very little. He recommended you, but we do our own diligence. You're not the only person we looked at. Whether or not Sam had said anything, you would have risen to the top of our list."

More knots loosened in his shoulders.

Greta picked up her case, then opened the door and gestured for him to proceed her. "It's been a long time since I've worked with Sam. It's a shame he'll be moving on."

"He has to, though. Part of the deal."

Greta nodded. "In some ways, he's too much of a go-getter to say put. Never willing to settle down."

That pretty much described Sam to a tee. They rounded the corner and returned to the lobby. On the far side, near the bar, Sam sat. He waved when he saw them, but it was stiff—calculated.

Michael hesitated for just an instant, his heart dropping to his stomach. Out of the corner of his eye, he saw Greta look his way. *I'm giving away too many signals.* He walked forward, keeping his pace casual. But God, the look on Sam's face. His smile didn't even touch his cheeks or eyes. Something was horribly wrong and Sam was doing his damnedest to hide it.

As they approached, Sam gestured at the other chairs around the high-top table. "Please. I need to speak to you both."

This time, it was Greta who paused, her expression frozen for just a second. Sam gave her a smile that was old and worn—the kind friends share—then she slid onto one of the chairs. Michael took the other. Sam's gaze was wary, sad, fearful, and defiant, all mixed into a blur.

Michael opened his mouth to speak, but Greta beat

him. "Oh, Randy. What have you gotten yourself into this time?"

Sam's chuckle was strained. "The usual."

Michael found himself being studied by Greta in a way that made heat rise to his face. It wasn't sexual by any means... but it was knowing. Very, very knowing. Sam's two words seemed to have told Greta everything. *Shit*. Had Sam changed his mind?

"I don't buy that," she said. "If this were the usual, he wouldn't be here. Or you wouldn't."

Michael's ears felt like they were aflame. She certainly knew they were a couple. And if Greta did... Michael's innards twisted. *Oh, fuck*. Everything they'd talked about moments before might be gone.

This time, Sam's laugh was more open. "Oh, now that's true. I always ran, didn't I?" He sobered quickly and lowered his voice. "I don't want to run. William is trying to blackmail me."

A burst of prickles raced down Michael's back. Sam wasn't running and they were in a fuck-ton of trouble. Elation and horror. "How did he—" His brain caught up and he swallowed. "I guess it doesn't matter how."

"Because indiscretion is indiscretion." Greta said the words without emotion. "One of you reports to the other."

Sam nodded.

A stabbing pain formed behind Michael's eye. "It's not —" His throat threatened to close tight. "He didn't take advantage of me. It just—" Jubilation to despair.

"Happened?" She finished for him. "That's fine. Well, no, it's not, but for this, it doesn't matter."

"I'm sorry," Sam said. "Truly."

Michael wasn't sure if the apology was for him or Greta

or both of them. He reached across the table and gave Sam's hand a squeeze. "What I said before still holds."

Greta blew out a puff of air. "You never make things easy, do you?" She raised a hand to catch the attention of the barkeeper. "I'm ordering a Bloody Mary and you're paying, Randy. Then you're going to tell me everything."

"Deal."

They added two waters to that order, and when the drinks came, they started. Everything meant everything, apparently, because Michael found himself telling her about Curaçao in general terms, but also the stupidity of the former CEO and what led up to Sam taking over Four Rivers. Sam filled in his own details—the financial corruption of Michael's old boss, Taylor, his suspicions about William, though not what Fabian had passed along. Then he told his account of Curaçao—and how he and Michael both tried to be on the up and up.

"I take it that failed?" Greta's amusement was evident.

Sam actually blushed, and that was answer enough. He cleared his throat. "Now William wants the site manager position."

"Why?" Michael tapped a finger against the brushed chrome surface of the table. "He doesn't know a damn thing about routers."

"That's the part that baffled me. He's hardly qualified and hates that kind of work. He said something about using it as a way into Sundra, but that makes no sense. Unless he has his fingers in something else."

Greta toyed with the celery in her drink. "Well, William won't get the job even if you were to sing his praises. It's a position for someone with a technical background, not a venture capitalist. And we don't take well to bigots."

Sam winced. "So you heard that part of the conversation this morning."

Greta scowled into her Bloody Mary. "The man needs a muzzle."

"He also tried to sink Four Rivers," Sam said. "I'm not so egotistical as to think he's just getting back at me." Sam shook his head. "From the way he acts, he's a homophobe, but I can't think this is all about that, either."

Michael still reeled from some of the information Sam had spilled. "What do you mean 'sink'?"

"He wanted to give you a week for testing after freeze."

Michael sat back in his chair. Sam had gotten him three and he'd been furious. If they made it out of this, he'd owe Sam. Big time. Now more than ever. "Well, shit."

Greta put her drink down. "I saw your test plans. That's — No way in hell you could have done your testing in one week."

"It's all very hinky," Sam said. "And I was dumb enough to give him an opening." He scrubbed his face.

"We." Damned if he'd let Sam take all the blame. "You didn't act alone."

The corner of Sam's mouth twitched as if to smile. "No, I didn't."

Michael stared at his water. William had never been kind, had always been an ass to him, even from the day the board took over. Michael still had no idea what Rasheed and Susan had told the board about him. He looked up. "Do you think he knew about me? From before?"

"I don't know," Sam said. "The paperwork I had access to was scrubbed clean."

"Before what?" Greta's question had the snap of irritation.

Well, she had asked for everything. "I helped found

Four Rivers. Why I'm not on any of the paperwork is screwed up and entwined with personal reasons, but I was there."

"From day one," Greta said.

"Yes. Except I was also—" Michael's throat tightened. Because he still couldn't betray Rasheed. Not even after all these years.

Greta took another sip of her Bloody Mary. "You and Rasheed Esfahani were lovers."

"How did you know?" It was Sam who asked the question Michael wanted to. Good thing, because Michael couldn't. Not through lungs so tight he could barely breathe.

"Mr. Esfahani told us." She set her glass down. "I told you we did our diligence."

Michael found his voice. "You *spoke* to him?"

"And his wife, yes. You were demoted when they sold the company. We wanted to know why."

Wife. Susan. *Shit*, they had gone and done that, then. "You knew this before we sat down back there."

"They think the world of you."

Michael reached for his water, wishing it were something much stronger. Sam wasn't the only one who'd need therapy when they got back to Pittsburgh.

Rasheed. Susan. His heart twisted into knots.

"They confirmed that where you ended up was not where you should have. It speaks volumes to your loyalty that you stayed. You care quite a bit about Four Rivers."

That was an understatement. "Yes, I do."

"Good." Greta turned to Sam. "You have lunch with Dr. Malik, yes?"

"At noon. With William. Whereupon I am to warble

about his wonders or William will toss Michael under the bus."

Michael nearly choked on his water. "Me?"

Sam studied his hands. "He guessed that threatening me wouldn't do anything. So he chose another target, one he thought I might protect." He looked up. Lines of anger and worry marred Sam's face. "It was a very good guess."

That heartened Michael, as did the sudden realization of one of the other reasons they were sitting here. "You don't want to see everyone back at the office screwed over by William."

"No. Neither of William's outcomes is acceptable." Sam leaned back. "So I'm doing the only thing I can."

Greta snorted. "You're changing the rules."

"I'd prefer to think of it as blazing my own path." He paused. "But it's not just mine anymore."

It was also Michael's. "I'll take my lumps for... this inappropriate relationship," he said to Greta. "I want what's best for my team and the office. You can't let William run them into the ground."

Greta rubbed her forehead, then took her cell phone from her blazer pocket and stood. "Let me make a call. I'll be back." She walked away from the table.

Michael laid his hand on the table, palm up. Sam hesitated for a moment, then covered it with his own. Sam's palm was sweaty and his pulse nearly as fast as Michael's own. "He was in the locker room."

Hell. "He couldn't have seen anything."

Sam shook his head. "But he very well might have heard quite a bit."

"Or guessed from the clothing by the lockers."

"Does it matter?" Sam sounded amused, but there was sadness layered on top.

"No. And I don't regret that day at all." He squeezed Sam's hand.

Sam's expression was thin. "I don't want to regret it, but we did break the rules. A case could be made that I took advantage—"

"Hush. One could as easily be made that I came on to you. Especially since I did in Curaçao." He paused. "I don't regret that either."

Sam exhaled. "Neither do I. That night was the second best night of my life."

Curiosity got the better of Michael. "What was the best?"

"Last night." Sam's smile took on depth and warmth.

Just you wait. "There will be more."

A redness tinged Sam's neck and he coughed. "You're not bothered by this at all, are you?"

He was. The position Sundra offered was everything he wanted—what he had once been. A correction for injustices done. But Sam—was more. Mornings and nights and all the times in between. Laughter and dinners and biking in the park. The job was, in the end, a job. Sam was everything Michael wanted in his life—someone to share it with. "Chance gives and chance takes. You cling to what's important."

Sam shook his head. "When you say things like that..."

"What?"

"I realize just how far I've fallen for you. Michael, I—" He looked up and froze.

Michael turned to follow Sam's gaze, slipping his hand free in the process.

Greta had returned, but not alone. Dr. Vijay Malik stood beside her, looking none-too-pleased. "You two chose quite the interesting time for revelations."

Michael stood. The sound of a chair scuffing carpet told him Sam had as well. "To be honest, I would have preferred a different venue," Michael said. "But it seems someone had other plans."

Sam stepped forward. "Regardless of us and whether we remain at Four Rivers, there are things you should know about William Vandershoot."

"So I hear." Dr. Malik gestured that they should follow.

Time to face their decisions.

CHAPTER TEN

DR. VIJAY MALIK WAS AN UNASSUMING MAN, UNLESS you'd seen him in action. Sam had. Shorter than Sam and wiry, Malik had a quiet, watchful demeanor until he had something to say; then his presence expanded to fill an entire room. Intense was one way to describe Malik's conversational style. Commanding was another.

Sam's heart lodged itself in his throat. This meeting would probably ruin him, which was fine. He had more than enough money to live off of for quite some time. Sam had no idea how Michael would survive. However, Michael hadn't even shown a touch of fear at Malik's appearance.

God, what a mess. A glorious, wonderful, and horrible mess. Sam's fault, too. He couldn't think around Michael, not in the way he should. He'd nearly confessed his love to Michael... should have. Shit.

Sundra had known about Michael—his past with Four Rivers. It showed a competency that made Sam feel a bit inadequate. But then, he'd only ever headed up smaller companies. He still had much to learn, apparently, if he even wanted to continue along that path. Consulting started to look better and better... he might be able to support them both, if it came to that.

Malik entered a small conference room and they all followed—Sam, Michael, and Greta. Sam glanced Greta's way, but her expression was the same one she wore while playing poker—utterly unreadable.

Not even an inch, G?

Then again, he wouldn't give her leeway in the same situation. It wasn't personal, just business.

Fuck that. Everything was personal now. His life. Michael's life.

Malik closed the door and gestured at the table. "Please have a seat." It wasn't a request.

They all obeyed. Malik remained standing. "Greta has told me you two are involved in a relationship with each other, yes?"

"Yes," Michael said. "And it's my fault. I—"

Malik held up a hand. "Fault, no fault. That's not important."

No, it really wasn't. Still, there were details that were. "It's mutually consensual," Sam said. "And began prior to us knowing we'd be working together."

"Ah," Dr. Malik said. "That's good to know." He gripped the back of one of the chairs. "Though a workplace relationship with an employee is not very politic. Your record speaks better of you, Mr. Anderson."

That was a bit of a punch to the gut. Sam took a measured breath and ignored the warmth in his face. "It does. This situation is—unique. Unexpected."

Michael shifted in his chair. "He didn't, in any way, take advantage of the situation."

"Did you?" Malik had golden-brown eyes, sharp as a hawk's.

Michael didn't flinch under that gaze. "No."

"You're both lucky that this is a case of prior engagement and that Mr. Anderson has a short-term assignment." He turned to Michael. "He was never going to remain your boss."

Michael nodded and a look of understanding passed over his face. "Of course. He's not part of the merger."

"No. That was a particular sticking point with the Four Rivers board of directors, though we would have liked him to join us."

News to Sam. It was a struggle not to speak, but something told him caution was a better approach. Maybe the weight of Malik's stare, or the indentation his fingers made in the seat cushion he gripped.

"Which brings us to William Vandershoot, the man who would out you, in more ways than one."

Michael smiled. "I go to Pittsburgh Pride every year. I don't make a big deal of my sexual preference, but he's only outing me to nonobservant folks. If they have an issue, that's their problem."

"Perhaps it's not a worry for you, Mr. Sebastian, but for Mr. Anderson?"

It was Michael's look, not Malik's, that pressed against his heart. "I—made the decision recently to remain in Pittsburgh." He swallowed and added. "To be with Michael. I was going to come out anyway." His face must be red from the heat he felt all over his body. "I'm tired of hiding my sexuality, but I'd rather it be for Michael, not because William is trying to blackmail me." Anger and pride were a potent mix. He clung to those rather than the fear. He'd been afraid too long.

Michael leaned back in his chair, his confidence so breathtaking Sam focused on Malik instead. Getting turned on now would be even less politic than having sex with Michael in the first place.

But he knew Michael approved of what he'd said. That was what mattered.

Malik nodded once. "And William?"

"He wants in on Sundra," Sam said.

"William Vandershoot will not be an employee of Sundra Networks, regardless of what personal information of yours he places on the table, nor what recommendation he might try to extort from you." Malik pushed off the chair and paced the length of the room. "I am tempted to let him follow through with his plan so that the both of you face the consequences of your sloppy behavior." He turned. "But then you are doing that right now, aren't you?"

"Better a crisis managed than a disaster allowed," Sam said.

"Ah, yes. And what would you do, Anderson, in my position?"

Sam tented his hands and placed them against his lips. He hated these kinds of questions. Malik might as well have asked, *How should I punish you?* His spine hurt from all the tension in his back. "Announce the merger as planned. Have me leave early. I won't object."

"And Mr. Sebastian?" Malik said.

"I can't be site manager." Michael's voice was soft, but firm. "You should pick someone from Sundra for that position."

Malik nodded. "Very good and nearly correct. Officially, your exit date remains the same, Anderson, but you will make yourself scarce at the office earlier."

"Done," Sam said.

"Mr. Sebastian, as you surmised, you will not be promoted."

"Understood." Michael sat firm in his seat. Calm, as if this were but a summer breeze blowing over him and not yet another chance at his rightful position being snatched away.

That was far better than Sam managed. His legs trembled underneath the table.

"Greta has agreed to work at Four Rivers and manage the transition on-site. Mr. Sebastian will work directly with her. We'll revisit your role at the office once the merger has been completed and integration is underway."

Not a closed door, then. Sam let out a breath.

Malik's expression softened, which was unusual. "If all goes well, this will be a mere bump in the road for you, Michael."

Michael nodded. "I'll do my best to earn back your trust."

"You have my trust. Both of you. This was not an easy thing to bring to us, especially considering all you've been through, Michael."

A crack in Michael's unflappable armor appeared and he nodded, his lips pressed thin.

No, it hadn't been easy. But it had been the correct move. Slowly, Sam's ability to breathe normally returned.

"Now, if you'll excuse Mr. Anderson and me, we have another topic to discuss." Malik nodded to Greta. "Thank you."

Greta and Michael both rose and filed out at the obvious dismissal. Sam had no time to say good-bye to Michael. He'd have to catch him later. And Greta. He owed that woman a drink. An entire month of drinks.

When the door closed, Malik took a seat. "A unique situation?"

Sam folded his hands on the table. "Unexpected and unique." A chance meeting in a hotel, an odd twist of fate, and exactly the man he needed. "We were both surprised to see each other at Four Rivers."

Malik's mouth twitched in a way that looked suspiciously like the start of a smile. "Michael will be fine. Believe it or not, this is not the first time such a situation has happened. We have protocols and procedures for inter-office relationships and neither of you broke any written rule. Four Rivers' human resource policy is silent on workplace relationships, and you're not Sundra employees yet."

And Sam wouldn't become one. More of the tension leaked away. "You looked this all up? In"—he glanced at his watch—"ten minutes?"

"Greta has access to a good deal of Four Rivers' paperwork. She did the legwork."

Wine of the month club for G. Two-year subscription. "Then why penalize Michael?"

"We're not. No one outside this room will think anything of what will happen. It'll look like he was groomed by Greta, rather than promoted because of your relationship with him."

It made sense, a great deal of sense. "I should have seen that, considered that." If he'd been less emotionally involved, he might have. Or perhaps, Malik and Greta played at a higher level.

Malik leaned back in his chair. "I hazard to guess that your head is not screwed on very straight when it comes to Michael Sebastian."

Sam cleared his throat. "No, not at all."

Malik waved that away. "I'm more interested in William Vandershoot."

William. The equilibrium he'd lost when William had threatened Michael snapped back into place. Sam leaned forward. "How much do you know about the financial dealings of Four Rivers' last CEO, Taylor?"

"Only what the report said." He tented his fingers. "You know more?"

Oh, did he know more. "I'm not sure how William is connected to this, but my instinct tells me he very well might be."

"Do tell."

Sam did. All the details he remembered. The discussions with the board around the shady dealings of the last CEO, what he could recall of William's reactions to the discovery. William's stunt of trying to shorten the test cycle and his reaction to Sam's fighting against that. All of what Fabian had told him about the potential Ponzi scheme. He spilled everything he suspected about William—and how he'd planned to verify Fabian's information.

"And if this becomes a legal investigation?"

"I'm more than willing to help." He pressed a hand against the table to prevent himself from curling it into a fist. "I don't appreciate being blackmailed." He hated how this all had come out. God only knew what Michael thought.

"Nor do I like being manipulated," Malik said. "The recent audit didn't turn up any odd dealings with William and Four Rivers, but if he's involved in other endeavors..."

"He may need a place to duck and cover."

"Or a new source of income."

That hadn't occurred to Sam. Perhaps William had burned through cash? It only took a few venture capital deals going south to take out a pile of money, but the Four Rivers buyout should be pretty large. "I'll find out what I can."

"Good." Malik rose. Sam stood and followed him to the door.

Malik paused. "I will be having lunch with William on my own. I suspect there's a more important conversation you should attend to."

Sam stared at Malik.

The other man chuckled and held out his hand. "I saw the look on your face when we walked up. Some expressions are universal, Sam."

Sam shook Malik's hand and spoke around the gratitude lodged in his throat. "Thank you."

"You're giving up quite a bit for Mr. Sebastian."

"No," Sam said. "No, I'm not."

Malik's smile was small, but warm. "Good man."

MICHAEL SAT AT THE BAR, STARED AT HIS GLASS OF water, and contemplated the twists and turns that had brought him to this place. Starting Four Rivers with Rasheed and Susan, then having them walk away—so maybe they hadn't screwed him over. All the years he'd thrown himself into the work—poured his heart into the company that wasn't his anymore. And then a chance vacation.

Had he not stayed in that particular hotel in Curaçao, not spent his last night in the bar, he'd not have met Sam... not the way he had. They would have met at Four Rivers. Would there have been sparks then? Would they have fucked in the gym shower? Probably not.

Or maybe they would have. There was no denying the instant attraction he'd—they'd—felt. Certainly once he had gotten to known Sam, Michael's desire had only increased—especially the way Sam loved the pain and release Michael gave him. They could have ended up in the same situation.

He'd kept his job and Four Rivers. Even held on to the promise of promotion that would put him back where he belonged. And he still had Sam. God, at least he hoped he still had him. He loved that intensity, the frenetic energy in Sam that Michael could tame with a touch and the promise of pain and pleasure, but it came with Sam's ability to turn on a dime and rationalize away his own feelings. Michael loved Sam anyway. Every ounce of his body wanted to be with Sam, to share his life, to learn more and more about him. Maybe they would last, maybe they wouldn't, but damn it, they needed to try.

"Hey." Sam's voice, soft in his ear, startled Michael out of his thoughts. Sam slid up to the bar, but didn't sit.

There was that nervous energy again. "Don't you have lunch with Dr. Malik and William?" He'd seen the latter in the lobby, looking smug. William had stared while Michael had crossed to the bar. William was also a large part of the reason Michael sat with his back to that area.

"Malik told me to spend my time with you."

What? Michael swiveled in his seat to get a better look at Sam. "Are you serious?" Dr. Malik had seemed unaffected by the news of their relationship, but it was quite a different thing to actively support it.

"He didn't use those words, but the meaning was clear." Sam's leg seemed to vibrate. "And there's something I've been meaning to tell you." A flush crept up Sam's neck and his Adam's apple bobbed as he swallowed.

Sparks traced through Michael's limbs at the sight of Sam's anxiety. He couldn't tell if this was good news or bad news. "Shall we go grab something to eat? Or find somewhere private... ?"

"Both. But privacy first." A faint smile touched Sam's face.

Not bad news, judging by that expression. The tingling surged down into Michael's balls and his cock shifted. He stood, so close that he towered over Sam. "My room, then?"

Sam tilted his head back to meet Michael's gaze. "Yes." His response was breathy. Then he grinned.

Maybe they could skip lunch. There wasn't a presentation Michael wanted to see until two. He gave Sam a nudge with his shoulder. "Elevator."

Sadly, they shared most of the ride up with an older couple obviously in New Orleans for sightseeing or Michael would have done far more than stick his hands in Sam's pockets and watch the flush on his neck grow. That changed, the instant the door to Michael's room clicked shut behind him. He caught Sam and pulled him backward, pushing his erection into Sam's crack. "What was it that you wanted to tell me?"

Sam groaned and pressed against Michael. His words came out as a gasp. "I'm in love with you."

Those words set every inch of Michael's skin aflame. He kissed the back of Sam's neck and rocked his cock against Sam's ass. "Say that again." He needed to hear it once more, just to be sure.

"Oh fuck." Sam twisted in Michael's arms, increasing the friction between them. "I'm in love with you, Michael."

He loosened his hold on Sam and turned him around.

Sam shook with need, the flush now coloring his cheeks. His lips were parted. "I love you." There was no hesitation in his expression, only open honesty.

Michael brushed his thumb against Sam's lips, his fingers trembling. "I love you, too."

"Do you?" Sam's smile was dazzling. "Well, good."

"Why the hell do you think I want to be with you? See if we can make this work?" Michael tugged at the knot of

Sam's tie, loosening it. He kissed Sam's neck. "It's not just your sense of style, you know."

Sam's voice was deep and full of gravel. "Well, thank goodness for that." Sam cupped the front of Michael's pants, and massaged the length he found there. "I wouldn't want to think you love me just for my taste in suits."

It was Michael's turn to moan. "If you keep that up, lunch won't happen." Nor much in the afternoon, either.

Sam opened a little space between them. "You're right. And lunch would be normal. A date, even."

Even though Michael's dick ached, he nodded. Very normal. Something a couple would do. "I suppose we could turn in early instead." If he had to wait all day for Sam, he was going to spend all night making Sam thrash and moan.

Sam reached up and pulled Michael's head down for a kiss. Not a burning or hard one—a taste of lips and tongue that was too short. "You have more tricks in that bag of yours?"

That didn't help the state of Michael's cock at all. "Just you wait and see." He had more than enough toys to keep Sam just like he enjoyed him—breathless and shaking.

"Promise?"

"Yes." For as long as Sam wanted and needed. "You sure about lunch?"

It was Sam's stomach that responded, growling loudly. "Sorry," Sam said. "I guess crises make me hungry."

"I meant going out with me. In public. Together."

Sam hesitated, but his smile didn't falter—just softened. As did his voice. "I've wanted to be *me* for so long. I should have told my colleagues to go fuck themselves years ago. Yes, I'm sure."

Michael took Sam's hand and pulled him toward the door. "Then let's go."

"I bet the concierge can recommend a place with authentic Cajun cuisine," Sam said. "And maybe something French for dinner."

He'd like that, except there were other considerations. "I'm still here to work, Sam. I should probably network. Go to dinner with Sundra folks." They headed back toward the elevator.

Sam shrugged. "Invite them. Greta, too. I'd rather that than some lame strip joint." He paused. "But lunch is for us." He pressed the down button.

After dinner? That would be for them, as well.

The elevator doors opened, and Michael followed Sam. Career, promotion, and Sam. He had it all, but the most important was Sam. "I'm glad you said yes."

Sam furrowed his brows for a moment. "To the brandy in Curaçao?"

Michael nodded.

"Best decision I ever made in my life."

Michael fiddled with the solitary cuff link at his wrist. "Should I give this back to you? I don't need a remembrance when I have the real thing."

"No. It's yours." Sam paused. "Just like me."

Sam was his. A lover. A boyfriend. Perhaps more in the future. Only time would tell.

The doors opened, and the hotel lobby lay before them. They stepped out of the elevator together.

THANKS FOR READING!

Dear Reader,

Thank you for reading *Takeover*! I hope you enjoyed Michael and Sam's story.

If you read on after the acknowledgments, you'll find *A Private Merger*, a bonus short story I wrote to bridge the gap between *Takeover* and the next book in the series, *Just Business*. The events take place directly after *Takeover*.

You'll see Michael and Sam again in *Just Business*, the story of Justin White, a barista and MBA student with aspirations of becoming Sam's assistant at Sam's consulting firm, and Eli Ovadia, Sam's CFO, a prickly man with a heartbreaking past.

I wrote *Takeover* in 2013, and it was my first contemporary romance. At the time, there was no marriage equality, and it was rare for CEOs to be out as gay in the business world unless they were highly acclaimed.

The world has change a lot since then. I hope we can change it even more for the better in the future.

To find out more about my books and new releases, you

can follow me on BookBub, join my facebook group or sign up for my newsletter.

Thank you so much!
    -Anna

ACKNOWLEDGMENTS

While writing is, generally, a solitary pursuit, it's not a lonely one. I've been very lucky to be surrounded by friends, family, coworkers, and fellow writers who encourage and uplift me.

First, many thanks Jennifer Udden for realizing this story's full potential and prodding me to push past the limitations I'd set for myself. Many thanks also to Cindy and Kristine for their enthusiasm, as well as the edits that made this story shine.

L.A. Witt deserves a tiara for friendship above and beyond the call of duty. Many thanks also to the AbsoluteWrite and the Seton Hill Writing Popular Fiction communities for their unending support.

And to my parents and my brother for their love and understanding. Yup, writing really is a job. It also happens to be the best job in the world.

A PRIVATE MERGER

A TAKEOVER SHORT STORY

Sam couldn't eat another bite of flourless chocolate cake. Thankfully, he and Michael had opted to share, so there wasn't much left. They sat too damn close together in the cafe, touching, holding hands, laughing, and smiling.

It was bliss. Pure heaven. He'd stepped out of the closet and into Michael's arms, damn all the trouble that would cause. He'd deal with that later. "I wish I'd met you years ago."

Michael squeezed his hand. "I was messed up in the head back then. We wouldn't have done well."

From the little he knew of Michael's past with Four Rivers and his ex Rasheed, if he'd met Michael before now, he'd have been stepping into a minefield of broken hearts and promises. Exactly the worst time to meet. "I suppose I regret living like I've been." Running from company to company. Hiding. Always hiding his sexuality to keep his business contacts intact, even as the world changed around him. The higher you got in business, the more conservative the values.

Michael nodded. "I understand."

They were interrupted by the waiter bringing the check. Sam snatched the billfold before Michael could, dropped his credit card inside, and handed it back to the waiter. "My treat."

"I could've expensed it."

A trace of cold ran down Sam's spine. "No. Not this dinner." Not a date between them. They were nominally boss and employee, though that would change very soon.

Michael colored and nodded. He must have realized that paying on the company dime wasn't the best idea. "What will happen when we get back to Pittsburgh?"

Thank goodness the waiter brought back the receipt. Tipping and signing gave Sam enough time to think of an answer to *that* question. "Well, I'll pack my office and what little I have in the apartment, since that vanishes with the job. I'll find another place to live... then I guess we'll figure out the rest."

Those dark eyes studied him. "If you're not averse to the idea, you could—" The ringing of Michael's phone cut him off. He snatched it up.

Just as well, since the thought of living with Michael stole all of Sam's breath. He wanted that. Feared it, too. He hadn't lived with anyone—well ever. Not since his freshman year of college in Boston.

"Hello?" Michael spoke into the phone. "Gretchen?" He glanced at Sam. "Drinks? When?" Conflict played across his features.

Sam relaxed. Good. Sundra was pulling Michael into the team. He laid his hand on Michael's wrist and spoke low. "Say yes."

Michael furrowed his brow, but nodded. "Yes, I'll be there. Thanks." He finished and set the phone down. "The top management is having drinks at a bar a couple blocks from the hotel. They've invited me to join them."

"Thought it was something like that, which is exactly why you should go."

There was hesitation and wonder in Michael. "They're really courting me to stay on, aren't they?"

Sam snorted. "Michael, you built Four Rivers and kept it together for years, at a cost to yourself. You're a tremendous engineer and a valuable asset. They'd be fools not to keep you." Made absolute business sense. Sam nodded toward the door. "Shall we?"

They rose and headed out into the muggy, packed streets of New Orleans.

"I was hoping to have a nice long night with you." Michael pressed a hand to the small of Sam's back and lightning shot through every vein. He'd left his suit jacket back at the hotel and Michael's touch burned through his dress shirt. It was a wonder he didn't catch into flames.

"We'll have time later," Sam replied. Hours and days and weeks. Perhaps a lifetime, if all went well. "I'm not leaving." Not anymore.

Michael stroked his thumb against Sam's back and his smile said *everything*.

Oh yes, he wanted to spend the evening with Michael. Naked and screaming. Or crying. Whichever Michael preferred. But they both couldn't drop their careers just because they'd fallen in love. His was in shambles. Out of a job, out of the closet, but hardly out of choices.

Sometimes you needed to change the game to play it.

"You're thinking again," Michael murmured.

"Always." Except when Michael made him soar, made him forget the world in a haze of pleasure and pain. "I have so much work to do if I'm going to start a consulting firm.

Find the right people to work with. And then there's the situation with William." Sam had no doubt William would make it known that Sam was gay *and* had been fucking an employee, especially once William figured out who dropped the financial information into Sundra's lap.

"William's done." Michael waved a hand. "He can't touch you."

"I wish that were true." They stopped at a curb to wait for the light. The hotel loomed nearby, as did Michael's drink date. "He and I know many of the same people. Run in the same circles." In fact, there was one phone call he needed to make soon, before William did.

"He's going to get nailed for the financial shenanigans." There was hesitation in Michael's voice. "Isn't he?"

"Depends on how much they have and what it means." So hard to catch people like William. Might not be worth it for Sundra to delve into. God, he hoped he'd given them enough.

The flick of Michael's thumb on his back was both calming and exhilarating. Sam could barely walk straight when the light turned green. "You'll come out on top, I'm sure." Michael's tone changed to one of finality. "People know you. Doesn't matter who you're sleeping with."

Another thing Sam wished were true, but the world had changed. Maybe Michael *was* right.

When they reached the hotel, Sam faced Michael and looked up into those brown eyes. "While you're off getting to know your new team, I'll let my colleague in Boston know I'm turning down his offer."

Michael reached out and straightened Sam's tie. The tugging, pulling and tightness around Sam's neck sent a sharp bolt of lust straight to his balls. "I'll text you before I return." Michael spoke softly. "When I get back, I want you kneeling on the floor of my room, wearing only this." He gave the tie a subtle pull, then stepped back. "See you in a couple of hours."

No kiss, but that was fine, since Michael's touch and his words set every part of Sam alight. So much so that he wanted to run up to Michael's room, strip and kneel right then. "I—yes." He was so fucking hard.

Michael's smile was wicked, he winked and headed off down the street.

God, that man. It was a very *very* good thing they wouldn't be working together much longer. He liked being under Michael a hell of a lot more than being above him.

When Sam could breathe again, he entered the hotel and headed up to his room. He keyed himself in and tossed the card on the bed. Jacking himself off was tempting, but Michael liked him on edge, and to be honest he loved that too. He did loosen his tie. If he were going to call Fabian he needed breathing room.

He stared at Fabian's contact information on his phone, then tapped connect. Three rings and there was Fabian's gritty voice saying his name.

"Fabian, it's—Randell." He *almost* said Sam. Another thing he'd change going forward. *Sam* fit him. Sam *was* him. "I know it's outside business hours..."

"Never a problem with you, Randy, you know that."

Such friendliness in his voice. Sam sat on the bed, heart in his throat.

Fabian continued. "Calling to tell me you're signing that contract?"

"I—No. I'm sorry, I'm not." Despite everything, he felt sadness there. It would've been an exciting job. A good fit, had he wanted to continue running.

"Ah, damn. Got a better offer from someone? We can renegotiate..." There was Fabian, the business man.

"No," Sam spoke with care. "I'm changing directions. Staying in Pittsburgh and starting my own consulting firm."

A creak from the other end. Maybe a chair? Hard to tell. "In Pittsburgh?" A cough. "I understand wanting to settle down, but why there?"

"Life got complicated." Sam's chuckle was bitter. "Then William tried to blackmail me."

The silence stretched and Sam shifted. After that line, a whole host of questions could pour from Fabian. Finally the other man spoke. "Does he have something on you?"

The truth stung. "Yeah, he does. I fell into a relationship with one of the Four River's employees. We kept it quiet, but..."

"Not quiet enough, eh?" Sympathy there. "You aren't the first, Randy."

"Oh, I know." Several others in their circle had wound up in compromising situations. At least Sam was single.

A grunt. "So you're staying in Pittsburgh for her? Hope she's worth it."

Sam tensed and this time, he was the one lengthening the silence. Finally, he croaked out a single word. "He."

An intake of breath on the other end, but nothing more.

God, his throat was dry. He spoke anyway, each word rough and jagged. "He. And yes, he is. Enough to stop running from job to job. Enough to stop hiding." He swallowed, trying to find some moisture to wet his throat. "I know you're not particularly fond of... gay... queer... people, but you've been kind to me. I wanted you to hear this from me, not William."

"Randy—"

Sam kept going because his heart wouldn't stop

slamming against his chest. "I gave Sundra all I had on William. The financial irregularities. Everything. Once William figures that out..." Sam spit out a harsh laugh. "We'll see how many contacts I have left to start a business."

"Randy—"

"I know this isn't what you wanted to hear."

A long pause from the other end, then quiet words. "Are you going to let me talk this time?"

"I—sorry. Yes." God, this was *hard*. Waiting. Listening for inevitable rejection. Or the condescension.

"You're telling me that what William has on you is that you're gay and you slept with an employee?"

"Yeah. He wanted me to sing his praises to Sundra or he'd tell all to everyone." Would still tell, regardless. Sam was sure of *that*.

A laugh. "So, you didn't play his game? You gave Sundra the dirt you had on him, and came clean?"

His skin itched. "Yeah. I can't see all of what William did, but it looks like a Ponzi type thing." He paused. "And yes, I told Sundra why William was blackmailing me."

"Good thinking."

Sam didn't know what was going through Fabian's head, but damn he was going to need a drink after this call.

"The man you're with, what's his role at Four Rivers?" Curiosity there.

"He's the head of their QA department, and was instrumental in founding the company."

"So, a direct report to you."

"We met in Curaçao. Neither of us knew where the other worked until I walked into the all-hands when I arrived in Pittsburgh."

Fabian coughed. "That must have been a shock."

"You have *no* idea." Sam rolled his shoulders as tension

leaked away. Fabian hadn't hung up in disgust and the conversation was remarkably... *friendly*.

"What does Sundra think of him?"

"They're grooming him to lead the office there—since he's more or less been doing that for years."

"No repercussions, then?"

"Other than outing myself, no." It was damn lucky for both him and Michael. "To be honest, it's a relief not to be living a lie, even if I do stand to lose a host of friends and contacts."

When Fabian spoke again, his voice was unusually soft. "My nephew Derrick graduated from high school last year. Got into MIT, but even with scholarships and financial aid, he wasn't going to be able to afford it. My sister and brother-in-law do fine, but college is so expensive now."

The itching under his skin grew. He didn't know where Fabian was going with this story, but Fabian never spoke without a reason. "It is, yes."

"I offered to pay some of it. Keep the kid out of debt, you know? Those loans are poison." He paused. "Gave him a big check at his graduation party and everything. Not for the whole amount, of course, but enough to start."

"That's really kind of you."

"He's a great kid. Smart. Well-behaved. Gets good grades." Fabian sighed. "The day after, Derrick stopped by my place and gave me the check back."

Oh. *Oh.* Tightness in his chest.

"You were right, Randy. I didn't care for gay people. Said hurtful things." Sadness in Fabian's voice. "Derrick... my nephew... a kid I love like my own kids... he stood in my entryway, shaking like a leaf and told me he was gay. Said he couldn't accept my check, since he was one of 'those people' I always went on about and couldn't live that lie, not even to go to MIT."

So many emotions. Pride. Anger. Relief. "It's different when it's someone you love, isn't it?" Sam said. Sharp words, but maybe Fabian needed to hear them.

"It is. And it made me face things about myself. Reflect on who I *really* was. How much hate was in me. I didn't like what I saw." Another squeak over the line—definitely a chair. "I apologize for the things I said, Randy. They were unconscionable. I know that now. When you get your firm set up, contact me. You're one of the best. I'll do what I can to scare up business for you."

Not at all how he expected this phone call to go. "Thank you for telling me that, Fabian."

"It's truly the least I can do."

His turn to probe. "What happened with your nephew?"

Fabian took a deep breath. "We talked for a very long time, and in the end I apologized for hurting him so deeply and I promised to do better. He's a sophomore at MIT and doing great."

Fabian was putting his apology to work. That was a start, just like his offer for contacts.

"I think you'll find you have many more allies than William," Fabian said. "You're right that some of the circle will drop you, but let me ask you this, Randy. Would you want to work with those fools?"

That was a formidable point. "No." He had options. Could pick and choose clients. Sam ran a hand through his hair. "I wouldn't want to work with *anyone* unwilling to work with me."

A chuckle. "There will be plenty of people willing to

work with you. Build a stunning team and the contracts will come. I'd lay money on it."

Normally, he'd take that bet, but not when he was sitting on top of improper financial dealings, even if they were Williams. "Well, you've set my mind at ease."

"Good."

They finished the conversation and Sam stared at his phone, a giddy stream of euphoria racing through him. Of all the people. If *Fabian* remained a contact, then this ridiculous consulting idea might work.

He needed that drink, though. A quick check of the time told him he could grab something from the hotel bar before Michael called.

He needed Michael more than anything else. His touch, his orders, his passion and love.

This is real. This is happening.

He was changing his life.

The bar wasn't crowded—probably due to the proximity of the French Quarter outside its doors. Still, it housed a few convention-goers not willing to brave the streets. Sam ordered a gin and tonic. There'd be enough alcohol to calm his nerves, but not enough to go to his head even if the bar poured heavy.

When the drink appeared, he took a careful sip—heavy it was—but with a generous helping of ice. If he nursed the drink, he'd be fine.

"Randy." Anger, deep anger, wrapped the enunciation of the name Sam wanted to shed.

The voice and the hatred belonged to William. Sam's

breath caught and he rotated to find William seething behind him.

"Where's your fuck buddy, Mike?" William's voice was loud enough to turn heads.

For the first time since college, Sam didn't care that he was being outed. He picked up his drink and stared at William. "He's off having cocktails with the executive staff of Sundra Networks."

That wasn't the answer William had been expecting. He started and fear twisted his features. "But I— What did you do? What did you tell them?"

Sam sipped his drink and was glad for the gin. "I told them the truth, William. All of it."

Such an angry, ruddy face. "So they approve of you fucking an employee?"

"Of course they don't, and I don't blame them." Sam shrugged. "But we didn't break any actual policies and he's not my employee anymore." He swallowed another mouthful of gin and tonic. "And I'm the one being fucked, if you *must* know the details."

William gaped like a fish.

Sam gave another shrug. "I don't like being blackmailed, William. If it means the world finally learning I'm gay and I like taking it in the ass, well—you're welcome to shout it from the rooftops." Yeah, *definitely* the gin talking.

An edge of fear crept into William's expression. "You *know* something."

"I know many things, Billy," Sam said. "I've been in this game as long as you have." He drank the rest of his gin and tonic and set the glass down. "But as long as you've been on the up and up with your business dealings, I couldn't possibly have anything on you, right?"

One horrifying moment later, William was in his face,

hands grabbing at the fabric of Sam's shirt. "You fucking *fag!*"

Sam fell back and struck the bar edge, lancing pain up his back—both from the impact and from the bruises still left from Michael's flogging. His curse was loud, but was drowned out by the bartender. "Hey! Get that guy off him!"

Someone steadied Sam and someone else—security—grabbed William. But only for a moment. A twist and a shove and William was heading for him again.

Fucking asshole didn't know when to stop.

All the rage and anger and too many years of pandering to people like William rushed into Sam and his fist connected with William's face. Fire flared against Sam's knuckles, but the crunch that sent William staggering back into the security guard's arm's felt *glorious.*

God, that was wonderful. Except for the throbbing in his fingers, Sam felt alive and light. He shook out his hand and opened and closed his fist. Nothing broken.

More security arrived, but William stood in the grip of the first guard, looking down at the rug like he didn't quite know what had hit him. There was blood on his lip.

He'd done that. Hit William. No blood on the back of his hand, but he'd be bruised there. Already, his knuckles were red. No way to hide that from Michael.

"Are you all right, sir?" That from one of the guards.

"Yes." He took a breath and met William's gaze. "No harm done."

For his part, William was pale and shaking. "I don't suppose there's a way we can settle this without paperwork?"

One of the guards rolled his eyes—but also looked like he wasn't about to enjoy the incident report or the potential for calling the police. "Sir?"

Sam was tempted to say no, dial 911, sit in some office somewhere, and detail every last second of that exchange, but he'd gotten what he'd wanted. More than that. "If he gets out of my face and *stays* out of my face—I'm satisfied."

"Want to get back to your boyfriend?" Venom in William's voice.

"God, will you give it a *rest*?" The words poured out of Sam. "Jesus, if you weren't such a pig with women, I'd think you were jealous."

William didn't say a damn thing. The guard who'd spoken raised an eyebrow.

Sam waved the look away. Maybe William *was* jealous, who knew? Sam didn't care. "You know, Michael's twice the businessman you are, William." He turned back to the bar and nodded at the bartender. "I'd like to settle up."

"On the house," the woman said. "He's been trouble all weekend."

When he turned around, William was still there. So were the guards. "Do you need me for anything?" he asked the guard who'd spoken earlier.

"If you're fine, sir—"

"I am."

The guard pulled William away from the bar. "You should head back to your room."

William let himself be led away, but not before he threw more words at Sam. "If Mike really was twice the man as me, he wouldn't be where he is now."

"You mean out having drinks with the top executives at Sundra while you pick a bar fight?"

William glowered, but the guard pulled him away.

Once out of sight, Sam sank down onto the bar stool. He doubted that would be the end—this little incident would only encourage William. "Fuck." There'd be months and months more of this before William—and his shady dealings—were behind him.

"Excuse me." A woman's voice shook Sam from his fugue.

He took her in—short red hair and multiple ear piercings. Surprisingly, they worked well with her stunning blue suit. He'd never seen her before and if she had a conference badge, she wasn't wearing it now. "Yes?"

"Are you S. Randell Anderson?"

He let out a huff of a laugh. "I am. Please call me Sam." It was a start. One person at a time.

She held out her hand. "Alexa Brown. I'm with TelCom Today."

Oh *hell*. A journalist. He shook hands with her anyway. "I suppose I gave you a huge amount of fodder."

She snorted. "We're not a rag sheet, so no, you didn't. I'm working on an article about women and other minorities in the industry."

Sam was glad to be sitting, because the realization hit him hard. Gay. Minority. He let out a breath. Things *would* change and not everyone would be like Fabian. "I—I don't—"

She perched on the bar stool next to him and her voice was gentle. "Sounds like you came out recently."

That was pretty much the heart of it. He scratched the back of his head. "I did, yes." Today. *Jesus.* Michael needed to call soon, because Sam was slipping and twisting and falling into panic again.

Whether Ms. Brown noticed, Sam didn't know. But her smile was kind. "I'd love to hear your thoughts about that, when you're ready." She pulled a business card out of her blazer pocket.

Sam took it, studied it, and flipped it over in his hand.

"I'm not ready yet." Everything was raw and new and ached. He'd done this before—been out—but the Sam of his high school and early college years was gone, replaced by someone with far more to lose. Far more to gain, too.

Her nod was solemn.

He tucked the card into his pocket. "When I am, I'll contact you." He stuck out his hand. "Very nice to meet you."

She took it, and her grip was strong and warm. "Good luck, Sam."

He rose and took his leave. Time to retreat to Michael's —their—room and strip off everything from his old life. He wanted nothing more than to start anew.

Drinks with Sundra had gone remarkably well. Sam had been right—Michael had needed to rub elbows with his soon-to-be colleagues. He nursed a dark beer the entire time, both to show restraint to the people who would decide the fate of his—and all of the employees at Four Rivers— career and also to stay sharp for what he had planned to do to Sam the moment they were alone.

Which would be very soon, now that they'd all retired from the bar. On their walk back to the convention hotel, Michael texted Sam two words:

Knees. Now.

The power, the shiver, and the desire flooded through him. He tucked away his phone, and fell into step next to Gretchen.

She gave him a quick glance. "How do you think the people in Pittsburgh will react to the buy-out?"

A good question. "Some will fear it at first, and we'll lose a few since Sundra is so big, but after a week or so, I think most people will be glad for it. It's been a rocky year."

"And how will they react to you and Randy?"

"Sam." It came out automatically. Sam was... Sam. At Four Rivers, in Pittsburgh, and on his knees in front of Michael.

The rhythm of Gretchen's steps faltered. "Sam, then. That's going to take me a while to get used to. He was Randy for so long." He picked up her stride again. "I'm guessing no one at Four Rivers knows about you and him?"

"Not that I know of," Michael said. Wouldn't take too long for folks to put it all together and figure out Michael had been fucking the boss. "Honestly, I think most won't care, not when they see the offer Sundra is making. Sam did exactly what he came to Pittsburgh to do."

A nod. "We'll watch the situation, then."

They'd have to.

The air conditioning in the hotel was a welcome treat from the humid hot air of the New Orleans night. Michael said good night to the Sundra executives and headed up to his room, his heart and mind full of Sam.

His Sam, the one none of the others saw, the Sam he'd have when they returned to Pittsburgh. With a quick slide of the keycard, he unlocked the door and opened it. There was the sight he'd been waiting for all evening: Sam on his knees. Naked and hard, wearing only his tie, tight like a collar around his neck.

He'd even clasped his hands behind his back, though he didn't drop his gaze. Bright blue eyes held Michael's attention. Still proud, even in the guise of submission.

Michael stopped and admired the view. Damp hair meant Sam had showered. Excellent.

Pity they weren't back in Pittsburgh. He had only a handful of toys here and nowhere near enough rope. He wanted all of Sam. Every last ounce of his will and determination. Wanted to give Sam the high and freedom he craved. Michael stepped forward and tilted Sam's chin up. "You were right about the drinks."

"I know this business." His reply was breathy.

"So you do." He ran his thumb over Sam's jaw. "Pity I can't flog you again tonight."

Sam's breath hitched, but any words were lost when Michael slipped his thumb between Sam's lips. What came out was a low moan that curled the desire in Michael's core. Such a perfect sound. Sam sucked and licked as if Michael had given Sam his cock to swallow.

The welts and bruises across Sam's back were stunning. Had it been earlier in his life, back when he'd been in practice with BDSM, maybe he could have added to them. But too many years had passed since he'd been at his peak as a Dom, and Sam was too new to this. More would only risk injuring Sam.

Luckily, there were other ways to torment a man. He pulled his thumb free of Sam's delightful mouth and stepped back. "I want you kneeling on the bed, as you are now." He turned to his tote bag of toys, not bothering to see if Sam would obey.

Sam would. Simple as that. He could order Sam to lick his dress shoes and Sam wouldn't hesitate if it got him what he wanted. Following orders was its own type of control— one of willpower and desire—and Sam delighted in control.

So, how to break that? Pain managed it, certainly. The sting of hand or crop of flogger eventually broke past that wall. Even then, Sam seemed to be able to hold himself still when given a choice. There was freedom in being able to obey or not.

So, take that away, as he did that first night when he looped a belt around Sam's wrists.

Michael took out a pair of leather wrist cuffs, lined so they wouldn't leave marks. They did, however, clip together easily and were extremely hard to wiggle out of. Yes, they would do. He turned back to Sam.

He'd obeyed perfectly, not resting on his heals, but balancing on the bed, his back to Michael. Once more, Sam's hands were clasped at the small of his back, but this time, his gaze was down, exposing the long line of his neck, broken only by the bright red and blue striped tie. Somehow, the dim light of the room seemed to highlight where Michael had bruised and beaten Sam the day before. Eying the matching bruises and lines tightened Michael's balls. His marks on the man he wanted to share the rest of his life with. He'd forgotten this part of himself, the feel of the flogger, the pride in bringing his lover to new heights of pain and pleasure and the joy of seeing the aftermath.

It'd been so long.

"Very nice," he said. "You like this, don't you?"

"I love this," Sam whispered. "I love you."

More fire in his blood, but this ignited bone and marrow and his soul. He stepped close and wrapped his hand around Sam's throat and pulled backward until Sam lost his balance and the only thing keeping him from tumbling was his head against Michael's chest. A small sound—the edge of fear—slipped from Sam's throat and he looked up, eyes wide, his pulse thrumming under Michael's fingers.

"I adore you." Michael ached for Sam, had since he sent the text. Having Sam under his hand, that flicker of both fear and trust in his face was *intense*—he wanted to come right then. Could with just a stroke or two. "I love every moment with you."

"I have a long way to go before I deserve the man you are."

Michael tightened his grip. "Don't you think I should be the judge of that?"

Sam's pulse quickened and his throat worked beneath Michael's hand. "I—yes?" Sam's dick jutted up, hard and tempting, pre-come glittering on the crown.

"Good answer," Michael whispered. He released Sam's neck and tipped him forward. "Shoulders on the bed, Sam."

Sam prostrated himself as ordered and displayed his lovely whipped and bruised ass perfectly. A nice sight, but that's not what caught Michael's attention. He took hold of Sam's right wrist and lifted it gently. The knuckles were purple-red and swollen. "What happened to your hand?"

A muffled grunt. "William's face."

Twin emotions of anger and pride erupted in Michael. "You *punched* William?"

Sam seemed to sink into the mattress. He rolled his head to one side, to speak without mumbling into the bedspread. "Yeah. He came after me. The first time, security pulled him off. The second time—well—I didn't let him get close enough to do anything." He filled Michael in on the rest of the story.

Seemed that William had realized things weren't going his way, the little fucker. Michael was utterly proud of Sam, though. However, the knuckles put a damper on the evening.

"You should ice it." He let go of Sam's wrist.

"And you should fuck me." There was annoyance in Sam's voice.

Well, if Sam wanted to play it that way, he obviously wasn't damaged that much. Michael swatted each of Sam's ass cheeks—hard. Sam's pained yelp sent lust straight to Michael's cock. "Maybe. If you behave."

A hiss and a moan. "I did ice it. Before you arrived."

"Good." Despite the pain in Sam's voice—or rather *because* of it—Michael spanked him again, just as hard.

This time, Sam cursed and groaned. "I'm sorry," he panted out.

Michael ghosted his fingers across the raised welts from yesterday—now even more red. "For what?"

A shudder ran through Sam's beautiful prone body. "For asking you to fuck me."

Dark desire spread warmth down Michael and he swatted Sam's ass again, eliciting a pain-filled moan. "You didn't ask at all."

Sam's breath was ragged. "I'm sorry for demanding you fuck me."

Not yet, he wasn't. "Better." Sam's flesh beneath Michael's fingers radiated heat. "When your ass is in the air for me is probably the *worst* time to demand anything."

He squirmed, then whispered the truth. "I don't want William to ruin this."

"He won't." Michael took Sam's wrist again. "Wiggle your fingers for me."

He did, and with ease. "It's not broken, just sore." He gave a hiccup of a laugh. "My ass hurts more."

Oh, how he wished he wasn't so out of practice with a flogger or that Sam's back and ass weren't already beaten. He didn't know Sam's limits—and he didn't know his own any more. There'd be a few calls he'd have make when they got back to Pittsburgh. A rusty Dom could be dangerous and Sam deserved better than that. Hopefully, all the old connections were still there.

Of course, that also meant calling Eli. Which meant explaining to Sam who Eli was. *Before Rasheed, there was Eli.* After Rasheed—well, he'd fucked up his friendship with E pretty damn well *during* Rasheed. But Eli remained a phone call away. One Michael very rarely made.

Eli never called him at all.

God, he'd let Rasheed take so much from him, then let so much go himself. He certainly wouldn't let William take this night from Sam.

Leather on those wrists then. Strip everything from Sam. Michael slipped on one cuff and buckled it tight and then the other. Sam's breathing shifted, became tighter and faster. Michael clipped the cuffs together and let go. "There."

A little moan from Sam, but no words. Michael stepped back.

Sam's ass was ruddy from being spanked. God he loved doing that, his hand against Sam's tender flesh. They could start there—it would be easy enough not to go too far.

Michael cocked his head. There was also the long lengths of Sam's trembling thighs. Bare and untouched. Flogging there *hurt* and Sam *had* been obstinate and needed a little disciplining. Delight rose in Michael and he adjusted himself in his pants.

"I'm not pleased with your mouth, Sam." He stroked a welt on Sam's ass. "I think you need a reminder of whose in charge when we're together like this."

Sam shifted, but kept his lips together. Smart man.

Michael stepped away, took off his watch and cufflinks and stripped off his shirt before returning to his bag of toys. He could use the crop again, but there was another option.

He pulled out a small cane—simple acrylic and eighteen inches long. Perfect for travel. Also stung like hell, especially against trembling thighs.

He took a deep breath to keep from moaning. This would be *fun*, at least for him, though Sam might think otherwise.

Sam was a picture of humility, forehead pressed into the bed spread, ass up, and hands firmly cuffed in leather. Not the most comfortable position, judging by Sam's breathing. "I know you like control. Crave it." He brushed the side of the cane against Sam's left thigh and Sam gasped. "I also know you want that taken from you." He stroked the other side. "And when we're here, where you want to be, you damn well will relinquish every bit of power to me." He cracked the cane quickly against Sam's thighs, first the right and the left.

Sam jerked his head up, his inhale sharp. "Oh fuck!" Pain deepened his voice.

Michael's balls ached and a dark fire bit into his blood. He placed a hand against Sam's back. "Head down."

Sam's breathing was ragged and harsh, but he bent.

"Three more, each side."

A moan from Sam. "Please."

"Please *what?*"

A cough of a laugh. "I guess I shouldn't ask you to be gentle."

He caressed Sam's ass, then kissed it. "That *was* gentle." He waited until he felt Sam tremble, then laid two more blows to each thigh a little harder this time. Sam's cry was guttural and part moan. Faint red lines rose where he'd struck.

"You going to give me lip again?"

Sam croaked a laugh. "Probably."

At least he was truthful. The last two strokes were hard, not anywhere near what Michael could throw, but had enough force to raise a line across each thigh and bring Sam close to tears, judging from his shattered breathing. But his body was relaxed. Pliant. All Michael's.

He drew a finger over one of the welts. "I'll have to remember that you like the cane."

"I don't," Sam said, a slur in his voice. "I really *really* don't like that thing."

"Mmmhmm." Michael pressed his lips to Sam's ass, and wrapped a hand around Sam's hard cock. "Like, loathe. Same thing for you."

A whimper.

"True?" Michael whispered against Sam's skin.

"True." A ghost of a word.

He let go of Sam's dick and slid both palms over Sam's ass. "Never get tired of this." Another kiss, then another. A nip, a lick. Over bruises and welts. He spread Sam's cheeks apart and worked his way inward.

Sam twisted beneath him, shuddering and gasping. "Michael? Michael!" Panic there.

He backed off. Wasn't a safeword, but something wasn't right. "Yeah?"

"Please, I..." Embarrassment colored his voice. "You're not going to..." Sam trailed off.

Now *that* was interesting! "Never had your ass eaten?"

Oh, the squirm and the whisper. "No." His whole body was red, and not from the beating.

He kissed close to Sam's hole and delighted in the gasp and the wiggle. "You know how to make me stop."

"You're a fucking..."

Michael tongued Sam's hole and the next word was lost in an intelligible cry that ended in a moan so heavenly,

Michael couldn't help palm his own straining cock, still covered in his dress slacks.

Sam's breathing turned into a litany of groans and whimpers and curses. He loved that sound—Sam being turned inside out.

He didn't let up licking and sucking Sam's hole until the timber of his moans changed. "God." Sam's words were mostly air. "I wanna come so bad."

Good thing Sam's hands were nice and restrained. Even as he twisted in the leather, they held fast. Michael couldn't wait to see him hung up on a rack or draped over a horse.

"You like that?" He didn't give Sam time to answer before he tongued his hole and pushed inside.

Sam's answer were the words *Oh*, *Fuck*, and *God*, repeated over and over, like beads on a string. So very nice. Such a simple, pleasurable way to take every bit of Sam's self-control away.

"I want to hear you beg, Sam."

A choked sob. "Please."

"That's not even close to begging."

"Fuck, Michael, I can't!" Tears drenched Sam's voice. No doubt if Michael looked, he'd see mortification on a wet face.

So, rimming both turned Sam on and utterly shamed him. Things like that were gold. Only one thing to do, really...

"Sam." Just his name, but laced with every ounce of disappointment Michael could muster.

That had almost the same effect as the cane. A deep inhale, then a moan. "I—Michael—Please."

"I'm waiting."

Sam pressed his head into the mattress and shook. "Fine." Pain and tears there. "I want you to eat my ass." It was a whisper, but his voice grew bolder. "I want you to lick my hole. Fuck me with your tongue until I can't see straight. Please—" Desperation in Sam's voice. "God, I fucking love it." The next sound was a sob. "Please, Michael."

Poor Sam. He was going to get everything he'd begged for. Michael redoubled his efforts until Sam was a shaking moaning mess on the bed. Michael almost expected Sam to come from the rimjob, but he didn't.

Micheal nearly did though, from the timber of Sam's cries. Finally, the need to be buried deep inside Sam overrode the desire to turn him inside out solely with his mouth. He stumbled back from the bed and shed the rest of his clothes. Didn't take long to get a condom and lube on. Sam was so pliant, he slid right in, balls deep and they both moaned. God, he needed Sam. Wanted to give him every ounce of pleasure he could. Take away everything then return it, tenfold. Michael pulled back and thrust in again.

No more words. They didn't need them. Sam's cries and hungry moans, the way he met Michael's every stroke, spoke for him. *Take me. Use me. Give me what I want.* So Michael did, fucking him hard and fast, stroking him off until Sam was coming and cursing and yelling Michael's name. His own orgasm, that blinding piece of pain and bliss, stole his breath and his heart, and he thrust into Sam until the world came back into focus.

Collapsing on Sam wasn't an option, but Michael's arms and legs were barely holding him up. He pulled out of Sam, breathless and dizzy and fought against both. Sam had melted against the bed, but in a position that couldn't be comfortable at all. "Let me get the cuffs off."

Sam shook both arms. "Just—free them?" A dusty voice.

What Michael could see of Sam's face was a mess of tears and bliss. He'd done that. Again. Warmth flooded through him, and he unclipped the cuffs from each other, ditched the condom, then sat down next to Sam on the bed.

Sam pulled his arms up and laid his head on his hands. "Like the leather." Sleepy words.

"Looks good on you." Beautiful. He wanted to wrap Sam in leather. Or rope. Not all the time—but when they needed it. When Sam wanted it.

"Have matching ones at home?" Sam lifted his ankles and wiggled his feet.

"I have matching ones in the bag. But no rope or spreader bar."

An inhale. Sam rolled on his side and peered up at Michael. "Spreader bar?" Excitement in his wrung out face and frame.

This man had no limits. Michael stroked Sam's cheeks. "Keeps your legs apart."

"Mmm." Sam pressed into Michael's hand. "I think I have a lot to learn."

They both did. Now they had a chance to do that —together.

"Let's get some sleep. We can talk about it in the morning."

Sam nodded, eyes closed.

Michael stripped the bedspread and gently untied Sam's tie. Both were wet with Sam's semen. He tossed them aside, and helped Sam under the sheets. No way Sam was moving any farther than that. He was practically passed out, even now.

Michael took a quick trip to the bathroom to wash his hands, face, and brush his teeth—then he crawled into bed.

He still couldn't quite believe he had Sam, but there he was, snoring softly on the pillow next to his.

Perfect.

When Sam woke the next morning, every bit of him ached in glorious ways. He hadn't been this well-fucked in... Well, never. Not like this. Some part of him wondered if he should feel remorse for liking the pain, for enjoying and craving being bound and spanked and flogged. He didn't. It seemed as natural as every other part of him—something that *was* him.

It was Michael who had unlocked it, those months ago in Curaçao—Michael who slept next to him now. He rolled onto his side and found Michael wasn't asleep at all. "Been awake long?"

A sleepy, but bright smile. "Not too long. Just laying here thinking I have to be the luckiest man alive."

Warmth flooded through Sam. "Ditto."

"Come here." Michael opened his arms and Sam scooted over into them and pressed his lips against Michael's neck.

The brush of hands against his ass sent a spark of pain and memory racing through Sam. Michael's hand slapping his flesh. Whatever the hell Michael has used on his thighs. The rim job.

God, the *rim job*. He whimpered into Michael's flesh.

A deep chuckle. "Did you enjoy last night?"

"Oh hell, yes." Eyes closed, he breathed in Michael and the vague scent of sex and starch from the hotel sheets.

"Everything?" Amusement in Michael's voice.

He knew what Michael was asking. "Yes." A whisper. That was all he could manage.

Michael stroked his hair. "Tell me."

It was a command, even though it was gently given. Sam gave in to it. "I've never been rimmed before. It's not something that I ever thought I wanted." Now he both desired and feared it—mostly because it cracked his brain open and he lost everything to a different pleasure than pain brought.

"And?"

Sam snorted. Typical Michael. Digging for more. "It's... intimate. I mean, fucking is one thing, but your mouth on my asshole is... really beyond that." He paused. "You trust me. A lot."

"Likewise—since you let me beat you." Michael cupped the back of Sam's neck, his hand warm and firm. "There's quite a bit that could go wrong with that."

"I loved everything last night." He shifted and winced. "Well, except for the part with William." Even in the diffused light peaking in from behind the curtains, his knuckles looked swollen. Could move his fingers, though.

His wrists were still encircled in the leather cuffs Michael had buckled onto him. He'd lost the tie afterward— and probably would have to trash it, as it and the bedspread ended up absorbing all of his load when he'd come.

Michael caught one of the loops on the cuff. "I like seeing these on you."

Desire pooled deep in Sam. "I like them on me." At least here in bed with Michael.

"I'm going to guess a collar is out, though." He let go of the loop.

Sam considered it. "I don't know, to be honest." He didn't mind the tie, but then he wore those all the time. "I don't want to be your sex slave."

Michael laughed and propped himself up on his elbow. "I don't want that either. I meant what I said. I don't want to run your life."

Just make him fly. He'd flown so very high last night, all

of his barriers stripped. Pleasure he hadn't expected. And the pain, the glorious pain. "Good." He paused. "Maybe a collar. We'll see."

Warm fingers stroked his neck. "I love you." Michael's voice was unexpectedly soft. "Whatever you want."

"Oh, *now* it's whatever I want." Sam flopped on his back and regretted it instantly. "Fuck!" Pain lanced up his back and his thighs throbbed. So good. So bad. Sitting on a plane for a couple hours was going to be *hell*.

A snicker from Michael. "Serves you right."

"What the heck did you beat me with, anyway?"

"Want to see?" Michael sat up, then slipped off the bed. The sight of his naked back and ass, the way his muscles moved as he walked and the broadness of his shoulders were a balm of desire against the ache in his back. The two mixed in a way that tightened his balls and hardened his cock. Michael pulled a thin cane with a black handle out of his duffle bag.

"It's purple."

"I *like* purple." Michael returned to the bed and handed the cane to Sam. A tiny plastic thing.

"Of course you do." Sam smacked the rod against his hand. Not hard, but it still had sting to it. With more force behind it, those swings would hurt. *Had* hurt. Holding this did nothing for him. But imagining it in Michael's hand was something else.

"Acrylic," Michael said. "Bit of a beginner's cane, but good for travel."

Sam sat up, wincing as his thighs rubbed against the sheets. "You're hardly a beginner." He handed the cane back.

Michael held the handle in his right hand but kept a grip on the end with his left. "Not a beginner, no. But I *am* out of practice." He shifted. "How much do you want to get into BDSM, Sam?"

Good question. He adored what Michael did to him. Had done to him. He certainly wanted to explore more. "I have no frame of reference to answer that. I don't know what's involved." Other than what he'd seen in porn. And he knew better than to trust that—even the amateur stuff. *Especially* the amateur stuff.

Michael toyed with the cane. "You like pain. Quite a bit of pain."

Sam nodded. "Seems I do."

"I can give you what you want, but..."

"You're out of practice." Sam studied Michael. Unusual to see him so hesitant. "How do you get into shape?" It wasn't like there were courses for whipping people... where there? He pulled his legs up and hissed. "Shit."

Michael gave another one of his deep, appreciative chuckles. "Love seeing that, too."

Sam snorted.

"There are clubs. House parties." Michael shrugged. "Mostly parties in Pittsburgh. I used to go, but when I started dating Rasheed—"

"You stopped." Another thing that asshole took from Michael. If he ever met the man... Probably a good thing he wouldn't.

Michael *thwapped* the sheets with the cane. "Exactly. But I still know people from that time. I can find out about parties. Demonstrations. If you wanted, we could go."

Sam sat still, because his whole body tingled. "I'd be your—what?"

"Partner," Michael said. "Submissive, at least in those spaces."

Submissive? Well, he *did* submit to Michael. "Only you?" Maybe he'd watched a little *too* much of that porn.

"Yes." Fast and firm, that reply. "I'm not good with sharing."

"I'm not good with being shared," Sam said.

Michael let out a breath. "Good."

This was really happening. He was in a relationship with Michael. Planning a life. Dating. Talking about weird sex parties. He laughed, reached over and pulled Michael to him. Sam took Michael's mouth and kissed him like he'd never ever kiss another man again.

When he broke the kiss, Michael took a deep breath. "Not *always* submissive."

"No. Not at all. Don't you forget it."

Deep brown eyes and a smile that lit eternity. "Oh, I won't. Not for an instant."

"Can you live with that?"

Michael cupped his face. "Yes. For as long as you'd like."

He'd no idea what the future held—so much was unplanned and unwritten—but he had Michael. And Michael had him. "This is love, isn't it?" Sure felt like it.

"Yeah." Michael spoke against his lips. "It is."

He certainly could live with *that*.

ALSO BY ANNA ZABO

Close Quarter

Close Quarter

Slow Waltz (a Close Quarter short story)

Takeover

Takeover

Just Business

Due Diligence

Daily Grind

Twisted Wishes

Syncopation

Counterpoint

Reverb

Standalone Works

CTRL Me

Outside the Lines

Weave the Dark, Weave the Light

Cinnamon Roll

ABOUT THE AUTHOR

Anna Zabo writes contemporary and paranormal romance for all colors of the rainbow. They live and work in Pittsburgh, Pennsylvania, which isn't nearly as boring as most people think.

They can be easily plied with coffee or a chance to see the Pittsburgh Penguins.

Anna has an MFA in Writing Popular Fiction from Seton Hill University, where they fell in with a roving band of romance writers and never looked back. They also have a BA in Creative Writing from Carnegie Mellon University.

Anna uses they/them pronouns and prefers Mx. Zabo as an honorific. They can be found online at annazabo.com.

twitter.com/amergina

instagram.com/amergina

bookbub.com/authors/anna-zabo

amazon.com/Anna-Zabo/e/B00A7LA6OC

www.ingramcontent.com/pod-product-compliance
Lightning Source LLC
Chambersburg PA
CBHW052039240626
47153CB00006B/2160